SKIP THE FIRST AMENDMENT

Marlowe J. Churchill

Order this book online at www.trafford.com
or email orders@trafford.com

Most Trafford titles are also available at major online book retailers.

Printed in the United States of America.

ISBN: 978-1-4669-8458-5 (sc)
ISBN: 978-1-4669-8457-8 (e)

Trafford rev. 03/19/2013

 www.trafford.com

North America & international
toll-free: 1 888 232 4444 (USA & Canada)
phone: 250 383 6864 ♦ fax: 812 355 4082

Also by Marlowe J. Churchill
"The Riverside National Cemetery Story:
A Field of Warriors."

For all my former colleagues during those golden years of newspaper journalism.

PART I

CHAPTER ONE
Tacoma, Wash. Feb. 6

Linda was vacuuming her apartment living room rug as she did once a week, Listening to Tom Petty and the Heartbreakers blaring over the racket from the old Hoover sweeper, when someone grabbed her around the neck and squeezed hard. Then, she felt a piercing pain in her arm.

The last thing Linda heard was the muted barking of her Yorkie she called Tootsie. Looking through a crack in the bathroom doorway, Linda's girlfriend watched the man remove the syringe from Linda's arm. He was gone before she found her voice and screamed.

I didn't have anything better to do that day, but it was still a pain in the ass to make this interview for my newspaper. I was reading in the car as I drove—why not?—and the story still wasn't waking me up. A woman named Linda had been killed. So what? People were killed constantly in a city like this, and nothing made this case any different from others.

Sure, the killer reportedly subdued her with some kind of a drug, but this was a cruel world filled with drugs and addicts.

I could barely remember the woman's voice. It sounded shaky and young, but that's all. She wanted to meet at a coffee shop in Gig Harbor and talk about what she insisted where "irregularities in the entertainment industry." It was a place my mom had taken me every week, but I hadn't been there since I left home after high school and joined the Marines.

Inside, I found a table and before I could pick up the menu and remember times and things I didn't want to remember, I heard a woman's voice, maybe the same one that had called me for this interview.

"Are you Skip?"

I guess my slacks, pressed shirt and tie left little doubt that I was the reporter she was supposed to meet. I was conspicuously over-dressed here. Funny how this place never changed—even the menu—since I was last here, probably 18 years ago.

She wore a heavy jacket that covered a baggy sweater. I couldn't tell whether she had a figure or not. She was a topless dancer, she said, but that could have meant anything. The bottom cuffs of her jeans were soaked from the rain and she wore clunky leather hiking boots with red shoelaces. Probably she was an outdoorsy gal who walked to the cafe.

When she sat down and unzipped her jacket, I first focused on her rain-splattered face and frizzy, wet hair that she tried to put back into place with a sweep of her fingers. Her cheeks were splotched with red because of the cold. She appeared to be a mix of African-American, maybe Asian or Pacific Islander. She looked great even without makeup or jewelry. Possibly in her early 30s, this woman really didn't need to wear make-up.

"You have a little jam on your cheek," she said. Was that faint smile she gave me a little flirtatious? I asked if she wanted any breakfast, although I was nearly finished with mine. She just wanted orange juice.

My chair creaked like the legs were going to snap as I searched for a pen in various pockets to start taking notes. "How did you get my name?"

"I told you before. I worked with Natalie a long time ago. She said you were cool."

Sure, Natalie thinks I'm cool. I couldn't remember Natalie or what newspaper department she worked in. I pulled out a Seattle News business card that read Skip Easley, Staff Writer and handed it to her. All I needed was for her to make some remark about my first name and I'd have to tell her why I never use Ralph Jr., the name I got from my dad. I changed it from "Skippy," what my mom called me until I left home. Mom called me that because I loved peanut butter so much.

"Before we get started, can I get your name?" I asked her.

"Listen, I'm not going to give you my name. I already told you that when I called yesterday. If you want to give me a name, just call me J.J."

I made a big show of writing "J.J." into my notepad, and noted the date and time of the interview. I could tell the woman was watching me carefully.

"Look, I don't know what you are going to tell me, but my editors are going to need to know your full name if I have any chance of getting your story into the paper."

She thought about that for a minute. I could tell she was sizing me up and wondering whether she could trust me.

"I'm not giving you my name. You still wanna' hear my story?"

"Sure, but I don't know what I'm going to do with it once I hear it."

"I think you will," she said. Then, she smiled. "Do you ski?"

That was a funny question. Guess she saw my sunburned cheeks and forehead from the outline of my ski goggles. Hope my boss isn't as observant. "Yup. I'm on the Mt. Rainier ski patrol. I was just up day before yesterday for a search and rescue. I do that, too."

"That's cool," the woman said. "You look like you're in pretty good shape."

"Old habits." I was tiring of this. But I just couldn't resist tossing in some macho background to impress her. "Former Marine. I work out every day."

"I work out every day, too," she cooed back in a sexy tone. "I can't afford the lift fees like you. I'd like to learn to ski, though. You ever get shot? You ever been to war?"

I'm often asked that when people hear I was a Marine. "Yup, I've been shot."

There's no way I'm going to tell her that I have a good-sized scar on my buttocks, plus a permanently bruised ego.

She looked around the room, as if to check whether any of the patrons were paying attention. "You know what a hotshot is?"

Never heard the term, I confessed. The waitress was moving about the diner and stopped by to top off my coffee cup and handed her the orange juice, interrupting the interview at a critical time. I handed the waitress my Visa so she could tally the bill.

When the waitress got out of earshot, "J.J." finally answered: "It's a good way to murder somebody. Just OD 'em on pure heroin."

That got me interested. "Hey, you wanna' take a walk? Find some place out of earshot of everybody?" I wanted to hear more. Mostly, I wanted to talk to this woman who was beginning to interest me.

She thought about it for a moment and agreed to leave and get some fresh air.

I left too much for the tip after I totaled the bill on my credit card. I have a thing for tipping waitresses more than they expect to get. I still identify with the blue collar folk, perhaps because of my dad who worked so hard for so little and hardly ever was around when I was a kid.

"What do you know about the topless dancing industry?"

"Not much." I lied. Topless joints were favorites among young Marines with a free weekend at Camp Pendleton.

"You need to visit a few," she advised. "Go to some joints in Seattle, Tacoma, Portland, Spokane, Vegas. You will begin to recognize the girls. There's a circuit. If you're a good dancer who goes along with the program and doesn't make waves, you can make $500 or more a night. And there's ways of making lots more money. I know, I mean I knew, somebody who wasn't a good player," the woman said

I pulled out the news clip that my editor gave me. It was just a long-shot. Maybe she knew the dead gal, maybe not. "Did you know her?"

The dancer held the news clip and studied it, reading every word. It was a shot in the dark. Maybe she knew about this; maybe she didn't., She was reading so slowly that I was watching to see if her lips moved as she pondered each word in the short news story. Speed reading is not an occupational requirement for topless dancers, I thought.

Then her expression hardened. "Yeah, she's who I'm talking about."

The dead woman, according to "J.J.," was killed by a hotshot overdose administered by a biker dude who was a vicious killer. The dancer, who the woman said was named Linda and whose name I had earlier got from the coroner, refused to follow the rules from various club owners. She hinted at a lot of illegal things that dancers did, but she never got specific. I guess I'm no different from most guys in figuring that most exotic dancers were involved in prostitution.

This was all mildly interesting, just as I suspected all along. The only problem was that I really didn't see any banner headlines in this story. The cops would eventually find and arrest the killer and that would be the end of it. The life of a topless dancer on the sordid dance circuit was a feature story that had already been written dozens of times over the years.

"So what's the big news here? What do you think I can do to make this a big story?"

Maybe I could have said that more diplomatically, because she just stared at me.

"You'd be pretty damned interested if you knew who the killers are." She was getting defensive and angry. I could tell she was reading my mind about this so-called story.

"Okay. Okay. Tell me," I told her, with a big smile.

Then her beautiful face turned as cold as the rain coursing down the street gutter next to us.

"I just don't think you appreciate how big this shit really is. This is dangerous shit! And I'm not about to get a hotshot or beat up so bad I can't look at myself in the mirror no more 'cause I got careless and told some idiot dude like YOU something I shouldn't!"

That was it, she announced.

"I'm done."

She said that with a pissed-off look that appeared more shocked and hurt than I thought was really necessary. I watched her walk briskly with head down, shoulders hunched, hands in pockets and with an attitude that clearly said she was gravely disappointed in me. I thought she liked me, maybe we could have coffee again under different circumstances.

What did she expect? She thinks she has the story of the Second Coming of our Savior?

I tried to light a cigarette, but a raindrop landed perfectly on the end. This was not going to be a good day and I was reluctant to return to the newsroom empty-handed. My boss doesn't like failure.

It was hard to leave Gig Harbor, one of my favorite places on a sunny summer day when my mom I used to comb nearby beaches looking for shells and clams. The rain worsened as I crossed over the Narrows Bridge into Tacoma, marveling over the new eastbound span that was recently finished. I drove back toward work, thinking of the old bridge that twisted and jumped in 1940, then fell into the deep, swift-moving waters—something that came to mind each time I traveled to the peninsula.

It was a newspaper reporter who was the last to escape before the bridge twisted and dropped into the Narrows. I always wondered what I would do in that situation. I know I wouldn't ever leave my 1985 Camaro.

My mind moved back to figuring out how I could salvage this interview. I could lie to Dave, my editor, and hope the matter would be over. But I also could ask a few of my police sources about the dead dancer as I passed through Tacoma going back to the office in Seattle.

I drove into downtown Tacoma and pulled into a designated visitor parking space behind the police headquarters. The cold wind coming off Commencement Bay made me shiver. I walked in the back door with some other cops returning from their patrol shifts, all of them happy to be out of the elements.

One of my old Corvette buddies had been promoted to sergeant and I was pretty sure he was still working the day shift. I found Kenny with his feet propped on his desk, talking to two of his officers. Five years earlier, Kenny had painted my 1963 Corvette coupe and did such a great job that my ex-wife claimed it in the divorce.

"Skip!"

"You wouldn't believe who we picked up early this morning," Kenny laughed. He tossed me a copy of an officer's report that was written with such precise printing that the officer could have been a human typewriter. I scanned the top of the report, looking for the suspect's first name. In the box designated for AKAs, the officer printed "Fast Eddie."

Fast Eddie, now revealed as Frederick Johnson, 62, was legendary for always doffing his clothes and flashing people, the more shocking and unexpected the better. I remember he flashed a funeral procession for a beloved and respected city councilman.

I read the report and chuckled at the police officer's narrative in which he tried to inject humor in a poor imitation of Joseph Wambaugh. According to the narrative, Fast Eddie had scampered across the street about 10 p.m. the night before, but was just not fast enough and was flattened by a car. The driver was an elderly, white-haired grandmother, who promptly suffered a heart attack upon realizing what just happened. Fast Eddie was discovered bruised, bloodied and hiding in a city park about 100 yards away. He was crawling toward a spot where he had left his clothes in a gym bag beneath a big rhododendron bush when he collapsed. When found, Fast Eddie was suffering from hypothermia.

I felt sorry for the poor man handcuffed in the squad room, a towel draped around his privates. The cops didn't know what to do with him. They knew the county prosecutor's office didn't want the case unless the frightened granny pressed the issue.

"Kenny, this is a sickness for guys like this. It's not a sport."

"Bullshit! I'm gonna' teach him one hellava' lesson," the sergeant answered.

I didn't want to talk any more about Fast Eddie. And Kenny could see I was here about something else more important. I asked about the dead woman found several days before by sheriff's deputies. "There's nothing to it. Just some dancer who got whacked."

"Do you have a report?" The cops and sheriff's departments swapped reports of any cases of unnatural deaths or homicides as a matter of professional courtesy.

"There's nothing new that you guys didn't already report." As much as cops hate the media, they still keep an eye on the headlines.

"My editors want me to do a follow-up on the babe, maybe talk to her neighbors or employer, you know, do a sob story about how she was victimized."

Kenny understood immediately, and I knew him well enough to tell his mind was working on coming up with a poignant quote.

"What a tragedy," said Kenny, suddenly very serious. "I hope we can determine how she died. I know her family would want to find some closure as soon as possible."

I reached for my notepad and scribbled down Kenny's quote. "I don't know how you can read that chicken-scratch handwriting, Skip. You got the worst handwriting of any reporter I've ever dealt with."

"I have photographic memory."

"The detectives told me she had some fresh bruises on her arm and neck. I don't know nothin' more. You gotta' talk to the sheriff's guys. Hey, I've gotta get back to the desk, man. Good seeing ya, Skip."

"Later."

I drove to the sheriff's detective bureau, which was not far away. Detectives are a different breed from patrol officers. They are not very friendly to reporters and lock their doors.

I knocked on the door and Lt. Jurgensen, a big Swede who loved to wear expensive cowboy boots, opened it and seemed shocked to see me. He ignored me as he walked out with a woman who looked like she had been crying.

"We'll call you as soon as we get anything," Jurgensen told her, then looked at me like I was a blood-sucking vampire. He quickly disappeared behind the locked door.

I decided to follow the tall woman in skin-tight Levis and calf-length black boots with stiletto heels. I called out to her when she turned the corner away from the detectives' offices. When she stopped, I noticed a faded blue tattoo on her left hand as she dabbed her eyes with a tissue.

She was attractive and looked Gothic with her black lipstick. After I identified myself, I asked if she were seeing the cops about the dead woman whose body was discovered several days before.

I know how to turn on the charm and show my sensitive side when it's perfect for prying information from distressed people.

"We will not be making any statements to the press at this time," she said. "I have no further comment."

"Can I get your name and relationship to the deceased?"

"Just a friend," she answered and walked off.

That was weird. She sounded like a corporate spokeswoman, not a close friend.

I went back to Jurgensen's office and waited for him to come out again. The lieutenant would have to go to the men's room eventually. Just as I suspected, the lieutenant finally came out in a hurry, dress shirtsleeves rolled up and tie loosened around his neck.

"Why you still here, Easley?"

"Who's the babe, lieutenant?"

I followed him into the men's room as he tried to escape further questions. "Screw you! Leave me alone Easley. I don't have time for this crap. Call me in the morning."

I picked a urinal right next to him and kept up the banter as we urinated side by side. I knew that would irritate the hell out of him. "Good lookin' gal, lieutenant."

"Skip, I'm so tired. Let me pee in peace. I haven't been home in 24 hours. I don't ever have time to spend all the money I make on overtime. I work so many hours I could never find a girlfriend. For God's sake, I still live with my mom!"

He was pleading like a baby. But I knew for a fact that Jurgensen was shacked up with one of the most beautiful court clerks in the courthouse. I saw a clandestine photo of the two screwing in a hot tub at a Cascade resort.

"Lieutenant. Tell me this story about the dead woman is nothing and I'll never bug you again. Gimme a break. Tell me this is just a routine homicide and I won't have to call you again."

"Skip." He drew out my name in a long whining plea for peace. "Look, I don't know what this case is, but I don't think it's routine. Call me tomorrow."

"Oh, man, I'm off tomorrow. Gimme a break." I always use that day off routine to push sources to give me information.

"Gimme a cigarette." Jurgensen snapped. "Let's walk."

We walked out of the building and huddled in a covered area reserved for lunch breaks and smokers on sunny days, which in the Pacific Northwest can be cause for major celebrations. Jurgensen smoked his cigarette quickly, crushing the butt beneath his shiny boot, then lit another.

"She's got a record," he said.

"Which one?"

He snorted. "Actually, both of them. The dead gal is who I meant."

"For what?"

"Drugs, solicitation. Petty shit. She was a topless dancer, you know the type."

I was pulling out my notepad, but Jurgensen stopped me. "Don't write any of this shit down. You can get the official stuff from the department's public information officer later. I'm just helping you out a little bit because I think you can help me."

The dead dancer's murder was made to look accidental, he explained. It appeared she was given a drug overdose, but it looked as though she tried to resist her attacker who came up from behind. Whoever did it was very strong and easily subdued the woman, Jurgensen said.

"Did anybody see or hear anything?" I asked. Jurgensen paused before answering.

"A neighbor saw a strange guy who looked like a weightlifter or body builder walking out of the apartment building about the same time we think the woman was killed," Jurgensen said. I sensed he was withholding other information.

Jurgensen begged off giving any more information, and promised to help next week as detectives pursued more leads.

"What's so unusual about this case, lieutenant?"

"Skip, we've seen other cases like this just a couple months ago. There's nothing to connect the cases—yet. But I have a hunch they're connected."

Well, maybe the whole breakfast date with J. J. wasn't a total waste. I had a story, but nothing solid to print tomorrow or any time soon.

"Thanks, man."

When I got back to the newsroom, I figured I would have to work later than usual because of the two shifts I missed earlier in the week after I broke up with Donna, the paper's education reporter who thought she could teach me about commitment. I would never tell my editors I ditched work and went skiing, which was my perfect therapy to forget any woman, and there were more of them than I preferred to remember. I hung up my dripping raincoat, and moved toward my desk, which was not far from Donna's. She probably had seen me come in because her chair was turned away and she was busily talking on the phone.

I had more to do than I figured after I went through some press releases from various police agencies. I was hoping to cruise at slow speed for the rest of the day. I figured out which ones deserved brief stories that I could bang out, and which ones needed more reporting that the night police reporter could pursue later. People are always getting stabbed and shot. Drunks are always wrecking their cars. There is so much crime news that reporters just pick the worst cases and ignore the rest. At least, that's what I do.

The day metro editor was getting ready to turn over his duties to the night editor. Dave, my immediate editor, hurried toward my desk. "Hey Skip. What's with the gal you went to see this morning? I've got you on the news budget for a follow-up story on the Tacoma woman. Are you going to file that?"

"Dave." I could tell he didn't want to hear my excuses.

"Skip, save me the details. Follow or no follow?"

"This chick refused to go on the record or give me her name. I don't have a thing I can use from the interview, and the breakfast cost me $12.32."

"Put it on your expense report. What can you write for tomorrow's paper?"

"I talked to the sheriff's department, to a detective I know. He told me there's a story, but wants me to hold off on any official comment until later. Maybe tomorrow. Gimme another day and I promise to have something decent."

I know Dave was tired of reporters who begged off of stories. He had no patience for lazy people and the endless coddling that went with his job. "Gimme two 'grafs (jargon for two paragraphs) that the investigation is continuing. Call the coroner and get an update and file it within an hour."

That was about what I figured. I'd make it up to him tomorrow.

CHAPTER TWO

After disposing of that dancer garbage, Deuce and the Pinkie, the dude who ordered the hit, headed back to the topless joint where Linda and J.J. were employed. Deuce also could use a beer and he was entitled to a free one after finishing this particular job for the boss, whoever he was. Even Pinkie had no clue on the identity of the shot-caller.

Predictably, for somebody who had just committed murder, Deuce was a bit "adrenalized" and was ready for a little repast—maybe knock down a few beers and have a few tequila chasers, and get a freebie from one of the dancers.

At 6-foot-2 and 253 pounds, Deuce was an imposing figure, particularly with all the tattoos he loved and all the accessories necessary for keeping up the image of being a bad dude in the biker world.

Deuce, fresh from the merciless kill of poor Linda, walked into the Tacoma joint and sidled up to the bar. He was thirsty, and killing people made his thirst ever more important.

"Dude, beer for me and my buddy and tequila chaser," Deuce said. He expected full service and the bill sent directly to his employer.

Deuce's thirst, however, managed to upset a handful of other dudes gathered at the bar. He muscled one very short white guy with close-cropped hair, and caused the man to lose half of his beer. Now, normal guys might say 'cuse me" or something more genteel.

Deuce didn't apologize, and he never looked at the offended patron. In fact, Bobby Joe Stevenson of Lexington, Ky., had just been promoted to staff sergeant in the vaunted 2nd Battalion, 75th Rangers at nearby

Fort Lewis in Tacoma. At these prices, Bobby Joe was not going to let this insult go without comment. He had killed dudes in combat under more tense circumstances.

"C'mon man, you spilled my drink," Bobby Joe complained to Deuce.

"Fuck you, you little turd," Deuce replied.

Bobby Joe was not unlike the 600 or more in his battalion, all trained to kill silently and quickly as the Army's elite force who didn't have the language skills of the Green Berets. Dealing with an adversary twice his size was no problem for Bobby Joe, who was strengthened with four hours of drinking in anticipation of just such an occasion. In fact, Bobby Joe and his fellow NCOs came to this bar because it had a reputation of providing a little extra excitement, other than the chicks who danced without any clothing.

Bobby Joe looked at Deuce and offered a silent prayer for his soul before he busted his nose, tore off one ear, broke every finger on both hands, and kicked Deuce's nuts so high into his body cavity that doctors later advised that Deuce change his name to Suzy and immigrate to a colony where physical violence is strictly prohibited.

Deuce's companion, who pointed out Linda's address for the Neanderthal Deuce, suffered a broken back, two crushed knees and would never walked with a normal upright motion.

The five Rangers waited in a semi-circle around the fallen biker dudes, all limbering up for some more action. Bobby Joe ventured an invitation. "Anybody else?"

No, the half-drunk crowd returned to their cheap beer and the dancers kept moving to the music, a bit more cautiously in case they had to dodge a flying barstool.

"Get outta' here 'fore the cops come," the bartender finally said.

And, they left, Bobby Joe, taking up the rear and backing out in case somebody tried to jump them.

This short brawl, after the cops took a report, eventually was the talk of all the bars in western Washington. The Rangers' commander shrugged his shoulders and professed no knowledge of any offenders in his ranks when later questioned.

This was not going according to plan, whatever that was. The head cheerleader of all topless dancers had just returned from the sheriff's office and was not happy to amend her report to the bosses about this latest dust-up.

Deuce was done. Where was J.J.?

After deadline, I headed toward the paper's reference library, carefully avoiding walking past the editors' desks and nervous about anybody noticing my sunburned face. Today's modern newspapers are like space-age reference centers with sophisticated computer programs that allow journalists access virtually to any source of information from their desktop computers. Databases also contained lists of registered voters and lists of previous residences. There were old file cabinets that contained clippings pre-computer age that had not yet been transferred to the computer database.

I walked through the tall file cabinets in the drab library to look for what had been written about the topless dance industry decades earlier. I was surprised. The librarians had accessed clips of stories that ran in competing newspapers over the years, and I began to see a pattern of young women in the dancing industry that occasionally met an untimely death. There were three brief news stories about suspicious drug overdoses involving dancers, but no other follow-up stories.

My desk was always a mess, but I tried to clear a spot for my dancer project story, knowing that within a few days it could buried beneath a pile of papers and notebooks. I'd make a few more calls in the coming days when I had time. I always promised myself to be more disciplined and not procrastinate on projects like these, but old habits are hard to change.

The next morning I was scanning my newspapers over coffee, thumbing through the competing Seattle Post-Intelligencer when I spotted a story on Linda, the dead dancer. I knew instantly I was in trouble back at the office. The P-I had something that I had completely overlooked in my brief follow up story. That reporter had obviously gone out to the neighborhood and talked to neighbors, something that, frankly, never occurred to me. If this had been a big deal, I'd be knocking on doors until my knuckles were bloody, but this was some two-bit hooker who pissed off the wrong people.

The P-I reporter got information from some unidentified neighbor about a very muscular fellow with a tattoo on his neck leaving the area near the dead woman's apartment. The tattoo on the neck was important. Could the neighbor identify the tattoo? That bothered me so much that I decided to drive down to Tacoma again in the rain and canvass the neighborhood to find that particular witness before I checked in at the paper.

Dave interrupted my hasty retreat out of the apartment, asking if I had seen the P-I story.

"Yeah, Dave. I missed that. But I'm on my way to Tacoma to jump that angle. I'm almost there." Actually, I was dashing out the front door.

"Good. Call me," Dave snapped, and hung up without another word. Clearly, Dave was not happy. One more screw-up and I'd be selling pencils in Seattle's historic Pioneer Square.

The drive to Tacoma that morning was just as bad as the previous rainy day. Interstate 5 traffic never seemed to lighten regardless of the hour or day. I wasn't sure I could remember the address of the woman's apartment because I left my notes at work. I did manage to find the place with this dandy GPS gadget I keep for times like these after checking the online coroner's website from my laptop.

A detective's beige Ford sedan was parked on the street outside the apartment complex. The thrifty hubcaps always give them away. I decided to just wait for a bit to see what developed. It was unusual for detectives to spend so much time on what seemed like a routine overdose case or homicide.

Within a half hour, the detective wearing a green jacket with SHERIFF printed on back climbed into the Ford.

I knocked on doors of some small homes on the street and a few downstairs apartments. Few residents had anything new to offer, but everybody knew about the murder. I was kicking myself for not being a little more aggressive when I got to an apartment across from the dead woman's place. There, a middle-aged guy in a T-shirt and sweatpants, invited me into his warm, cluttered apartment.

"Yeah, I saw the guy," said Swen who didn't mind turning down the television and chatting. "Big, mean-lookin' muther."

Swen, who went on and on about all his dead-end jobs as a logger, fisherman and finally a welder, noticed the guy because he had developed a fascination with the comings and goings of his neighbor before her murder.

"Lotta cute chicks visit her all the time," Swen said, giving me a wink. "Nice tits showin' through tight sweaters. You pray for a cold day just to see them nipples stand out."

I had to get Swen to focus on the strange visitor instead of the girls' tits.

"I tole the other reporter about the guy," he said. "He was real interested. He asked me what he was wearing. You know, everybody wears a coat and jeans around here this time of year. Nothin' unusual."

"What about the tattoo?" I was getting impatient.

"I've gotta' few tattoos myself," Swen answered. "I notice them things. It was a faded Iron Cross. Right on his neck." Swen pointed to a spot on the right side of his neck. "Here," he said with certainty. "No, meebe it was here," he said, pointing to the left side.

"Did you tell the other reporter what kind of tattoo?"

"Nah. He never asked."

That made me feel somewhat better about my blunder.

Swen couldn't add anything more useful, except the guy climbed into a pickup parked on the curb with its engine running.

"You know," he paused and scratched his head. "There was somebody else in that truck. Dunno if it was a gal or guy, but definitely somebody sitting in the passenger seat."

Swen was on a roll. "You know, that dead gal had a real looker over at her apartment 'cause I saw her leave in a hurry after the big guy."

"You sure?" I asked.

Swen nodded.

I called Dave, my editor, and quickly filled him in on what I'd been doing. He sounded friendlier this time. We agreed that I still had nothing solid, and needed to question the lead detective about the neighbor's information.

"Give it another two hours and come back to the office," Dave ordered.

I was soaked from the rain, but continued to wander the neighborhood and rounded up a handful of quotes. Linda the dancer had mostly made an impression on the men who apparently watched her come and go with some fascination.

I headed back to the office and began piecing the story together, padding it to a fair-sized feature with all the neighbors' observations, mostly using Swen's, quotes. I sent the story to Dave and waited for his inevitable questions as he edited the story.

Within a few minutes, Dave messaged me on the computer to come up to his desk. I knew something was up.

Dave didn't look too happy.

"Bradley wants to see you now." He then glanced back at his computer screen without another word.

I walked slowly down the hall toward the offices of the managing editors and the executive editor, Mike Bradley.

Bradley was as tough as my old Marine Corps drill instructor and, in fact, had been a D.I. in the Army. He was waiting for me, and jerked his head to come in before his secretary could buzz him that I had finally arrived.

"Close the door."

"Hey, Mike, what's up?"

"Sit down," the editor ordered.

Bradley's huge office was lined with walnut paneling and huge banks of bookshelves containing books and mementoes from his distinguished career. He was nearly 65 and preparing for retirement.

His office had enough chairs and couches for the endless parade of politicos who came to see him. The office also served as a meeting place for senior editors who gathered for a noon status check of the day's major stories. I had last been in Bradley's office a year ago when I sat in on an interview with some politician running for governor.

"Skip, I want you to quit before I have to fire you," Bradley said.

It was like a sucker punch to the stomach. No, even lower. And then Bradley got mad and his voice was growling. "You're a cancer and I can't keep you any longer. You're a bad influence on the younger reporters out there and most of my young editors are afraid of you. They can't manage you, and that's not good."

"Oh, Mike, that's bullshit and you know it."

"Skip, you're a good man, you can be a great reporter when you want to be. But you're a loose canon. This crap between you and Donna has divided the newsroom. It's embarrassing. I've got people digging up more dirt between you and Donna than they are on their own assignments. You disappeared for two days without checking in or getting approval for time off."

He was on a roll. I didn't know whether to interrupt and defend myself or wait until he finished.

"As soon as you get some emergency call, you dash out of here for your fucking mountain rescue work and ski patrol bullshit. Getting a story out of you on all your rescues is like pissing into the wind. All you give me lately are a few inserts into rescue stories the backup cop reporter is doing for you. I can't let every one of my reporters do whatever they please, whenever they please.

"Besides, you screwed the goose. You think I'm an idiot. I've seen the stories in all those outdoor and car magazines that you're freelancing under some weird byline, and it's against company policy. You always think there are rules for you and other rules for everybody else. Not at my fucking paper!"

Bradley was running out of venom.

"Mike, you're blowing this way out of proportion."

"The fuck I am!" Bradley snapped. "You've screwed half the women in the newsroom! I can't let this go on!"

"Mike, not nearly half of the women," I protested. I was joking, but Bradley took it seriously.

The editor's secretary probably could hear us screaming behind the closed door and was taking notes on my screwing half the women in the newsroom, worried that her name might come up. She was one hot date, and was pretty cool about the casual sex we both loved.

"Skip." Bradley's voice interrupted my walk down memory lane. He had cooled down, speaking slowly and quietly, like this was a secret conversation that should not leave the room.

"I have a buddy in California I'm gonna' call for you. You are a fuck up, Skip. Do yourself a favor and admit it. But you were a goddamned good Marine. That counts more to me than any fuck up you ever did around here. You were tops around here. Then, you get a big fuckin' head about how good you are and start chasin' pussy. It all went downhill cause you think you're hot shit. You were, but no more. I tell you what I'm gonna do. I'm gonna' call my buddy, but this will be your last chance in the news business. Trust me. You fuck me over and mess up again, and I'll find you and twist your balls off with rusty pliers."

Ouch.

"Now get out of here and go home," Bradley ordered, handing me a piece of paper with the phone number of The Press in Riverside, California, along with some guy's name. "I'll have a news assistant pack up your stuff. I want you to sign a letter of resignation and leave with some dignity."

I saw the typed letter that amounted to my resignation. It was the only piece of paper on Bradley's neat desk. Fumbling for my ballpoint pen, I signed below my name. Just to fuck with Bradley, I scribbled something illegible, although the first letter did look like an S. Bradley stood and shook my hand, then sat down again at his computer, my signal that I'd better leave without another word. As I left the editor's office, I rolled my eyes at his secretary and her terrific legs.

I went into the men's room that served the team of editors at that end of the newsroom. I was wiping my face with a wet paper towel when one of the editorial writers walked in.

I needed to make my exit as soon as possible. I quickly went to my desk, noticing that my computer terminal was oddly blank. The computer techs had already pulled the plug. I picked up my day calendar, a notebook with source names and numbers, my Marine Corps coin I got from the Commandant, then went to the coat rack to get my jacket. I saw my old black umbrella I had left hanging there for at least five weeks. Screw it. Let the fuckers figure out what to do with it. I knew there would be a memo about the unclaimed umbrella as soon as the rainy season was over.

As I headed back to my apartment, I tried to assess the next course of action. The paper owed me a paycheck, plus all my accrued vacation. That would carry me for a couple of weeks. I had some savings, thanks to the advance I got from an East Coast magazine that wanted a piece and photos about sailing around the San Juan Islands. It was time to plan my next move.

I could barely remember Riverside, California when I was stationed at Camp Pendleton. I remember the place was a furnace in the summer with a lot of smog. My other option would be to phone one of my ex-girlfriends at Crystal Mountain Ski Resort and see if I could get a seasonal job as an instructor. That would only be for a few more months.

The phone rang, interrupting my review of all my limited options for the future. It was Dave at the paper.

"Skip, I'm sorry but I just couldn't cover for you any longer. You missing those two days, then you couldn't get a decent follow to that murder story. I just couldn't ward off the dogs any longer."

"Dave, I really appreciate your friendship." It felt good that Dave would call, the only one from the office so far. "I'll be okay."

"Listen, bud," Dave said. "I got you a kinda' buy-out from the paper. It's not much, but it's enough to get you going down the road. Mike told me he hooked you up in Riverside. You've gotta' try it out. Get outta here. Those chicks in Southern California are very, very hot, I hear."

Short skirts, halter tops, deep suntans. I could learn to surf in no time.

CHAPTER THREE
Riverside, Ca., April 26

It took nearly two months to pack, wiggle out of my apartment lease and finally nail down the job in Riverside, plus get packed for the move of my lifetime. Mostly, I skied and took some long hikes when the weather warmed, and just procrastinated on what appeared to be the inevitable move from my comfort zone. I still had some misgivings about leaving a place where I spent most of my life. A couple of my friends took me sailing in the San Juan Islands so I could finish this freelance piece that paid a thousand dollars, plus another $250 for two nice color photos.

I began to analyze how I ended up in this predicament, and I knew I had just fucked up a good thing. My dad was a Navy enlisted man who died in an accident loading a ship in Bremerton, where he was home-ported. My mom raised me on the insurance money she received, and I always felt that I just didn't fit in with the other guys around Bremerton, and later Port Orchard. Maybe I over-compensated for my insecurities. I certainly felt like somebody when I won a journalism award soon after I got to the Seattle News. I nailed a story about a crooked cop who protected all the whores in downtown Seattle for a cut of their wages and hot sex. I got cocky, careless, egotistical and made a nuisance out of myself. And all my colleagues were anxious to see me fall off my proverbial pedestal. The self-analysis had helped me focus on my next move.

I made a quick trip to Riverside to meet the editor, Milton Dozier, who seemed tougher than Mike Bradley, and that worried me. This guy actually was intimidating. But he appeared to be more afraid of my old editor Mike. I later learned that Milton owed Mike a big favor because of an incident a few years back when Milton got totally shit-faced at a national editors convention in Las Vegas. Mike rescued Milton from a transvestite hooker who had dressed the tough editor in pink women's panties and a bra, and was spanking him inside Milton's hotel room. More embarrassing, it seemed, was that Milton seemed to be enjoying it. I heard Mike never lets old Milton forget that debt, and keeps winking at him whenever he meets him at a journalism function. An image of Milton in panties ought to be worth sharpening Bob Woodward's pencils at the Washington Post. But that's the reason I was able to get this job so quickly at a time when newspapers were beginning to downsize and trim news staffs.

I had no choice but to sign a contract that required me to produce a huge project piece f my own choosing that would be good enough for Page One within six months of my probationary period. It was clear that I would be out of a job if I failed probation. I spent only a few hours searching for an apartment. The $900 monthly rent for a decent one-bedroom was steeper than I budgeted, but I had little choice unless I wanted to find some dump an hour's drive from the newspaper.

For the first time in a while, I used my reporting skills to the max and did some research on Southern California. I found lots of maps on the Internet that helped me orient myself to a region that seemed like a foreign country.

I was getting more confident about making this big change. I knew it was time to change my bad attitude and get serious about my career. I don't know how my attitude became so rotten, but I guess it did. I got complacent and thought I could do anything I wanted in a newsroom where egos constantly clash and people are constantly trying to climb over the wounded warriors. I kicked myself for not seeing this coming. I needed to care more about what I did and what I said.

Within a week, I was on the road for a three-day drive south in a 24-foot rental truck that contained all I owned and towed my Camaro on a trailer. The scenery on the drive south on Interstate 5 was slowly turning from the familiar forests and fast-moving rivers I knew all my life to something different. Ginger, my Pomeranian who had been so excited to take off on the road trip, tired of straining her 12-pound fur-ball body, all 20 inches of her, as she perched her hind legs on the rental truck's seat, craning her head to look out the window at the passing cars and scenery.

I pushed on as the scenry changed from thick stands of Douglas firs and evergreens along Interstate 5 to the more interesting California Sierras. I stopped to gaze at Mt. Shasta, which looked almost as high as Mt. Rainier, but in the April weather sat elegantly alone as the Cascades morphed into the Sierras. And then I floored the heavy rental truck up the steep Grapevine leading into the Los Angeles Basin. It was at that point that point where I almost called the paper and headed on the most direct route to Colorado or Texas or New Jersey or Alabama. The basin's sky turned from clear to opaque.

The I-210 freeway from Pasadena heading toward Riverside was making me nervous the farther east I headed. Housing tract after housing tract, one strip mall after another, every conceivable car and RV dealership filled the space between freeway off-ramps. The mountains had no trees. Just big boulders. No rivers.

My job as backup courts and police writer was just what I needed to get a fresh outlook and re-launch my career. Everybody on the staff seemed friendly and helped me adjust to the new routine. The regular courts beat reporter was a 29-year-old journalist who had graduated from law school, but never took the bar exam. He was a snob. My resume was bullshit compared to his, and he let me know that he was a superior journalist. But he decided to spend the necessary time to train me on the beat, knowing that if he didn't, he'd never cut down on his own workload.

I felt like a raw recruit fresh out of boot camp in a newsroom dominated by mostly young people with graduate degrees and a burning desire to be the best journalist in Southern California. For what? Maybe 40 grand a year?

I learned about journalism from college extension courses at Pendleton because I got tired of going to tittie bars in Oceanside every night. I felt out of place. But I also thought I could learn something here and compete with the best of them. I kept my mouth and zipper shut. I didn't need a girlfriend—just yet. I even began listening to editors—and actually liking a few of them.

A copy editor, at least 15 years older than me, a shy and sensitive 34, invited me to a nightclub to hear some jazz., Ed Michaels, was an unusual face in this mostly lily white newsroom. An African-American, Ed was a decent guy with an incredible background at big newspapers all over the country. He had lots of stories that gave me some hope that I could change my luck. Hell, I needed to change my fucking life.

Ed, who worked the night shift, always came up to my desk as soon as he showed up for work, smelling of cologne and dressed in a crisply pressed sports shirt. Ed always looked dapper and young women seemed to love talking to him, although they suddenly disappeared when I showed up. He could help me organize a news story I was working on with just a few suggestions. I felt my writing and reporting skills were improving every day I listened to Ed.

I was thinking about Ed's story about investigating some Mafia guy as I waited outside a courtroom to talk to a federal judge.

I noticed this big man in a blue suit, white shirt and red tie sitting on a bench across the hall from me. I figured he was a cop, because the white shirt seemed too starched and the tie too tight. He looked bored and appeared to be waiting to testify in some case inside the courtroom. Each time his cell phone rang, he'd flip open the phone and mutter something.

I watched him casually check out all the defendants who had these worried expressions on their faces. He smiled and nodded at a few attorneys loaded down with paperwork walking past the courtroom. He then bored in on me when he noticed I was staring at him. Maybe he thought I was a familiar suspect.

At that moment, a redneck biker type walked up to the courtroom door near where we were waiting. Dirty jeans, T-shirt and a Levi vest with the sleeves ripped off. He wore no gang colors on his jacket—an omission that immediately caught the cop's interest. The guy had a bushy beard and wore a blue do-rag on his head. On the backside of his left arm was a faded blue tattoo that proclaimed White. The right arm had Power. On the right side of his neck, an Iron Cross.

The cop glared at the man. Uncomfortable but too stubborn to back down at any perceived threat, the man stared back for a moment trying to look tough, then turned away as if he had been recognized from a post office wanted poster. The tough guy walked up to closed courtroom doors and looked through the windows to check out what was going on inside. An older federal bailiff quickly opened the door from the inside, surprising the man.

"Can I help you?" the bailiff asked.

"What trial's this?"

"Court is not in session," the deputy answered.

The man just wheeled around and walked off to the bank of elevators down the hall.

The bailiff at the door nodded to the cop on the bench, who retrieved his cell phone from his belt and pushed a button. I clearly heard him say "One," which probably referred to the elevator.

I had to know. "What was all that about?" I asked as I walked over to the guy on the bench.

"Who are you?"

"Hey, I'm Skip from the Press."

"What's that?"

"It's the local paper."

I handed him my business card. He pulled out one of his and gave it to me.

"I don't like talking to reporters," said Deputy Marshal Franklin S. McLaughlin.

"I wouldn't talk to one, either."

He smiled and I took a chance at small talk.

"You a Marine?"

"Former."

"First Regiment, First Division," I answered, knowing that former Marines always helped one another.

"Semper Fi," he said, his face softening—somewhat. "I'm still not talking to you, dude."

"Yeah, but you want to. I can tell. You've got a great story and you want me to write your memoirs some day."

"Hey man, we could make some big bucks, too," McLaughlin laughed.

Turned out we had some things in common from our Pendleton days. One infamous dancer at a local topless joint got us laughing like we were old buddies. A bailiff came and interrupted our war stories and said the judge had a few moments for me. McLaughlin and I saluted each other and promised we'd see one another in the courthouse again.

The U.S. Marshals Service has a long and illustrious history in law enforcement that dates back to George Washington's first term as president. But everybody only remembers "The Fugitive" with Tommy Lee Jones. It became the best recruiting poster the tight-knit agency ever received.

But the marshals service is one of those federal agencies, like U.S. Customs or Bureau of Alcohol, Tobacco and Firearms, that employs some of the nation's best investigators who work long hours for lousy pay just because, as one Army Ranger once told me in Recon School, it's more fun than a slow hand job from the girl of your dreams.

I kept Deputy McLaughlin's card in an index that was slowly filling each day with my new sources. Days later I met another source who seemed more receptive to helping me get oriented on my new beat. She was a lot better looking, too.

An assistant U.S. attorney who prosecuted mostly white-collar crime, Angela Gonzales was a friendly Latina who actually took the time to chat with me, unlike some of the other stiff-neck prosecutors. Each time I prowled the halls of the courthouse I looked for Angela, and when I spotted her, I walked with her to chit-chat about legal cases she was working.

"Have you seen this?" Angela asked. She handed me a press release about one of her colleague's cases that discussed conspiracy and attempted murder charges that would soon be filed against a suspect, who was in custody. The release had a color mug shot of a guy who bore a tattoo on his neck. He was accused of nearly killing a prison guard with a shank, a knife-like weapon.

I was seeing more guys with tattoos on their necks lately. Guys who sported White Power tattoos were even more unusual. Angela told me there were lots of notorious biker clubs, but the white racist gangs were deadly enemies to the Mexican Mafia types and some of the black gangs.

"The Iron Cross is a white power icon to many gangs," she told me.

I immediately remembered that biker who was suspected of killing the dancer in Tacoma. I was trying to remember where I had placed that damned cardboard box that contained all my old notes and that one clipping about Linda.

"Can I keep this?" I asked her.

"Why else would I hand it to you?" she smiled.

Angela said her colleagues might be interested in sharing more details with me.

"Don't do a cowboy number just yet," she warned. "There's some people I want to introduce you to first. Give me a few days to set this up, but I think it's going to be worth your while. There's a story here that my office is interested in getting out to the public, but doesn't want to appear to be campaigning for a lot of publicity."

"Angela, this guy here looks and sounds like some character I was checking out in Tacoma before I came down here—some homicide of a topless dancer."

"Well, Scoop, that's why you are being handed this little piece of paper. You still interested?"

Is the Pope Catholic? Do I look like a moron? Shit yes, I needed a hot story and I only had five months and two weeks to nail it. I watched Angela in her tight skirt walk away. God, I loved salsa.

I didn't see Angela for a few days, and she never returned my phone calls. I left her a message on her voice mail.

"Angela, you tease me shamelessly with the promise of a good story, then you tell me to cool my jets. It's not fair. If I don't hear from you soon, I'm going to start doing a little research."

"Don't," Angela warned when she returned the call within an hour. "Please don't work this until I tell you. Stuff will get screwed up really bad if you nose around prematurely."

Sources are always putting me off on good stories. I really get tired of this game, but I needed that story. Like now. I decided to play hard ball, something I never had to do in Seattle because I never had to work that hard for a story.

"Angela, I can't wait much longer. Call me back soon."

I know Angela did her best to avoid me for a few days because I made it a point to hang out at the courthouse and scan the docket for her court appearances. I stepped into an elevator and there she was.

"Skip, don't talk to me. Please," Angela whined.

"No problemo, mi amiga." I thought I would impress her with my Spanish that I picked up at the local car washes and taco stands.

"Your Spanish is . . . muy . . ." She then used those luscious brown eyes to speak for her. She looked me straight in the eye and asked:

"Hablame, para vier que podemos hacier?"

What the fuck did that mean? She saw my confusion.

"Talk to me when your Spanish is better," she said.

A nurse will be spoon-feeding me oatmeal at a nursing home when that happens.

CHAPTER FOUR

Angela, a seasoned veteran of the ponderous federal bureaucracy, was too bright to be pigeonholed in white-collar crime. At 35, Angela had gained a certain amount of respect within the U.S. Attorney's office but really had not risen to the top tier for only one ironic reason: she did her job so well that she lacked sufficient trial work to pad her resume.

But she also sometimes rubbed her colleagues the wrong way. They felt she was too pushy, although Angela saw it as just trying to be helpful. Angela, all 5 feet of her without high heels, was so well prepared and demanded so much from her investigators that 95 percent of her cases ended with guilty pleas from beaten-down defendants.

Angela wanted to do much more than white-collar crime and pinch crooked businessmen. She wondered whether her being a Hispanic, growing up on the edge of the University of Southern California campus in downtown LA, was a factor in her being on the slow-track in her legal career.

Angela, only married two years, found some comfort in bitching to this one mean ass federal agent who always had an encouraging word and never breached any remark given in confidence. He also was a hunk. She could look but not touch, she told herself.

"Frank," Angela left a message for the deputy, "I need to see you about this case."

McLaughlin returned her call within the hour.

"What's up?"

He had little time to dink around with rookie prosecutors fresh out of law school, but Angela was different from the rest. He and Angela had first met six months earlier, and he recently sought her advice on protecting a federal witness whose testimony could either break a case or cause it to unravel and self-destruct.

"We need to get your witness deposed, like as soon as possible," Angela advised.

"I can get her set up for tomorrow." She was a witness that he had just been assigned to protect.

"If we get her on the record, we can use that as leverage to get other information from confidential sources."

"I already got permission from the lead prosecutor to conduct the deposition. They're too swamped to deal with your witness. Bring her downtown LA. Let's get this case off the back burner. The U.S. Attorney wants to keep this under wraps, but wants to make some progress on this case."

She also knew that aggressive reporter, Skip Easley, was now pushing her faster than the office was prepared to go at this point.

The next day, the federal agent, wearing a yellow knit golf shirt that barely stretched over his barrel chest and weight-lifter arms, ushered into a conference room an attractive, tallish woman, probably 5-foot-7, who wore a tan suit that featured a series of six prominent black buttons in front of her suit coat—three of which were noticeably undone.

"I'm Assistant U.S. Attorney Angela Gonzales."

"I'm Janelle Jones. You can call me J.J."

"This is our court reporter who is going to take down every word you say for the record. We need you to understand that this record may be used in court and you might be asked to testify in this criminal proceeding."

Janelle said she understood the process, but she appeared nervous and suspicious of the prosecutor.

"Okay, let's get started," Angela announced. She was curious about this beautiful woman who appeared to have more Anglo than

African-American or Asian in her blood, and could drift from very correct grammar to street slang within the same sentence. Angela felt this woman was purposely downplaying her education. She was probably a professional businesswoman who turned to dancing to pay for her college tuition.

"Today is June 1. The time is 2 p.m. We are conducting a deposition in the case of United States vs. John Doe, and individuals two through 50. Would you please give us your name and spell it?

"Janelle Jones. J-A-N-E-L-L-E J-O-N-E-S."

"Where do you reside?"

"Well, I'm kinda' in protective custody. I live where these guys take me. You want an address?"

"No, that's fine. We don't need the address."

"Why are you in protective custody?"

"I've got some pretty good shit on some pretty scary dudes."

Angela's expression lightened a bit as she prepared her next question.

"Why don't you start at the beginning of when you first became aware of events that pertain to this criminal investigation." Angela's officious tone came out condescending. Janelle picked up on that and answered appropriately. She was beginning to dislike this little brown princess.

"I'm in the entertainment industry."

Janelle coyly said she danced at a number of nightclubs, working for a couple of months in one location before moving to another club throughout the Seattle-Tacoma area. Sometimes, she just wanted to move because the money was harder to earn from all the idiots who normally frequented these kinds of clubs.

"Sometimes I stay longer if I like the club and the tips are good."

But she stated she always learned to keep her eyes open and mouth shut. "Dancers love to chat," she said. They picked up bits of information and traded it to people, including cops, for the good tips they collected. Dancers who earned the big bucks learned to confide in only a select few. One never made close friendships and one never dated anybody who came to the clubs if she wanted to stay employed and make a ton of money, Janelle said.

"You have previously described an incident with one female dancer. What happened?"

"The chick was murdered. Couple months back."

"Did the cops find out who did it?"

"I heard it was a biker dude, but as far as I know, he was never busted. The case just kinda' dragged out and died."

"Why do you suppose that is?"

"I'm saying there are some prison inmates who are running a big criminal enterprise, both inside and out of prison. That's what I'm saying."

Now, Angela needed to get on the record some issues that gave this case its urgency.

"What information do you have that would lead you to come to that conclusion?" Angela was doubtful about the woman's claims, but determined to press ahead on the record.

"I hear stuff," Janelle said.

"What did you hear and from whom?"

"I heard the dead chick tell several of us dancers this," she answered. "I only heard this from this chick who ends up dead."

Angela thought Janelle was lying.

"Ms. Jones. When were you taken into protective custody?"

"Couple months ago."

Angela decided this was a good time to call a break to let Janelle unwind and collect her thoughts. She and Frank went into the hallway to talk as Janelle left for the women's restroom.

"I think she's lying about what she knows. We have to keep pushing her." Angela said.

"Let me talk to her and go over some details before we start again," McLaughlin replied.

The feds were mostly interested about expanding spin-offs to their monumental racketeering case against the Aryan Brotherhood, one of the most notorious and powerful prison gangs in the nation whose reach easily breached prison bars and into the outside world.

The power of the "AB," as it was known, was to compromise prison guards or threaten them. That, at this point, was the key focus of the current probe. The feds were taking each case of threats against prison guards and trying to piece them together to determine the reach and influence of all prison gangs, and how guards may be intimidated into helping these gangs nurture their illicit activities.

The case that McLaughlin was working involved the attempted murder of a state prison guard by a self-described "hit man" for a little-known prison gang protected by the AB. He was believed to be a member of a San Bernardino outlaw biker gang before he was sentenced to a 10-year term for drug trafficking. So far, he had merely laughed when investigators interviewed him about his job as an enforcer behind bars. He was the one that Angela thought might fuel the investigation, but was thwarted by the U.S. Attorney Warren Frost. The feds were delaying any criminal charges in hopes of turning him into a government witness.

The deposition resumed after the break, but Janelle seemed like she wanted to share something more.

Janelle stated in her deposition that she felt afraid for her life soon after her meeting with a newspaper reporter in Gig Harbor. Angela, surprised by this admission, pressed Janelle about her meeting.

"The reporter wasn't interested in my story," Janelle answered.

"Why not?" Angela asked.

"Well, I couldn't tell him the whole story."

"Are you going to tell us the whole story now or must we cut you free and put you back out on the street?" Angela was getting tough and tired of this gal's bullshit routine.

"Either you tell us what you know or we fly you right back to Tacoma tonight."

"Do you know what a hotshot is?"

Angela confessed she had no clue. Maybe it's tequila, she thought.

"I saw that Tacoma dancer murdered. I was there in her apartment when it happened. The killer didn't see me 'cause I was working my hair and eyeliner in the bathroom. Linda was running the vacuum cleaner when this dude just walked in grabbed her from behind and jabbed her with a syringe."

"Okay, let's take a break," Angela announced. The court reporter picked up her notes and headed back to her office to begin transcribing.

When the reporter left the room, Angela startled everybody.

"Okay you little shit. If you're playing us, you better quit pretty damned fast or I'm going to twist that cute left boob of yours and make your silicone implant pop out!"

Janelle laughed, but inside she really hated Angela. Maybe it was time to confess her secret. Janelle admitted she wasn't an innocent dancer as she had initially told FBI agents in Seattle when she came to them for protection.

It poured out fast and almost matter of fact as Janelle made herself comfortable in her chair, crossing her long legs and leaning back to let her short skirt slip up her thigh, just enough to make Angela jealous of her figure.

Janelle, and probably as many as 20 other dancers she knew, were used as couriers for a nationwide drug operation, she began. She was allowed to continue dancing unharmed and not disfigured on the condition that she fly to a certain destination at a moment's notice, pick up an old car, and drive it to the next destination. Somebody would contact her and she had no choice but to drop everything she was doing immediately and comply.

Sometimes, she said she took a plane to Los Angeles, sometimes Ontario, sometimes San Diego or Las Vegas. She would be met by somebody who gave her a car key, plus $500 in cash for expenses, and would tell her to pick up the car from the airport parking lot, and drive it to the drop-off location. She had to commit the destination to memory, along with the name of her contact there.

Many times, she drove to St. Louis. Other times, the destination was Chicago. Linda told Janelle several days before her murder that she gave a blow job to the guy who handed her an ignition key and directions before she headed off to St. Louis. He confided that 20 kilos of cocaine were secreted inside the crank shaft of the Dodge she was about to drive. Nobody would ever find it because the cartel had welded the secret compartment shut, Janelle said.

Angela and Frank were stunned.

"Get the court reporter now! We've got to get this on the record," Angela ordered.

For hours, Janelle went over each trip she made during the past two years. She estimated she made about 30 runs. Some of the girls were doing weekly runs. And some girls were never heard from again, Janelle said.

As federal investigations tend to go, this case that had lost momentum was suddenly shifted into high gear. Janelle would no longer slide into oblivion, but would become a pampered and well-chaperoned federal witness.

Janelle was now being deposed in front of an entire audience of senior investigators and prosecutors, all deferring to Angela to ask the leading questions, some of which were scribbled onto paper and handed to her by her colleagues. The feds tossed her photos of suspects, some of whom she knew and many she had never seen before.

"So, Janelle, who's pulling the strings here? Who's the boss?" Angela waited for an answer to the million dollar question.

"Dunno. White Power dudes. That's all I ever dealt with."

Janelle had given the feds enough information to keep them busy for weeks. After the long day, she deserved to sleep until noon. McLaughlin drove her to the safe house in the suburbs of Riverside. It looked like every other home in countless housing tracts spread across Southern

California. Except this one was guarded by federal marshals and protected with hidden surveillance cameras.

The next day was to be more intense for Angela who hoped to hear whether her role would be expanded into this investigation. Still at home in the small Orange County suburb of Brea 40 miles away from the safe house, Angela was packing a brown bag lunch so she could scoot off on her court assignments in her four-door Honda Civic.

For a couple with two fairly good incomes as attorneys, Angela and her husband Dan had a pretty dinky house in a mostly middle-class bedroom community. They had saved for a bigger home, but never had time to browse the real estate listings together and start shopping for a more upscale home.

Through her open kitchen window, Angela heard a noisy chopper revving its engine outside. Turning from her lunch-packing task, Angela looked out the window and saw the shirtless rider with a Nazi like helmet staring directly at her as he slowly wheeled past the house.

He then revved the chopper a third time, popped the clutch and performed a neat wheelie as he raced off down the street.

Angela rushed to tell her husband about the guy on the chopper. Dan didn't say much, but she could tell that he was unnerved by the encounter, too.

Angela locked the front door and adjusted the blinds and left for work.

McLaughlin got very nervous when Angela called to tell him about the encounter.

"I'm scared, Frank."

His mind flashed to Janelle in the safe house. All kinds of bad things came to mind.

"Frank, you still there?" The agent hadn't said anything and she was hoping he would put her mind to rest by dismissing the incident as a weird coincidence.

"Give me a couple hours and I'll be right there," Frank said.

Angela hung up the phone wondering what this was all about. It didn't help that Frank was vague. In fact, his terse response was scaring her even more.

She was pretty worthless as she waited for the agent to arrive. Angela was engrossed in thought when her phone rang. The U.S. Attorney operator transferred the call.

"This is Angela Gonzales. Can I help you?"

"You bet."

"Yes?"

Dial Tone. Nothing.

Angela called the operator. "Who was that?"

The operator said the caller asked for her by name. No big deal, she said. She fielded hundreds of similar calls for prosecutors each day.

Angela resisted the temptation to call Frank again. He would be here soon. He would know what to do.

Frank was becoming increasingly worried by the turn of events. It was clear to him that somebody had leaked the identity of both Janelle and Angela and was trying to intimidate the feds to quit their investigation. He did not tell her that he suspected that he was being followed as he returned Janelle to the safe house from the deposition.

"I think we need to have another chat with Janelle," Frank said when he arrived at Angela's LA office.

Frank thought it might be better if he and Angela talked with Janelle at the Riverside safe house and discussed whether she had shared any details with anybody other than McLaughlin's people l. They went to his unmarked sedan in the underground parking lot, and headed toward Highway 60 before the rush hour traffic became gridlock about 3 each afternoon.

Frank couldn't help but check out Angela's legs as she rode in the passenger seat beside him as they drove to Riverside.

Frank had an evil thought. He turned the air conditioner on high. The vents in the dashboard blew her skirt a little bit. Not much. Just enough to raise his blood pressure.

They found Janelle was upstairs surfing the Internet in her bedroom. Her babysitter, an overweight agent nearing retirement age, was watching television.

"Frank," the agent grunted. Their eyes met briefly, and Deputy Manny Rodriguez turned his attention back to the old re-run of "Bonanza."

Within a few minutes, Janelle appeared barefoot with a pink tank top and faded, very tight jeans cut off for maximum exposure of her dancer's legs. She wasn't too happy to see Angela. She preferred their company to Manny's, however.

"Manny, you sex machine," Janelle purred. "You been fartin' in your chair again?"

She laughed to herself when she saw Manny actually sniff to smell any fart he feared may have carelessly passed. "Screw you, lady!" He had diverted his attention from the "Bonanza" re-run where Little Joe was about to kill a gunfighter.

Angela's interview of Janelle began with asking the dancer more about her background. Before dancing, Janelle had sold advertising and taught elementary school, something Janelle found hard to discuss without getting depressed over her stalemated lifestyle.

Frank and Angela let Janelle get back to her surfing the Internet.

Angela could tell Frank seemed distracted. "We've got a leak somewhere. I don't know how anybody knew about you and Janelle," he said. "But I'm damned sure going to find out. And I'll kill the fucker if he's a cop."

Frank's cellphone rang once and he answered before it rang a second time. His face flushed. Angela saw it. He glanced at her. And he stared at her face as he listened.

"Be right there," he said. "Angela, I've gotta' go, but some other agents will be here really soon to take care of you."

"Okay." Angela was confused. She watched the agent quickly exit the room. She heard him yell at Manny in the next room.

In a few minutes, she heard Frank's sedan back up quickly, tires squealing as he bounced from the driveway into the street. The big super-charged V-8 roared as he zoomed off.

Manny returned to the room where the women were still seated.

"We have a problem, ladies. I need you to go upstairs now." Manny instinctively touched his .40-caliber Glock that he had never fired in the line of duty. In fact, Manny had not qualified in the last quarterly shooting inspection and might lose his cushy assignment.

CHAPTER FIVE
Riverside, Ca., June 3

I was used to quitting any damned job when I got pissed off or couldn't get along with the boss. I'd never been fired before, and that episode with Iron Mike still played in my mind every day. I was feeling more confident, but I still felt like a rookie playing in the big leagues at my new job.

I was putting in a full eight hours at work and earning my paycheck for the past month, and poor Ginger, my Pomeranian, was feeling neglected. I was leaving her alone too much, and she was excited that I finally had the time to take her on a long walk after work. My cell phone interrupted our bonding.

"Skip, where the HELL have you been?" my editor, Stuart, seemed annoyed. I called him Stuart Little, but his last name was Donnelly.

"I'm walking my dog."

"Don't you ever think about checking in with the assignment desk?"

"I just got home! What do you want, a fucking umbilical cord? You want my left nut?"

I was ready for war with this asshole editor, but remembered I was still on probation. I was ready to apologize.

"Calm down. Calm down. I need you to work some overtime. Get your butt to Brea," the editor ordered.

Where the fuck is Brea? I got a brief explanation about a shooting that first reports indicated had involved an attorney. This had come from a tip at the federal courthouse. Nobody had called me with the tip, despite all my ass kissing the past month. My editor was hearing from a friendly judge source that this shooting had a Riverside connection.

"Skip, find out as much as possible, then call us so we can figure out if this is a story we want to chase or just leave to the Associated Press to cover," Stuart told me.

"Don't worry, I've got it covered." But I wasn't so sure. How many shootings had I covered? Lots. Just go by the numbers and crank out a story.

I could tell I found the right place because it appeared I was the last reporter to arrive on the scene. There were three LA television news trucks parked on a side street with power generators humming. Cameras were positioned on tripods and aimed at the house, ready for something to happen. It was getting dark. News crews were chatting among themselves. Reporters had already canvassed the neighborhood, talked to any cops who would comment, and were waiting for a press conference.

My job was to find out the identity of the victim, as much detail about the shooting as I could, and any connection to the paper's circulation area. And I only had about 30 minutes to get as much as possible before I needed to call the paper. All the TV reporters and the Associated Press reporter were working their cell phones.

I had to think. I walked around the block, lit a Marlboro and fished in my pants for a ballpoint pen to joint down some notes. Color stuff I can pad to the story if I came up empty.

A woman in a pink jogging outfit was crossing the street and joined me on the sidewalk. She had been out for a run. She wanted to bum a cigarette.

"You run and you smoke?"

"Yeah, I can run three miles a day and still smoke a pack of cigarettes." She seemed very proud of the accomplishment.

"Hey, excuse me ma'am, but what's with all the news media over there?"

"An attorney got shot. I think his name is Alexander or something like that. Been in the house a couple of years. Nice people. Real quiet. I see him running or playing basketball in the park."

"Did you hear anything, see anything?"

She took a long drag on the Marlboro.

"You're a reporter, aren't you?"

"I admit it. I'm Skip Easley from the Riverside paper."

"What's Riverside's interest in an Orange County crime?"

"We think there's some connection to the Inland Empire," I answered, trying not to look too desperate for information.

"Probably the killer was from Riverside. We never have anything like this in Brea. This is a quiet, beautiful little town." She looked up and down the tree-lined streets as she sucked another drag on the cigarette. Landscaped yards and nicely kept homes were the norm. You could leave a kid's tricycle on the sidewalk overnight and it would still there the next afternoon, she said.

I couldn't get anything more from her, but she thought she had seen some scruffy guy on a souped up motorcycle cruising around the neighborhood before the shooting. She wasn't sure, but nobody on the block has a motorcycle, she said. She agreed to let me use her name.

When I called Stuart, he seemed to know more about the shooting than I did. Old Stu, buddy, why didn't you go instead of fucking up my evening? But I bit my lip for once and listened politely. Stuart said several television newsbreaks had given updates on the shooting. I gave him the names I had heard from the jogger. Stuart had a list of California attorneys among his reference books and was looking for Alexanders. He also asked the reference library to run criss-cross directory check that listed owners of homes on that block.

I had to remember that trick if I ever needed to identify a dead person quickly.

"I think we have a match for a Daniel Alexander, a civil attorney, who resides at that house," Stuart told me. He promised to do more research in the news library to see if the paper had published any stories about him.

"Good work. You've earned your overtime already."

I returned to the shooting scene, as ordered, and waited for any press conference that may or may not occur.

I was hanging out with all the other reporters when I spotted a young woman who looked like she lived out of her car during the days and chased ambulances with a Nikon and tape recorder at night.

"Is that an 80mm zoom you have there?" I asked, trying to act nonchalant and friendly. Maybe she'd tell me some good tidbit I could relay to Stuart.

"Yeah. I just love this lens. I had to give two editors a blow job to buy it," she replied.

"Those were sure expensive blow jobs," I said.

"Easy money. The editors had pencil dicks."

I was about ready to wander toward the pack of television reporters to see if I could pick up any gossip. But she wasn't through jerking me around

"What do you do?"

"I'm a blow-job appointment scheduler at the Daily Planet."

"I bet you're busy."

"Busier than a two-peckered billy goat."

"I haven't heard that in a long time," she said, suddenly turning friendlier. "You look like you need some help. You want to buy my photos, any info?"

Shit yes! Finally, I was getting a break. I called Stuart and he agreed to buy whatever she had photographed, and take any information to insert into my story. Stuart didn't even talk money.

I got the freelancer's name, Dawn Adams, and put her to work after she sent one or two usable photos to the paper on her laptop. The skinny freelancer in a T-shirt and dirty jeans with a bad hairdo became my instant partner. Dawn felt a need to impress me.

"Look at this crime scene and what do you see?"

"Lots of cops." I could play her game.

"Can you figure out why?"

"Ummm . . .

"I guess you guys don't monitor the police frequencies like I do. This ain't no normal homicide, according to the chatter I heard on a couple of channels as soon as it happened. I didn't understand a lot of the communications 'cause they kept changing frequencies. Cited security reasons. The local yokels apparently contacted the feds. Then, everybody clammed up."

Slap me for sexual harassment, but I gave her a hug. "Good job, Dawn."

Why was this a federal investigation? We decided to walk the perimeter and try to spot any feds and try to get some names.

We headed up the alley toward the shooting scene as far as we could go. Dawn didn't recognize anybody. It was so dark that I couldn't tell which cop was a federal agent and which one was a local detective.

I could see through the windows people moving about inside the dead attorney's house. An Orange County Coroner's van drove past us and parked in the back.

Dawn was preparing for her "money shot" that she hoped would make her financially solvent this month. Any photo of the coroner's office loading a gurney into the van usually is picked up Associated Press. Dawn seemed to have the exclusive shot from the alley. The cops apparently knew the urgency of loading the van as quickly as possible before the horde of reporters out front caught on to the ruse. Within five minutes, the loaded gurney was inserted into the van. Skip could hear Dawn's motor drive click off 15 shots in rapid succession.

"It's pretty dark, but I think I have a shot," she said, not too optimistic.

She unloaded memory card in the Nikon and handed it to me. I didn't understand what was happening, but tucked it into my jeans. Dawn already had another card loaded into her camera.

One of the local cops approached. "Stop taking pictures!"

"Why?"

"Because I told you so!" He didn't like my attitude. Join the crowd. Nobody does, it seemed.

"This is a public street and we are standing outside the police tape. We have every right to be here," I told him. I saw the cop's nameplate. SMITH. Great. When I complain in the morning to the police department, I'm going to report an Officer Smith.

The cop ordered Dawn to give him her camera. Dawn apparently had been through this routine before. She offered to give him film, knowing that the cop probably didn't know she was using digital images as well as film. He took the roll, which actually was unused, then walked off.

"This is very unusual," I told her. "And you are a pretty devious person."

"I told you this is weird. I'm going home."

Dawn, retrieving her digital memory card from me, wrote out some notes on her reporter's notebook, mostly color information that I could stretch my story into a 10-inch piece.

I walked with Dawn to her car, and then went to the front of the victim's house for one last look before I called the paper. Several TV reporters were doing their live stand-ups. They didn't seem to have much more than me.

I called the paper, dictating a story the way I had been taught by old time journalists. I learned because I had taken dictation from these guys who could rattle off a story from their notebooks faster than I could type.

The phone rang at 8 a.m., and I was trying to wake up. "Are you coming to work today?" The tone was almost nasty from Stuart who seemed to have it in for me.

"Man, I didn't get home until 1:30 a.m. You wanna' pay me all the overtime you owe me?"

Stuart apologized and asked if I could do a follow-up story during the day. I turned on the radio and listened to the late breaking news flash as I made some coffee.

"This is just in. An assistant U.S. attorney's husband was gunned down in their home last night in Brea. More, after this message."

Oh shit.

CHAPTER SIX

The Brea Police Department was getting help on this homicide from all corners: LA County Sheriff's, FBI and U. S. Marshals. When completed, the reports would probably total hundreds of pages.

McLaughlin returned late to the safe house from the murder scene at Angela's house. He was hoping that she would not want to visit the murder scene. He showered and changed into fresh clothes that he kept in a travel bag in the trunk of his car. McLaughlin was anxious to get a full report from the investigating officers on the murdered attorney. Because it was not his crime scene, the deputy marshal was considered only a professional observer and he needed to be escorted by homicide detectives if he wanted to return to Angela's house.

When he arrived at the police station, all of the officers who had worked the scene through the night had gone home for some sleep. Nobody in the station knew more than the obvious.

"He was shot twice," the captain of detectives told McLaughlin. "First shot went through the front screen door. Hit him in the chest. Second shot was like a coup de grace. Right in the forehead. We checked the door for prints. Don't know yet if we have anything. That's all I know now. Neighbors heard two shots. Dogs were barking. Nobody saw nothing.' Nothin' suspicious before the shots. Nobody saw the killer or killers leave."

Lots of cases began with even less evidence than this one, and ended with quick arrests. McLaughlin knew Angela's husband was the unfortunate victim. She must have been the real target. But maybe this was just intimidation to keep her off the prosecution team. He knew that everybody associated with this case had to be protected before this thing unraveled any more.

It was about 9:45 a.m. when McLaughlin thought about calling Angela back at the safe house. A doctor had given her a sedative.

Angela was feeling like she could sleep forever. Why wake up? The soft cotton T-shirt Janelle gave her to sleep in was comforting somehow. She curled her legs up and rested on her side beneath the warm covers. The fairly new and barely used mattress was so comfortable. Even with the sleeping pill, she felt as if she were more unconscious than asleep.

Janelle heard the sobbing in the other bedroom down the hall. She also was beginning to wonder why she ever got involved in this case, and feared she might be the next target. Hearing Angela moaning in grief made Janelle feel even worse and more afraid, although she still found it hard to forgive the prosecutor for her rude treatment at the deposition.

She decided to don her Speedo and go for a swim in the backyard pool. Manny couldn't keep his eyes off her as she padded past him and into the patio.

Something she couldn't quite understand was why she loved the attention of perverted men who stared at her body; maybe it dated back to her father who fondled her and leered at her during puberty.

She liked to please her daddy, but now realized his attention toward her was far from innocent. She thought about her life leading to this frightening point, then felt guilty considering Angela was now in grave danger and suffering so deeply from the loss of her husband. She wondered if she could deal with Angela's grief. She barely knew the woman, and now she was confined in the same house with her. Janelle began wondering if her personality quirk boiled down to a deep distrust, maybe even disliking both men and women.

After her swim, she called Frank.

"What's going on? I'm scared."

"I'm still in Brea. Don't worry. The guys are gonna' take care of you. I hafta' stick with the P.D. here to get any update on the homicide."

"I wish you were here, though." And that was the truth.

McLaughlin, working on about three hours of sleep, was determined to hang out at the police department until the investigating officers arrived. He went into the squad room and found several detectives had already arrived from the murder scene.

"Whaddaya got?" The deputy marshal was short on pleasantries.

"Not much." This detective had been on the force for six years, and was working his first homicide. Nice lime green shirt, tan tie tightly knotted, pressed brown slacks, polished loafers. No paunch on his 6-foot frame. His police skills were being tested to the max on this one.

"Have the feds briefed you yet on this? Do you know the background?"

"I don't know a lot," the detective, John Schultz, admitted, saying he intended to get a summary as soon as possible. McLaughlin cut him short.

"Let me," the deputy marshal said. McLaughlin spent 30 minutes telling him what he knew, which was probably only half the entire story. So much was classified or scattered in the collective minds of a dozen agents working different angles on this case.

McLaughlin told Schultz about the 1956 pickup that he had spotted several days before in Riverside following him, and the biker who had earlier taunted Angela in front of her home. Those were tips the deputy marshal had shared with cops last night. They agreed these two leads needed immediate priority.

Schultz called his buddy who was the department's traffic sergeant. The detective wanted to spread the word among the traffic officers to see if anybody had spotted the pickup or the chopper the day of the murder. Within an hour, the sergeant called with a tip.

The California Highway Patrol had cameras posted at key interchanges throughout Southern California to keep track of traffic flow and assist in cases similar to this. One of the cameras at the Highway 60 and 57 interchange had captured something that might help. The other cameras recorded hundreds of thousands of motorists and would take days to process. This interchange was closest to the crime scene.

Schultz sent an officer to pick up a DVD of the footage. When he returned, the entire investigative team of six officers, plus McLaughlin, gathered to watch the disk on the detective's television.

The CHP's logo was superimposed on video of a steady stream of cars and trucks. The picture was divided into the four views of traffic heading north and south on Highway 57, and east and west on Highway 60. The time and date superimposed On the screen: 18:47 6/01. It was close enough in time to when the shooting was reported.

The frame showed a tiny figure of a guy riding a chopper northbound on Highway 57, and then taking the off-ramp eastbound on Highway 60. The guy was wearing one of those Nazi-styled helmets that bikers loved.

McLaughlin and Schultz thought it worthwhile to have the CHP scan other footage of eastbound Highway 60 to see if the biker showed up again. Maybe they would get lucky and find out which off-ramp the biker had taken.

Schultz said he was going to post a memo to get some help from Southern California gang experts.

CHAPTER SEVEN

By the time I got to the newsroom, the messages were pilling up. I was so worried and nervous I delayed reading them. The editors wondered why I had not discovered the link to the Assistant U.S. Attorney Angela Gonzales, wife of the murdered attorney. They also wondered why I had not used the dead attorney's name in my story.

I was wondering about that myself. Some night editor thought my story was pretty thin on the identification of Dan Alexander and trimmed that from the story at the last minute before deadline. I guess they wanted the identification to come from official sources, such as the coroner.

And then they blame me. Go figure.

This was a different kind of newspaper here. Maybe I was over my head. But I had to redeem myself. And pretty damn quick. After all those editors with their fancy degrees and experience went over everything that happened, they chalked up my performance on the story to my being so new on the job.

Stuart told me to call for help if I felt overwhelmed and they would put another reporter on the story. Nice guy. The condescension in his voice was not too subtle. If you suffer a heart attack, Stu baby, I might just forget my CPR training.

All these negative thoughts were fucking me up. I headed off to the courthouse to schmooze my sources and try to redeem myself.

I got some background on Angela and her husband, interviewed friends and associates about the murder and was feeling better about delivering a much better story than I had put together the night before. I even found a federal judge who was very complimentary and eloquent in his condolences to the couple.

As I was leaving the courthouse, I spotted one of the court-watchers who hang out at the federal building and who soak up gossip better than 90 percent of the news reporters in the business.

"Lyndon, what do you think happened?" I knew Lyndon would have a theory.

"Well, it's pretty obvious that it was a hit."

John was in his 70s, and had retired from the Air Force after 32 years of distinguished service as a chief master sergeant, the highest NCO rank. He spoke legalese and cop-talk better than attorneys and cops.

"Why do you say that, John?"

"It either was a disgruntled client of Dan's or somebody who was just pissed at Angela. I heard Angela is overcome by grief and hasn't left her bedroom."

"Where's she staying?"

"Feds got her in protective custody." That made sense. I gave John my home phone number and asked him to alert me to any new details.

Angela is in protective custody: that had to be the angle of my follow-up story: An assistant federal prosecutor is being protected from further harm after her husband was brutally murdered. This was fresh news.

I finally got the FBI spokesman to admit that Angela was being protected. It really was a no brainer, if you thought about it. Who wouldn't be in protective custody under the same circumstances? I hammered out my story and found an attorney who had a nice photo of Angela that he could use in the next morning's editions.

I was on overtime, again. That thought cheered me up because I really needed the money. No sooner had I entered the apartment than Stuart called, wanting to know what kind of follow story I could work on tomorrow.

Ten minutes later the phone rang again. It was John, the courthouse insider who had a tip.

"This is BIG," he whispered as if the CIA was secretly monitoring the call. "I heard the feds are going to have a big confab on this tomorrow. They are bringing people from all over the country to work this."

"C'mon John. What for?"

"Dunno, Skip, but this is huge."

Maybe I could survive my probationary period.

CHAPTER EIGHT

The meeting by the U.S. attorney for Southern California began promptly at 10 a.m. No coffee, tea or doughnuts. Meetings like this were strictly business with very little chitchat.

The top federal prosecutor turned to his lead prosecutor in the conspiracy case. "Bring us up to speed on the case, Ben."

Ben Duncan was a career prosecutor who now headed a section dealing with high-profile cases. This was one of about 34 on-going investigations that his team was handling in the Aryan Brotherhood spin-off. At 55, Duncan had no time for trial work. He was a tactical strategist who kept a tight rein on scores of federal agents and attorneys. He was the best at analyzing information and summing up the case with just the essential details.

"OK. First up, Angela is doing as well as can be expected. The coroner has not finished the autopsy, but the initial report is that Mr. Alexander was shot twice. One shot was fired through the screen door from about 15 feet, and the second shot was almost point-blank as he lay on the floor, face up. Square in the forehead. The first shot would have been sufficient to kill him outright. The second shot was a coup de grace by the gunman."

Duncan looked at each of the attorneys in the room, and then to U.S. Attorney Frost.

"The killing is an obvious message. To Angela and to us. It appears the house was briefly searched. We have no prints yet or any eyewitnesses. We have some interesting footage from the CHP showing a potential suspect on a motorcycle leaving the area not far from the murder scene. The locals, marshals and FBI are working that."

Duncan asked for an update from the FBI on the conspiracy investigation involving federal and state prisoners. The case had been brewing for nearly a year until Janelle's little bombshell deposition. The latest incident would either chill federal witnesses from cooperating or prompt more leads, the agents told Duncan.

"I asked the deputy marshal who has been working some aspects of this case to attend the meeting. He's out in the hall. You want to hear from him on his report?"

"I don't have time," said U.S. Attorney Warren Frost, abruptly getting up to leave. "Brief me on that later."

He was gone out a side door that connected his office with the conference room. Probably a Rotary Club meeting, Duncan thought.

"OK," Duncan turned to the agents and his assistant prosecutor. "Where do we go from here? Well, what are we going to tell the press?"

Back at the safe house, Angela, an only child, called her parents asking their help with funeral arrangements.

Dan Alexander, a Navy veteran who never served on a ship but earned his G.I. benefits as an enlisted personnel clerk for two years, was to be buried at Riverside National Cemetery, Angela decided.

The beautiful cemetery with its war memorials and sprawling green lawns was dotted with flat headstones. A berm running the length of the property kept the vehicular noise off Interstate 215 from marring the tranquility that was only disturbed by the occasional rifle volleys from honor details. She was told that Riverside's cemetery was the only national cemetery in Southern California now available for new burials. Angela thought this would be a fitting resting place for a husband she only had just begun to understand and cherish as her best friend.

June 10

"Motorcycle approaching slowly."

The message McLaughlin heard in his earpiece caused him to go into high alert status.

The funeral mass at a Brea parish had gone smoothly, but this was an ominous warning that McLaughlin had feared as he prepared his team of deputy marshals stationed around the burial plot at Riverside National Cemetery.

Standing near Angela, in her black suit that Janelle had purchased for the occasion, McLaughlin moved into action during the reading of Psalm 23. His actions caused everybody to watch him instead of the priest.

"He's still approaching," was the next message in his earpiece.

McLaughlin instinctively touched his Glock at his hip as an assurance it was ready if needed, then listened for any additional information as he caught the eyes of Angela and Janelle, whose expressions now reflected a near state of panic.

Four deputies converged on the roadway in front of the advancing motorcycle ridden by a shaggy bearded guy wearing dark sunglasses, a do-rag, white-T shirt, Levi vest and jeans.

The rider saw the four gun-toting men running toward him and stopped. Instead of finding out what was going on, the rider gunned the loud engine, popped the clutch and made a Steve McQueen wheelie and U-turn on the one-way street.

"Police! Stop!" The motorcycle's loud roar drowned out the men's orders.

McLaughlin could hear the bike roaring through the cemetery, and heard the orders via his earpiece from the security team to cut the suspect off at the main gate.

McLaughlin nodded to another deputy to take his place and trotted off to his sedan to give chase.

When he arrived at the main gate, he found the man sprawled on the pavement in handcuffs with police surrounding him. A funeral possession waiting to head toward their graveside service had parked on the side of the roadway with everybody in their cars turned from mourning a loved one to watching the startling and exciting chase.

"What's going on?" the scared rider was asking over and over of the dark-suited men who surrounded him.

"Who are you?" the deputies were asking him, but he kept asking what he had done wrong.

McLaughlin reached down and pulled the man's wallet from his jeans, removing his California driver's license. The photo was of a clean-cut man sporting a white dress shirt and tie. Same guy in the photo, but he now was sporting his shaggy beard.

"Are you Justin Clayton?" McLaughlin was beginning to relax just a bit from the adrenalin rush.

"Yeah, but who the fuck are you?"

"What are you doing here?"

'Hey, man, this is a public place! I come here all the time to visit my buddies buried here!"

Oh, this is just wonderful, McLaughlin thought. Either this is a distraction or it's a totally harmless vet out for a ride to pay his respects. McLaughlin admitted to himself that he was stumped and needed help with this case.

CHAPTER NINE

McLaughlin sat at his desk re-reading Janelle's deposition, looking for any lead that might give insight into another possible line of questioning. The word had come down from superiors to go over everything again with fresh eyes.

"You Frank?"

McLaughlin looked up and saw a character that under any other circumstances might prompt him to go into full alert status again. He felt safe because, after all, he was in a heavily secured federal marshal's office. Any civilian would be tagged and escorted by an agent, and no civilian could ever get this far inside the offices without a visitor's pass.

"Yup," McLaughlin answered, still scrutinizing the man standing before him.

"Dude. Name's Terry."

McLaughlin decided he liked this guy, obviously undercover with long, stringy black hair, a Fu Manchu moustache, orange tank shirt, colorful tattoos on both very tanned and muscular arms, and a deep scar running down his left cheek. A silver chain connected his wallet with a belt loop. His leather belt had a Harley-Davidson buckle. And next to the buckle was a badge.

McLaughlin scolded himself for not seeing the badge immediately.

Terry "Gunner" Crawford looked much younger than his 30 years. He could pass for 24. He had been a cop for 10 years and now was on special assignment with a task force of federal, state and local police agencies that only two or three within the task force actually knew about his identity. He was a Riverside County Sheriff's Department deputy on loan as a biker gang investigator for the task force.

This was Crawford's first meeting inside any police agency within the past two years. His normal lifestyle was on hold until he finished his assignment. Luckily, he was single and loved motorcycles.

"Dude, I'm all yours. Just for a few days, though."

"What the hell are you supposed to do for me?" McLaughlin told the grinning stranger.

McLaughlin was pissed that nobody had sent him a memo that any undercover agent was coming. Sometimes, he just wanted to sell used cars in this wacky world of law enforcement.

Crawford went to the coffee urn, found a clean Styrofoam cup, opened some sugar and cream packets to mix with his hot coffee and pulled up an empty chair near McLaughlin's desk.

"Lighten up, boss," Crawford said, sipping the cup of super-sweet coffee.

Crawford was under such deep cover that he was "arrested" at his favorite biker bar so that he could be brought to the marshal's office that day. His arrest was made in front of a crowd of surly fellow bikers when cops found a packet of suspicious pills stuffed in his jeans.

Gunner was whisked out of the joint in handcuffs and turned over to an FBI agent at the Riverside County Jail. Unknown to McLaughlin, Crawford was brought to downtown LA in a Chevy Suburban, and handed his badge and police identification only after being led into an elevator leading to McLaughlin's office.

To anybody but the special FBI agent who escorted Crawford, and now McLaughlin, Crawford looked like some felon who was being questioned about his drug dealings. The California Attorney General's office had invested a lot of time and money preserving Crawford's cover. That had been a miracle in the wake of the hugely successful operation against the notorious AB prison gang that had nabbed all the top ringleaders and resulted in a comprehensive indictment.

Crawford's intelligence in that case was incalculable. There were still a lot of loose ends, and Crawford, lean but a tough 165 pounds on a 5-foot-7 frame, was an asset who could not be compromised. A third-degree black belt in Shotokan karate, Crawford honed his fighting skills during two very tough years of bar fights where his new occupation was to hang out with extremely vicious people as he moved toward the fringe of the AB and its friends.

He was a trained observer who gathered intelligence to help law enforcement monitor the gang scene, both inside and out of prison. He already had served very brief stints in various state and federal prisons throughout the state. Each time he was in danger of being discovered by guards or inmates, Crawford would be mysteriously "beaten" by guards and transferred to another location. He kept in touch with cryptic codes he sent weekly to his "mother." She would also visit him occasionally, bringing him a new book that contained an encoded message in the acknowledgements at the back of the book.

"Why are you here?" McLaughlin asked, still suspicious of the character seated in front of him.

"Dude. I've been sent to help you with what you are working on. So let's cut to the chase and swap spit."

McLaughlin didn't know what to say. He looked at the special FBI agent who had brought in Crawford.

"He's cool, Frank. Where do you think we've gotten the Intel to launch this conspiracy case anyway?"

"Goddamn it! Nobody tells me shit around here." McLaughlin moaned.

"Just chill, dude," Crawford said softly. He had been in character so long he could no longer speak without expletives and slang. "I am your leader and I'm here to save you," he announced.

"Jeez, Terry. I'm so tired. I haven't taken a decent shit in a week and I'm still wearing the same socks I had three days ago."

The three men spent hours going over the case of the slain attorney, plus Janelle's earthshaking observations in her deposition, before Crawford offered his assessment: "Let's kick some ass!"

CHAPTER TEN
June 14

SERVICES FOR SLAIN ATTORNEY SET, was the headline Janelle had been searching for on the Internet. The byline on the story about Angela's husband was a surprise.

SKIP EASLEY, Staff Writer. Janelle still had his old business card somewhere. There couldn't be two Skip Easleys, she thought. After all this was over, maybe she could call him and invite him to breakfast again.

Why hadn't she seen him at the funeral? And why hadn't he seen her? Maybe she hadn't made a good impression on him in Gig Harbor. She was hurt that he hadn't approached her at the funeral. Maybe she was just fuming over nothing. There were a lot of people at the funeral, and Skip probably was too busy to notice her.

Janelle's protective custody had its perks. She was escorted to area shopping malls on occasion. And the feds gave her a new laptop computer that allowed her to comb the Internet for news and do some on-line shopping. She had managed to snare a free e-mail service about which she carefully avoided telling her handlers.

The bottom of Skip's story had his e-mail address, something most newspapers did to bolster readership input and keep reporters accountable for their reportage. Skip's name and e-mail address gave her a dangerous idea.

Closing the laptop, Janelle searched for one of her scores of bikinis ordered online, and decided to take a swim in the backyard pool. As she slowly swam laps up and down the kidney shaped pool, Janelle formed a plan to contact Skip. What would she write? "Hey Skip. Remember me? Great story. See ya' soon. J." Apparently, Skip had not seen her at the funeral. Maybe he'd forgotten her. That hurt.

From her vantage point, which was fairly close to the investigation, Janelle saw the federal probe at a stalemate. Poor Angela. She couldn't get back to her duties as a prosecutor, which was bad for Janelle. Angela was so grief-stricken over her husband's murder that detectives were probably spending more time on her murder case than on what information Janelle had confided. Nobody seemed to be taking an interest in her anymore, and she was tired of this routine and anxious to get on with her life.

Janelle floated in the middle of the pool like a bobbing cork, her eyes protected from the glaring sun by dark sunglasses. Her hair fanned out about her head and she felt outwardly relaxed yet deep in thought about contacting the reporter who she thought might be able to help.

Janelle unhooked her bikini top, and wiggled out of the bottoms, tossing the tiny wet wad onto the lounge chair next to the pool. Floating once again, Janelle felt better and returned to her plan to contact the reporter.

Janelle swam for a few more minutes, then climbed out, toweled off, grabbed her bikini and walked butt naked into the house. Manny, in his favorite chair and now watching CNN, saw her bare back and ass pass his chair, and he instantly took his attention from the stock market results to Janelle's physique as she disappeared upstairs.

"Jeez, Janelle! Cover yourself up like a decent woman," Manny yelled after her.

Janelle ignored him, as she usually did, and quickly went to her room and closed the door.

"Hello Skip," she began in the email. "You might not remember our meeting in Gig Harbor in February. I read your story about a friend's funeral for her husband. Hope you are well. I read your stories all the time. Love, J."

She re-read her message over several times, then toyed with the idea of canceling out the message. Was the "Love, J" too much? Instead, she pushed the SEND button after a long pause.

CHAPTER ELEVEN

Janelle got Skip's message—"Yes I remember you! What are your doing in SoCal? Can we get together"—and was wondering why it took him so long to respond when Angela interrupted her. Janelle worried that her excitement over Skip's message might be obvious to Angela. She was almost too distracted to understand what Angela was saying. You know, I feel like I really didn't know Dan that well," Angela told Janelle as they sat on the patio.

"I only met his parents at the funeral. They didn't come to our wedding. I don't think they liked him marrying some LA Latina. And my dad never liked Dan. He thought he was too Anglo. I think dad wanted me to marry some Cholo from the barrio.

"We just had ourselves, pretty much. Just work and dinner together every boring night." Her thoughts were delivered in a soft monotone. "We had separate legal careers, and I think Dan resented my work because it was more challenging and more interesting than what he was doing. He was just kinda' boring, not what I thought when we first met. I feel so guilty and ashamed telling you this," Angela said.

Janelle just nodded sympathetically. She had never thought of being married. She lost contact with her family in Seattle when they discovered she was moonlighting as a topless dancer. Her perverted father had tried to find out where she worked, no doubt to see her dancing. She was too smart to get involved with any of the goof balls that frequented the bars where she worked. After her attempt in the business world and stint at teaching, Janelle just liked to dance, and the money it provided was too good to be true at first. And then, she got mixed up with the drug crowd.

How could she relate to this professional woman whose important career had taken such a deadly turn?

She felt badly, but she really wanted to talk about Skip.

"Lady, you just need to kick back and let the dust settle for a bit. Sure, life's a bitch but the shit will stop flying in no time."

Angela laughed and turned the conversation to Janelle.

"So, you have a guy in your past?"

Without thinking, Janelle surprised herself by blurting out something that she instantly regretted.

"I knew this newspaper reporter up in Seattle. He's a decent guy that I thought I could get to know better." Janelle was concocting her story on the fly.

Angela, who knew her share of reporters, was interested. "The one you mentioned in the deposition?"

"I went to him about all this shit, and I didn't handle it right. And I wish I did it differently. And now I found out he's working here in Riverside."

"Who is it? I know some reporters here," Angela said.

"His name is Skip Easley."

"I KNOW him!"

"C'mon! Look, I gotta' tell you something. I saw the story he did about Dan's murder and I emailed him."

"Madre dios. Madre dios. Ayeee!"

Angela's suspicions over this dumb dancer chick were correct. Then it struck her. Skip might be useful. She could manage this situation and if it worked as she planned, she could still stay involved in this case.

CHAPTER TWELVE
June 15

Gunner walked into the same bar where he was busted the day before and found a stool.

"Dude. We took care of your ride," the bartender said. "Your bike's in the back storage room."

"Thanks, boss. I need a beer real bad."

Deputy Terry Crawford was now undercover again. His eye was still puffy from being smacked and his lip was swollen and cut.

"They worked you over," said the bartender, nicknamed "Change" because of his habit of palming all the loose change left on the bar for more than three seconds. Only a handful of people knew that Change was the owner of the biker bar in Jurupa known as "Kick's."

"Weren't no cops, bro. I got whacked in the tank by some Crips."

Change lowered his voice, vigorously scratching a spot on his side. "You take names and numbers and we can fix them ghetto bunnies real fast."

"Nah, boss. I don't want no mo' trouble."

Change wanted to know more about Gunner's bust. "Why you out so fast, Gunner. Thought they got ya' nailed with the dope. Thought we wouldn't see you for three- to five."

Gunner set the hook and needed to yank it into place or he would be coyote bait in the desert within the hour.

"Weren't what they were after, dude." Gunner sipped his beer as Change moved closer.

"Yeah?"

"Dude, they let me go. Said the bust weren't cool. They wanted information."

Change, who seemed cast right out of a bad Hollywood B flick, was truly interested.

"Yeah?" Change was no movie dummie, however. He was a man who Gunner heard enjoyed killing guys who were slightly dumber than him, and Change was begging for more information, scratching that same spot on his side so hard that Gunner feared he might draw blood.

"I know nothing, boss. Nada. Not one friggin' thing." Gunner finished the draft in one gulp. "Can you spot me another beer? I'm so broke."

Change poured him another draft, telling a customer down the bar, who also wanted a free re-fill, to go fuck himself until he was done visiting with his buddy Gunner.

"What they want?" the bartender slopped the glass on the counter and grabbed his towel to wipe up the suds.

"Boss, they's grabbing all bikers cause they're lookin' for one for this murder of some big shot in Brea, some attorney shit."

"Suck me," "Change whispered. "You the first I hear been busted."

"You hear 'bout that shit?" Gunner said, hoping to keep the conversation going but faring it may not be such a good idea.

"Not heard shit."

Gunner finished his beer and went out back in the storage shed to retrieve his old Harley, assembled from numerous stolen parts that had been collected and inventoried by the sheriff's department as part of his cover story.

He had to be patient. The word of his bust would spread slowly. Change was not as stupid as he appeared.

Gunner headed to his ramshackle duplex in Rubidoux, west of Riverside off Highway 60, to chill for a bit until he felt the time was ripe to head back to the hiker haunts in the evening hours. He had spent these two years winning the trust of dudes within the Hells Angels, Mongols, Vagos and Hessians motorcycle clubs. He wasn't a member, and was never trusted enough to join. He was just a tag-along who kept a few buddies connected with dope for which he always seemed to have ready supplies whenever he was tapped.

Gunner felt the pressure to produce something on this attorney's assassination although he knew the intelligence he already passed along to his superiors was sufficient for him to return to regular uniformed duty.

Gunner was tuning up his bike when he heard the rumble of choppers pulling into his driveway and park behind his old Chevy truck that had more primer than black paint.

"Dude!" one of the guys yelled to him as he leaned the bike onto the peg and swing his foot to the ground.

"Cool!" Gunner said. "Just trippin'"

Six-pack in hand, one of the guys ripped off a can and tossed it to Gunner who caught it in one move and flipped the top in a micro-second, tossing down the contents his throat in one impressive move.

The four sat in some old plastic lawn chairs around the driveway, pulling out cigarettes and chatting about nonsense.

"Angels are for real, dude," said Danny "Loco" Estrada who followed the baseball team with a passion that rivaled that of his five stolen motorcycles. "The Dodgers are fucked again, man. Them Angels, man, are for REAL."

"You say that every year, dude," Gunner teased.

They finished the beer and drank another six-pack Gunner had chilled in his little bar refrigerator in the garage. The men went to the side of the duplex to pee, instead of trudging into Gunner's unit, which took too much time.

Neighbors across the street and next door, mostly Hispanic, avoided looking over at Gunner's place when he had these visitors out of an honest fear that they would come over and beat them to death. What's the problem with a little public urination if it meant no problemo for them?

"Dude, what happened with the friggin' cops?" Danny asked.

"You heard?"

"Yeah, dude. Weird shit. You shoudda called, man, and we'd bail you out."

"Dude," Gunner told them carefully, "they just cut me loose. Asked me all kinds of shit. I dunno know shit. Nada. End of story, man."

"That's cool," Estrada said. "That's cool, you know, that you don't know, man, 'cause that shit is scary, man, and you keep, you know, yourself low profile, man."

"Dude," Gunner said with a worried look. "Maybe I should know shit so I can stay cool. I gotta' protect myself, man. Why am I a target, man? Have you guys been bounced, man?"

Estrada lit another cigarette. "Yeah, there's a few guys been yanked by the cops. Dude, all they want is some moron who whacked some attorney who's married to some fed. No worry, man. Just chill."

"Heard the shooter was connected, man," said Ernie Salas, who had a penchant for saying too much at the wrong time. He was a mechanic who occasionally worked at auto and bike shops throughout the area when he wasn't scoring and selling drugs.

"Godammit, Ernie!" Estrada interrupted, kicking out at the man. "Don't trust nobody. Who knows who's listening to us. Jeez."

"Piss on you, Danny. That shit ain't no concern. I don't give a shit who hears. I don't know shit, and I could give a holy shit."

Gunner thought the two might come to blows. But they calmed down, and returned to the heated discussion over baseball versus football until the bikers decided to leave.

Gunner needed to pass this information to his supervisors when he felt safe enough to leave the duplex. He scanned the neighborhood, a mess of untidy houses with cars parked on the dirt that at a better time were nicely kept front yards.

Gunner locked his duplex and headed toward his bike, and ran the engine for a few minutes, waiting for any sound of engines being started elsewhere in the neighborhood. He heard a motorcycle turning down his street. Gunner got nervous and felt for his pistol and the buck knife he kept in a scabbard on his belt.

Ernie wheeled up solo on his chopper and cut the engine.

Gunner nodded. "Forget sumthin?"

"Dude," Ernie finally said, sucking deeply on a cigarette. "Hey, listen, man. I don't want cha' to get hurt so I suggest you split real soon, like now, man, and don't come back for a few days. Meebe longer."

"Why's that?"

"'Cause you are in deep shit, man." Ernie looked somber and suddenly anxious.

"What did I do? What do you mean?"

"You marked, man."

Ernie Salas was loyal to his club, but also was loyal to Gunner. He considered Gunner a true buddy, although he hadn't known him that long. Gunner was just a funny character he loved to be around.

"Guys think you're talking to the cops. Guys are saying you might trade information to stay out of the joint."

"Man, that's bullshit and you know it."

"Yeah, I know it, man. But, you know, dude, guys are scared shitless that this attorney being whacked is going to rain shit down on them, too."

"Who's out to get me? What you want me to do?" Gunner wasn't playing a role any more. He truly wondered whether his assignment was blown.

"You've been in the joint, dude. Right?"

Gunner nodded.

"'Member some scary dudes who ran the joint from the inside?"

"Yeah, sorta. I tried not to know too much so I could just survive, man."

"This shit is coming down from inside, man. And you can't trust nobody. They got guards on their payroll. They be getting information from cops on the take. You know?"

Gunner tried not to get too excited and hunched forward as if eavesdropping on some conspiracy. This could turn out two ways, Gunner thought. He could solve this murder mystery and learn a ton more about what's cooking inside the prison system, or he could be exposed as a cop. How should he play this? If he rushed to his superiors with this insider tip, he could set in motion a sequence of events that could end with his being whacked. And Gunner knew it would be a painful death.

"I don't wanna hear no more," Gunner told his buddy. "This shit is too scary and it's not healthy."

It was a gambit that Gunner played on a hunch as if he were holding three aces and fishing for the fourth in a game of poker.

"Man, Gunner, I'm serious about this shit. You gotta' know so you can protect yourself. Someone prolly coming to get 'ya right now."

"Why me? man," Gunner played along.

"Cops are on to 'ya and they be twisting you 'til you squeal. Change says you are on the cop's payroll."

"That lying son of a bitch. Well, who's going to come after me?" Gunner fished again.

"They's a club in Hesperia, mostly skinhead types, like Nazis, you know them German guys from way, way back, and they been paid by this group inside the joint. They's trying to save one of their members who's inside the joint and needs to hook up to their organization or get whacked by the Mexican Mafia or AB."

Salas was on a roll. He just couldn't resist telling Gunner everything he knew. Ernie could never keep a secret.

Salas thought about telling Gunner more. He wanted to give Gunner the dude's name that killed the attorney and was bringing down all the feds' and their firepower to his little world.

"You gotta' watch out for this fucked up Nazi dude," Ernie said. He thought about telling more and silently brooded over the ramifications if he did. "He's scary, man."

Gunner felt like Salas was going to give up more information, and just sat there on his bike waiting for Salas to tell him more. Several minutes passed as Salas yanked on his gloves and fiddled with his sunglasses.

"Ernie, let me take care of this bad ass fucker. Tell me where I can find him. I'll whack him before he can whack me."

"Man," Salas whined as he debated telling more. "I dunno. This shit is going to hit me, I know it. I feel it. All I want is you to disappear and protect yourself. Get the hell out of Dodge."

"Ernie, my man, mi compadre. I hafta' kill this dude now. I'm going to be dead meat if I don't, man."

"Promise me this, compadre," Ernie finally said. "You won't give me up. You bleedin' in the dirt and you don't know me or never talked to me. Comprende?"

"Es verdad," Gunner said. He smiled at Ernie, and showed him his .357 Magnum. "I'll pop the dude in the nuts and between the eyes before he can squeal mamacita.

"I ain't gonna say it. Gimme some paper."

That was a rather odd request. Ernie would divulge what he knew, but his honor prevented him from mouthing the warning to his buddy. Have it his way, Gunner thought, walking into his apartment and fearing that Ernie would roar off by the time he re-emerged with the paper and ballpoint pen. Something told him to look at the pen. To his horror, it was from the Riverside County credit union where most cops bank. He tossed that into the trash and found another.

Ernie was still waiting impatiently. Gunner tossed him a cold bottle of water he grabbed from the refrigerator on his way out. "Don't look," he ordered Gunner, hoping this would justify his satisfy supreme club rules.

"Whatever, man," Gunner said, laughing at the ridiculous request.

Ernie scribbled something and threw the paper on the ground, then cranked on his chopper. He nodded at Gunner and backed the bike into the street, roaring off as if he were fleeing a horde of Mongols, Hells Angels and Hessians.

CHAPTER THIRTEEN

I was in the tank tonight. I had to work a cop shift. Although I loved working cops, I hated the long night shift where I was the sole reporter on duty. I wanted a good story, but really didn't want to work too hard at it. I was getting lazy again. I had to keep my ass clean and covered. No screwups—ever.

Gunner went over to the piece of paper that had blown a dozen feet from where Ernie had tossed it. For a second, Gunner wondered whether Ernie had even written something or whether this was the right piece of paper strewn among all the litter in the yard.

Ernie had written a name that meant nothing to Gunner. "Mongo" was the character Gunner remembered from one of his favorite movies, "Blazing Saddles." Mongo was the fearsome character played by retired Detroit Lions tackle Alex Karras.

In the fading light of this long summer day, Gunner went to the lawn chair in his carport and weighed all his options. He could disappear now and turn over this information to the feds. Let them take it from here. That would be the end of his undercover assignment. But that might endanger Ernie, his secret source.

The other option was to lie in wait for this so-called Mongo character that was bent on whacking him, then apprehend the killer for the feds, and resume his undercover role.

Gunner felt extremely vulnerable and nervous about leaving his place to check in with his superiors. It was inconceivable that this

Mongo would come for him that night. Better to be careful than sorry, he thought, grabbing his special cellphone that he hid inside the carport and text-messaged a code to his sergeant:"911. Text me ASAP." He rarely text-messaged his superiors, and the "911" reference would surely cause a few hearts to race inside the department.

Five minutes, then 10 minutes passed. Deputy Terry Crawford was ready to ditch his role as Gunner. He sat in his rickety lawn chair inside the carport, holding his cellphone in one hand and his .357 Magnum in the other. He wanted to be outside, not trapped inside the apartment in case Mongo arrived before the team of investigators he hoped would race to rescue him.

Finally, the return message arrived from his sergeant: "Ready."

The deputy texted back: "Hot tip. Need pickup @ Home. No sirens."

Two minutes passed before the message appeared. "Roger. En route."

Deputy Crawford relaxed somewhat and leaned over to get a bottle of water from his small second-hand garage refrigerator that he simply treasured amid the hovel he was forced to call "home."

As he sipped the cold water, he heard some dogs barking a few houses down from his place. He tensed up all over again. Sometimes, cops get a sense of something bad that could happen. Now very paranoid, Crawford went inside his apartment and found his fully loaded pump-action .12 gauge Remington shotgun and quickly resumed his seat to listen for Mongo or whoever else was being sent to kill him.

It was torture waiting, but the deputy knew he had no other choice. The dogs weren't barking as much as before. Crawford heard a board snap from the neighbor's rickety side fence. Gunner knew an intruder was moving toward him at the back of the vacant duplex building he shared with illegal immigrant neighbors that the cop had temporarily relocated to a safer place during his assignment.

Gunner knelt on one knee in the dark, watching the back corner of the carport for the intruder to move into the opening on the side of the garage. He planned to empty his revolver and then use the shotgun on whoever was moving toward him. The sun had set and it was dark with a Santa Ana breeze picking up. He knew the intruder would wait until it was pitch dark before making his move.

Gunner took aim at the open side of the carport.

The loud crash of splintering wood scared Crawford so much that he froze momentarily as he watched the old back door of the carport that he locked and never used come off its hinges and fall inward in pieces. Crawford, his heart pounding and the veins in his temples pulsating, heard himself cry out in shocked disbelief as he saw not one but two huge figures moving to squeeze through the caved-in doorway and enter the carport.

He fired six rounds at the doorway in rapid sequence, and dove to the dirty concrete while grabbing for his shotgun that he earlier placed against a cardboard box next to his lawn chair. Amid this gunfire was a deafening roar of a gun—not his—followed by the pain and jolt of being hit in the left hip.

Crawford heard screaming and cursing, not comprehending whether these words were coming from him or his assassins. He turned the shotgun toward the door entrance and blasted three rounds as quickly as he could pump a shell into the chamber.

Crawford's heart felt as though it was about to explode.

"Gunner! You mother fuckin' scum! You're DEAD!"

From the floor on his belly, Crawford pumped another round in the direction of the man's curses, although he knew he had missed the target. The man's screams were horrific.

The neighborhood dogs were going nuts when Crawford came to his senses from the extreme adrenalin rush that had not only dulled him into becoming a shooting machine, as he was taught from the academy, but dulled the intense pain in his hip and now the side of his face where a shotgun pellet had penetrated just below his left eye.

Neighbors too frightened to leave their homes were screaming from open doors. "Call the police! Call 911! What's going on!"

Yes, please call the police, Crawford thought. He didn't want to move just then. He heard a man crying in pain, his sobs were like a little boy calling for his mother. Where was the other one? He panicked, fishing into his blood-soaked jean pocket for any cartridges to reload his .357. It hurt too much to move, however. Crawford was losing consciousness, but seemed to hear what sounded like police sirens in the distance.

"Jesus H." Crawford's sergeant muttered as he ran up the driveway along with six other deputies with drawn pistols and shotguns.

"Crawford! Crawford! Crawford!"

The deputies shined their flashlights around the carport as they searched for their man and approached the mayhem in the dark.

"Two down! Two down! Medic!"

When Sheriff's Sgt. Joe Heacock found Crawford, he thought his young undercover deputy was dead. The flesh on his face was torn and blood was seeping from a wound beneath his eye. The wound on his hip had drenched Crawford's pants and was pooling on the concrete.

"This guy first!" Heacock told the medics who were running to the melee. But a rattled medic kept looking toward a huge man screaming in the shadows on the cluttered floor about 10 feet away. The senior paramedic medic was applying pressure bandages on the hip wound and bandaged the writhing officer's face. Another paramedic team arrived to tend to the wounded assassin.

"Secure this area and let's get some lights on out here," Heacock ordered the gathering throng of deputies.

Heacock heard a deputy yell outside the door. "We got a dead one back here!"

Heacock took out his cellphone and called his lieutenant. "Get ready for a shit storm. Crawford was hit. Two bad guys are down. One we think is dead."

The lieutenant told Heacock he was en route, and then Heacock called U.S. Deputy Marshal Frank McLaughlin as he had earlier agreed to do in any such emergency. McLaughlin passed the information up his chain of command, and motored into high gear on the 60 Freeway toward Riverside.

The next two hours saw the neighborhood quickly transformed from a the luckless spot where police patrols often were infrequent into a huge crime scene that featured a high-tech command post, a dozen volunteer deputies manning traffic barricades that secured a two-square-block area, a Red Cross van and volunteers to care for the evacuated neighbors near the shooting scene, portable outdoor lights to illuminate the crime scene, plus homicide and special investigations detectives, and lots of federal officers.

The body of the unidentified shooter was still sprawled just outside the back garage door where Crawford had shot him once in the forehead and once in his open mouth—two lucky shots that nearly blew off the back of his skull. The second shooter was being loaded up into the ambulance with medics telling the cops that chances are he might not survive the blood loss to his groin area.

"Terry! Terry! Terry!" Heacock yelled at the prone deputy whose wounds had sunk him into shock as medics tried to stabilize him before transporting him to the hospital. A fire captain radioed for a medevac helicopter.

Terry Crawford recognized his superior, but could not say a word. His mouth was frozen. His facial muscles twitched and he felt like his tongue had been blown to pieces.

Every word he tried to say would not come out of his mouth, even though he tried his hardest to utter a sound that came out only as a low moan. The shotgun pellet had entered below his eye, bounced off a molar and ricocheted out the backside of his jaw. It was one of those miraculous cases, doctors would later say, that occasionally happens in combat.

Bullets or pellets take weird paths as they tear through flesh, deflecting off a piece of bone and narrowly missing the brain. Crawford had fired so many rounds that one pellet had bounced off of something in the garage and struck him in the face, forensic experts would later determine.

Heacock needed to know his man was OK, but he desperately wanted to know what information the wounded man was so anxious to share before the shooting. This was too crucial to wait for Crawford to recover days later.

"Can you write on this paper?" Heacock asked Crawford in a loud voice. The gunfire inside the enclosed carport had been deafening, making it hard for Crawford to understand all the commotion that surrounded him as they lifted him onto a stretcher and wheeled him toward the helicopter.

Heacock held up his notepad and a pen. "See? Write what you got," he told Crawford, who grasped the ballpoint pen and began to write with a blood-caked hand. He paused and seemed as though he were in deep thought or about to croak. Actually, the wounded deputy felt like he needed to puke and shit his pants.

Heacock became excited seeing the man scribble something. "Thanks, Terry! You take care. I love ya.'"

The deputy was placed inside the waiting helicopter that adroitly avoided power lines and roared off toward the hospital.

Heacock glanced at his notebook. He couldn't make out the two words at first. He studied them for a minute.

"No 'membrrr."

Heacock screamed and threw the pad on the ground. "Shit, shit, shit!"

"My man can't remember what he had to tell us," Heacock told McLaughlin when he arrived.

"Hey, he's had a traumatic injury. It'll come back. Don't worry," McLaughlin reassured him. "Let's lean on the other guy. Let's find out who they are, maybe that'll shed some light on what we have." McLaughlin, for the second time, was an important "guest" at a homicide crime scene. Even Heacock was looking to the newly arrived lead homicide detective for permission to inspect the crime scene.

With the homicide detectives accompanying them to ensure the crime scene was not compromised, Heacock and McLaughlin turned their attention to the dead guy.

The detective recited what he saw to the two lawmen who stood about 20 feet away. The wounded suspect was en route to emergency surgery, and the prognosis didn't look good as the cops monitored the radio chatter from the racing ambulance. The detective lifted the dead man's I.D. from his wallet as they waited for the coroner, who probably wouldn't arrive for another hour. It was fortunate the dead guy even had a California driver's license in his wallet, along with scraps of paper and $356 in cash.

"It says Chester LeRoy Desmond," the lead homicide detective read aloud, studying the dead man's face and the mug shot on the license. "Sure looks kinda' like Chester. 'Cept this here Chester has two holes in his head."

"Even without the holes, mean lookin' muther," the other homicide detective observed.

"Who's the other joker?" McLaughlin wanted both names to check on warrants and records from the vast federal database.

"It says Mongo on his leather wallet," the lead homicide detective told Heacock, fingering the cheap wallet with the embedded sobriquet. "I hope Mongo has a last name. In fact, I hope he has a real first name."

Mongo's blood had soaked his wallet. The detective had to find a rag to wipe off the blood from his gloved hands and fish through it for the DMV license. He found it beside a Blockbuster video card as he strained to read them by flashlight.

"Harold Cross. DOB 11/11/80. Born on Memorial Day. Wonder what good deeds he's done when we run his I.D." The license had expired two years ago.

Chester and Harold, a.k.a. Ace and Mongo, were card-carrying members of the newly formed Nazi Warriors, Hesperia chapter, according to first reports from dispatchers who recounted their rap sheets in a typical monotone that showed no emotion. Hesperia cops hopefully would be familiar with this duo, McLaughlin and Heacock agreed. "Find out who these creeps are," the lead homicide detective told one of his men, handing him the licenses. "Need it ASAP."

"So piece this thing together for me," McLaughlin asked Heacock, impressed with the two homicide detectives.

"So when did you last actually talk to Crawford?" McLaughlin asked.

"We didn't talk. Actually, he text-messaged me that everything was cool, and then I got the 911 message just before this happened."

"Sergeant," a deputy interrupted anxiously. "We've got a bunch of TV and newspaper reporters out at the command post, and they've been walking around the neighborhood asking questions. The PIO needs help. We've got to give them something."

"Horseshit! Horseshit! Horseshit!" Heacock screamed.

There are moments during intense, draining times when cops find black humor in the strangest occurrences. McLaughlin wondered if the sergeant always cursed in triplet.

He was about to crack up and tease him about it but his mind focused on a dilemma if word of Crawford's undercover status ever were known.

"Heacock?" McLaughlin whispered. "Who knows that Crawford is undercover? Pass the word to all these officers to keep their mouths shut about any of these three dudes."

"I've already made that order, but I'm gonna' make it again. I don't think nobody knows Crawford except you, me and the lieutenant at this point." He turned to the young uniformed deputy who was told to back away from the conversation. "Any leak on what happened here will have dire consequences. You get it? You know nuthin."

The deputy, whose eyes were still bug-eyed from the unfolding events in front of him, nodded that he understood. But he really didn't.

Heacock and McLaughlin, now joined by a FBI guy and the sheriff's lieutenant, decided they needed to come up with a story for the press that would take the heat off them for a couple days. Whatever story they concocted would have to stand up as reporters began piecing things together and digging deeper into the shooting. The three lawmen came up with this: two bikers attempt hit on rival: one dead, two severely wounded.

"Let's hold off on labeling them bikers," McLaughlin suggested. "We can release their names through the coroner's office once next of kin are notified. So let's go notify their kin."

"The press will call them bikers when they do background checks," Heacock interjected.

"That's OK," McLaughlin said. "They can call them fuckers for all I care, but we keep as mum as possible for now."

"Agreed," the lieutenant said. "Where the hell is the coroner? We need to get people to these dudes' homes ASAP."

"Shit! Shit! Shit!" Heacock screamed.

McLaughlin couldn't help but laugh. "I liked 'Horseshit! Horseshit! Horseshit!' a lot better."

"Horseshit! Horseshit! Horseshit!" Heacock screamed, laughing at the folly of the weird set of circumstances.

The lawmen decided they needed to figure out what to tell the throng of press people gathering, now including a handful of freelance video people hoping to sell video to the networks before the 11 o'clock newscasts. McLaughlin and the FBI guys removed their vests that identified their agencies, and made sure they were out of camera view from the journalists' long lenses.

Sheriff's Lt. Timothy O'Malley, whose district covered the unincorporated area of Rubidoux, was picked to be the messenger for the press briefing. The department's public information officer, besieged by reporters and photographers, was told via cell phone to prepare the throng for a briefing in 15 minutes.

"Listen up! Listen up!" the PIO Leo Peters told the crowd. "I'll have somebody for you to talk to in 15 minutes. Get ready."

Lt. O'Malley went over the details in his head on what he intended to say. His cell phone rang.

"What the fuck is happening out there?" It was an assistant sheriff who normally couldn't find the doorknob on a bathroom door. O'Malley briefly explained the situation and said he was about to brief the press.

"Hold off, lieutenant. I'll be there in 45 minutes. I'll do the press briefing," the assistant sheriff ordered, hanging up before the lieutenant could protest.

"Fuck him!" O'Malley muttered.

O'Malley quickly found his sergeant and told him the bad news. "What!" Heacock screamed. "He's an opportunistic egomaniac who'll fuck up things even more. You didn't tell him about Crawford did you?"

"No, just what we discussed as our story," O'Malley replied, deciding then that he had no choice but to give the briefing as planned. "I'm gonna' do it now," he said, walking toward the PIO officer standing next to a patrol car that still had its emergency lights blinking.

O'Malley, in an official sheriff's sports shirt and unofficial blue jeans, walked to the semi-circle of cameras and reporters. "You ready?" he asked the group.

A television reporter interrupted him before he started. "Tell us your name and rank so we can do a quick sound check."

"I'm Lt. Timothy O'Malley, Riverside County Sheriff's Department, West Riverside district."

Somebody asked the lieutenant to spell his name slowly. The pause was helping O'Malley form his thoughts.

"Tonight, about 8:30, a shooting occurred in the house behind me," he began with the obvious. "We have one dead person, and two other individuals wounded. The cause of this shooting is still being investigated. We have few other details that we can give you at this point in time."

"Are they all men?" asked a female reporter.

"Yes," O'Malley said, thankful that was a softball question.

"Do you know who they are?" another reported asked.

"We do not have positive identification," the lieutenant said.

"A neighbor told me he's seen a lot of bikers coming and going there. Do you know anything about that?"

"No, I don't. We'll be interviewing all the neighbors as part of the investigation." O'Malley was getting nervous about the questions.

"How many shots were fired?"

O'Malley honestly didn't know the answer.

"Were there any witnesses inside the house or anybody else there when the shooting occurred?"

"Not that we know of," O'Malley answered.

"A neighbor said he's called your department several times about the rough-looking characters who hang out there. The cops didn't seem too interested. Can you comment on that?"

"We'll be looking into all that as the investigation proceeds," O'Malley promised.

"Are any other police agencies working with you on this case?"

O'Malley turned to the reporter who seemed to be asking all the questions. Who the fuck was that guy?

CHAPTER FOURTEEN

The New Guy always gets dumped on, and I was the newest guy who pulled the boring Wedneday night cop shift that runs from 3 p.m. to midnight, and a regular day shift on Thursday. You have to listen to the police scanner all night and make hundreds of phone calls to police and fire dispatchers about anybody stubbing their toes.

The Riverside County fire dispatcher's call for a medevac helicopter caught my ear. Something about three gunshot victims in Rubidoux. That was enough to send me to the scene.

I worked the scene like a pro, which meant that I talked to a lot of neighbors who spoke English as I waited for a sheriff's press conference. Normally, I would talk to the cops first and take their word if this was newsworthy. I needed to be more aggressive, and I felt great about how I handled this story.

Something was different about this shooting scene, and I wasted no time sending a pretty detailed story to the newspaper from my laptop. I decided to hang out as long as possible at the scene.

"Skip, you write that neighbors often see bikers at this house," Ed called me from the copy desk.

"Yeah." I got worried that old Ed was going to nitpick me to death.

"Skip, my friend, the only two cop stories you have done since you got here have something to do with bikers. What are the odds? Any connections?"

"Good point, Ed. I don't know, but I'm going to find out."

"Well, think about it. It's a wild notion, but the world's a weird place, my friend. It won't hurt to noodle around, will it?"

"Ed. That's a thought. I never considered any connections until now, but it's worth pursuing."

On a busier night, I would ignore the shooting or just deal with it by phone. It would be karma if the Brea shooting and this one had any connections. I couldn't help but see the Big Story unfold before my eyes.

Most of the other reporters had left, and the television reporters were busy doing their stand-ups in front of the video cameras.

I strained to look at the illuminated house, but couldn't see anything but a throng of people moving in and out of the carport. Lots of people making telephone calls. The coroner had finally arrived, but the detectives apparently were not letting them remove the body just yet.

I could see camera flashes of forensic people working to document the crime scene, but it was too far away and too dark to make out anything useful.

Soon a Ford Explorer approached the roadblock and was allowed to pass, then moved to the driveway where a big man eased out and appeared to be having some spirited words with the gathering of deputies.

I watched the man move toward the house, but he was blocked by what looked like a detective with a clipboard. Within five minutes, he was back in the Explorer and backing out of the driveway with wheels spinning up rocks and gravel. The Explorer that bore an insignia of an assistant sheriff sped past the spot where I was standing. The driver seemed really agitated as he glared at me.

Nothing else happened after the press conference, so I headed back to the newsroom, checked in and went home.

Just for chuckles, I checked my e-mails hoping to hear from "J."

"Hi Skip. You better check out a shooting in Riverside tonight. Stuff is getting kind of scary here. It's all related. Love J."

Hello! Gotta' meet this dancer.

PART II

CHAPTER FIFTEEN

Crawford awoke in the surgical ward of Riverside County Regional Medical Center, located in the eastern suburbs of Moreno Valley. He thought it was Heaven.

His head was wrapped in bandages, along with parts of his left side and hip. He had no recollection what had happened to him. He couldn't move. He couldn't talk. He couldn't make anything on his body function. He could only make one side of his upper lip work, but no smile or frown.

He was lying there for what seemed like hours, when a nurse came into the room to check on him.

"Glad you're awake, pard."

Crawford saw a uniformed officer peek inside the room and duck out again, then closed his eyes and fell asleep again.

Sergeant Heacock arrived as fast as he could and nodded to the deputy who was parked in an uncomfortable hospital chair while holding his latest cup of coffee.

A doctor told Heacock that his deputy probably would be unable to communicate for several more hours, but Crawford's condition was improving and he should fully recover from his wounds. The doctor was not as optimistic about Mongo who was still in a coma.

The lawman, who couldn't resist checking on the sleeping Crawford with a quick peek inside the room, decided to check on this Mongo character.

The floor above Crawford was reserved for high-security cases and served as a jail ward for inmates who needed medical attention ranging from an infected molar to stab wounds. Mongo was hooked up like a 22nd century robot. He looked dead.

"He's not going to last," a doctor told the sergeant.

"Anybody checking on him?" the sergeant asked.

Nobody was supposed to know Mongo was there, and no calls from family or friends had contacted the hospital, the nursing supervisor said.

It was time to get his team together for a status meeting. "Okay, ladies and gentlemen," Heacock began when they finally gathered that afternoon.

"Who the fuck is Chester LeRoy Desmond, aka "Ace?"

His team began filling Heacock in on what they had learned during the day after Terry's shooting. Chester had ridden as an associate with the Mongols years earlier, and had a reputation for shooting at a couple of Hells Angels tooling down Interstate 10 near Fontana. He had a prison record for drugs, motorcycle theft and assault with a deadly weapon. He had only served three years at the California state prison in Chino, however.

He had been known to associate with a so-called White Power club in Hesperia. Chester was married with two sons, aged 7 and 10 who all lived in a two-bedroom manufactured home on the outskirts and more rural part of Hesperia. He held part-time jobs as a welder, working only when he was too broke to pay his rent or groceries.

Mostly, he earned his steadiest money working two or three days a week at a Hesperia muffler shop that did much of its business for motorists who broke down either going to or from Las Vegas on Interstate 15. The big RVs were good money for Chester, but the shop manager said he had a couple complaints from customers about things being missing from their RVs.

"That it?" Heacock asked, impressed with the thumbnail profile the detectives had managed to put together so quickly.

"God, no," said the female sergeant. "We've been real busy. There's more."

Chester, although married to a gal named Mary for only two years, had a string of girlfriends and probably six or seven other children from different women, according to interviews conducted by a coroner's deputy.

Chester's mom was your basic trailer trash without a trailer. She had little patience dealing with Chester or any of his other siblings whose dubious parentage sunk her further into darker depressions.

Chester inherited his mom's ramshackle house after she grew weary of the domestic life and apparently just walked out the back yard and disappeared into the desert, leaving only a note for Chester to take care of his little sisters.

Chester's sorry life soon changed when he began riding with the rebel motorcycle clubs and learned to cook methamphetamine. His stint in prison connected him with valuable white supremacist gangsters who trained him to serve with unquestioned discipline on any mission he was given. The missions couldn't be too complicated, however, because Chester could barely read and never learned how to keep track of money.

The only problem with Chester was trying to coherently notify his widow about the circumstances of his untimely death. Mary, who once was a fairly good-looking biker chick, had left Chester Jr. and his brother Lester alone in the old bungalow on the edge of the desert while she sipped Tequila shooters with a pitcher of beer at a biker hangout down the road.

The coroner and two Riverside sheriff's deputies and a San Bernardino deputy hung out in front of the house until the early morning hours when Mary pulled up on her old off-road bike that looked like a cross between a Yamaha, Suzuki and Honda.

"She wasn't real friendly," one detective said.

Told that her husband was the victim of a shooting in Riverside hours earlier, Mary didn't look too surprised. "She asked if he had any money on him. We told her he had nearly $400 in his pocket and she wanted it immediately."

Mary had never heard of Mongo.

"Ace goes his way, I go mine," she told the lawmen.

"What about Mongo?" asked McLaughlin, who had just joined the briefing.

A detective, Josh Shanahan, known for his deadpan humor and often under-estimated for his exceptional police skills, took over the discussion of Mongo, also known as Harold Cross, 27.

"Sterling citizen. A devout Methodist. Works at Goodwill Industries and helps the orphans every Christmas with toys and candy."

"You're joshin' again," Heacock said. His team tolerated his bad puns.

"Both these guys have loads of tattoos—mostly White Power stuff and all of them pretty crude and cheap," Shanahan said.

Chester's best tattoo was "Mi Fuehrer, Su Fuehrer" across his hairy back in bold blue 42-point Gothic type. Mongo also sported lots of "Mongos," swastikas and Nazi emblems on his arms, back, chest and legs. Both men had tattoos on the backs of their triceps proclaiming White Power.

Mongo, still clinging to life support, would have to get a few tattoos touched up if he survived his wounds, Shanahan said.

"Basically, his love life is over," Shanahan said. "He's going to be pissing through a tube for the rest of his life, if he lives."

Harold Cross was a very big man, about 6-foot-3 and nearly 260 pounds. The address on his expired DMV license was out of date. His prison record showed he had a brother in Corvallis, Ore., and a sister in Winslow, Ariz. Investigators could find no record of any next of kin in the area.

"The Blockbuster video card you found in his wallet has an address in Hesperia that we're staking out right now. It's only about three miles from Ace's house. Just another shack in the desert," Shanahan said.

"What was the last movie he rented? 'Schindler's List,'?" Heacock asked . . . "God, I'm getting truly goofy."

Harold Cross, the son of a decorated Vietnam War airman, had grown up in Victorville not far from the old George Air Force Base, a former fighter base that was now wasting away in the desert since it was mothballed in the early 1990s.

Harold, according to prison records and interviews he had given to probation officers, had tried to enlist in the Army at age 18 but was rejected because he had flat feet and no high school diploma.

He repeatedly had tried to take the required recruiting test, but just couldn't score much better than 44 percent. Because of his persistence and his impressive physical size, recruiters had tried to prepare him to pass the test. Harold just wasn't sharp enough to retain all the answers, even if they were supplied to him in advance. It was a wonder that Mongo had passed the DMW test, and knew his left from right.

Harold was addicted to speed—both on the highway and in his veins. He had more suspended license citations and tickets than any NASCAR wannabe. Cross had also served time at Chino prison for auto theft and methamphetamine possession. Fellow inmates who thought he resembled the character in "Blazing Saddles" first coined his nickname in prison.

The White Power club, whose members and dealings were not too well known to cops, employed Mongo for various chores that didn't require too much sophistication. Mongo and Ace were valued for their talents in stealing and building choppers, and scaring the shit out of would-be competitors in the lucrative meth trade, and more recently, dealing with cocaine trafficking.

Neither Harold Cross nor Chester Desmond had any record of extreme violence other than the regular bar fights so common among their biker crowd.

"Has Angela Gonzalez had a chance to see Mongo's or Ace's mugshots?" Heacock asked.

"We asked the feds to show them to her, but she apparently cannot make a positive I.D.," Shanahan said. "We've got Brea P.D. circulating the photos, too."

It was clear that they needed to know more about the newly formed Nazi Warriors. It also was poignantly obvious that they were in desperate need of Deputy Crawford's expertise and were at a critical juncture in containing this investigation on a need-to-know basis.

CHAPTER SIXTEEN

To nobody in law enforcement's surprise, word of the shoot-out in Rubidoux was reaching the people most interested in the welfare of Ace and Mongo, and their intended victim. How quickly word spread, however, was not fully appreciated by those in uniform.

Change, the bartender, already knew what happened. That's because he helped plan the entire affair.

Change received word from Riverside County Jail from a trusty who picked up gossip like a pristine Micronesian sponge. His source was a skinny tweaker who owed him a ton of money, which he was forced to re-pay by providing tips from inside the jailhouse. He was not Change's only source of information, but he was the first to call his "momma" who happened to be one of Change's part-time bartenders when she wasn't busy turning tricks in Change's bar parking lot.

The tidbit was a coded message that, when translated, informed Change that two patients had arrived at the county hospital, while a third was missing.

Change, who read all the newspapers each morning, saw the brief story about the Rubidoux incident as he opened the local section

Scratching that pesky itch three inches below his left armpit, Change was disappointed that it wasn't a bigger story, however. It sounded like the hit on Gunner had not gone as planned. Typical fuck-up, he thought. It was a wonder Mongo found the attorney's house in Brea.

Although the identity of the victims was unknown at that point, Change knew this shoot-out was bound to bring heat from law enforcement. He didn't doubt that detectives would find their way into his bar sooner or later to hassle him.

Change went to his computer and logged into the Riverside County Coroner's website to check on the dead man's identity. It was a public record that Change had found most informative in situations like this. The description of the incident in Rubidoux was terse.

"Victim found face-up outside carport with two gunshot wounds to head. Victim, male apparently in early 30s or late 20s, was dead when police arrived. Identity being withheld pending notification of next of kin."

Change, always paranoid about the cops, knew he had to make contact with his friends up the hill in the High Desert. Change grabbed his briefcase and eased his 300-pound frame behind the wheel of his Toyota Camry that had given him 144,414 flawless miles with the only maintenance being regular oil changes.

Change, who shaved his head to take care of the few hairs that sprouted above his ears, didn't appear to the customers standing in line at the Hesperia In-N-Out that he could afford a Double Double with cheese. His heft and his scruffy clothes, stubbly beard and mean looks, made two teen-aged girls standing in front of him more than nervous.

When it was Change's turn to order, he was polite and gracious to the girl at the counter, ticking off two Double Doubles, a large order of fries and a large drink. He waited for his order, and found a small table with a plastic bench seat that sounded as though it might collapse under his weight.

Change saw the man get out of a 1956 Ford pickup and walk into the fast-food restaurant and order. Change was finished eating by the time the man he knew as Tommie brought his tray to the table.

"Double Double. The best."

Tommie nodded, and began eating with the appreciation of a gourmet who found the perfect béarnaise. They ate in silence.

"Let's go," Tommie said.

The packed restaurant watched the two men leave, thankful that these characters had not created a ruckus. Tommie, a rail-thin 6-footer in his 40s who walked with a slouch, wore a cut-off Levi jacket with no logos or colors on the back. His tattooed arms were heavily muscled with the triceps knotted as he swung his arms back and forth. His tanned face was barely visible from the sunglasses he never removed and the thick mane of black hair that fell past his shoulders.

They sauntered easily to Change's Camry unaware that a few patrons were still watching them from the windows.

"You gotta' love In-N-Out," Change said.

"I've tried 'em all," Tommie said.

"I hear Ace is dead, and Mongo may croak," Tommie said in a monotone. "The attorney shit and now Gunner. What's going on, dude?"

"Just chill it, man," Change answered. "I do what I gotta' do, and that's it. My people say jump, and I fly as high as I can, dude. You do the same, and we're cool. The heat is on, though."

Tommie smiled. "Keep it hanging, dude. Everything is cool. Sig Heil!"

Change wasn't so sure.

CHAPTER SEVENTEEN

"Hey, Ed, it's Skip."

"My friend, how's the ace reporter doing this fine morning?'

"You were right, Ed. The attorney shooting and the Rubidoux one are connected."

"How do you know this?" Ed asked.

"It's all unofficial. I got a tip from a good source I know." Yeah, and by the way, the chick will probably never e-mail me again, I thought. It was too late to back out of the blunder over telling Ed about a "source." That's a loaded term in the news business. A source means somebody who you can call back and get more information. Unless you piss them off and they sue.

"Look, Ed, I'm stuck. I really don't know what to do next."

"Skip, you're missing the obvious here. You cannot do this by yourself. I'm going to help you as much as I can. But it's your story, and at some point, you're going to need to get your supervisor involved."

"I don't think I'm nowhere near that point, Ed. That's the problem."

"Okay, let's work this out like a cop would. What do you know and what do you NOT know?"

I ticked off all the facts of the Brea and the Rubidoux shootings.

"Is that it?" Ed asked. "What about your source saying there was a link?"

It was time to tell Ed about the dancer.

"Well, it all began back in Washington earlier this year."

I told Ed about meeting this hot-looking woman for breakfast that identified herself as "J" I confessed that I pissed her off and did not follow up on her tip, and was fired from the Seattle newspaper.

"I'm confused. You mean she had information about another murder?"

Ed was asking more questions than I was prepared to answer. Do I tell him I really don't know the full name of this dancer source or where she is at the moment? I was more confused than Ed.

"Skip, I want you to promise me that you'll write me a memo with everything you know about all three of these stories. Don't leave a goddamned thing out! I'll be in the office shortly."

I was used to doing a story my way. I'm an independent guy. I know how to get stuff done. My way. Now, I needed help but I also needed an emotional shove because I was ready to blow this whole thing off and slink out of town.

"Always keep your sense of humor, Skip. You're a good journalist, but you got to be better. You've got a huge story developing here!"

"Thanks, Ed."

"Let's get to work!"

I needed "J" and none of this bullshit e-mail business:

I e-mailed her my cell phone and home phone numbers, plus my personal email address. Should I beg? Did I sound desperate enough? First time in my life I needed somebody's help.

I wrote Ed's memo and he later told me he took it into Stuart's office, no doubt to explain what I wanted to do. It was up to Stuart to give me some space to work this story, although I wondered what my next move would be. Just pull on the ball of yarn and let it unravel a bit at a time.

I was counting on "J" to meet me and lay the story out. When I got home that afternoon, her e-mail wasn't what I expected. "Skip: I can't meet you because it's too dangerous. Keep working the connections. The feds know more than they are telling. Love, J"

Love J? Did she really mean it?

I wanted this conversation to continue like in one of those weird computer chat rooms.

"J: I can't work this story without you! Keep e-mailing me tips. I need your help. Skip."

Within minutes: "Dear Skip. I need your help, too. I'll do what I can. But keep pushing the feds hard. Love, J."

Well, that was encouraging. Keep pushing the feds? That might be a start.

I caught U.S. District Judge Robert Nichols' administrative assistant on the first ring of the phone the next morning. It obviously was a mistake on her part because she never answered the phone until precisely at 8:30 a.m. I sweet-talked the woman whom I'd carefully cultivated as part of my routine beat work over the past few months. The judge was an important federal legal figure in the Inland Empire. But he was one of the friendliest guys I'd ever met. We loved to talk about sports and fishing.

Always giving me tips and story ideas, the judge had helped me build some credibility with the paper's other court writers who routinely got tips from attorneys and judges.

"Is the judge in chambers?"

"Only for a bit. He has a hearing scheduled at 9:15 a.m."

"I'll be over in two shakes."

Judge Nichols, wearing a red polka-dotted tie and suspenders that brightened his otherwise somber dress, was waiting for me outside his chambers.

"How's the Fifth Estate? I mean Fourth Estate." It was a corny joke the judge always loved to play with me, but I never forgot to laugh uproariously on cue.

"Actually, your Honor Bob, I'm getting a lot of heat from my editors about the Angela Gonzalez thing."

The judge leaned forward and actually looked over his shoulder as if somebody was about to overhear what he was about to say.

"You should be getting heat, Skip. That was just an outrageous attack on the federal court system. You need to get cracking on that. The sooner the better."

"Your Honor Bob. I'm stuck. Nobody is telling me diddly squat. I can't get a thing from the U.S. Attorney's Office, the FBI, local cops. Nothing. Nada."

"Skip, it's out there. Go get it."

"Your Honor Bob, I've heard that Angela's husband's shooting is related to the shooting a couple nights ago in Rubidoux.

"No shit?" the judge said.

"No shit," I replied.

"Well, that might explain what I found on my desk this morning," the judge added.

The judge went to his desk and picked up the two search warrants that needed his approval. He held them up high at eye level, and then placed them back down on his desk at an angle.

I might not be a mind reader, but I've learned how to read upside down over the years. I walked over to the judge's desk and glanced at the framed photos of his grandsons and two beautiful, blonde daughters.

"Gawd, your girls are just cuties," I told the judge.

The judge picked up the photos, looking at them lovingly as I peeked at the warrants. I could make out one name, Harold Cross and the first name of another person named Chester, plus some address in Hesperia on the warrants.

We sat back down in our chairs. The judge risked being admonished for such a breach, but as a long-time federal judge he was used to moving his caseloads and justice down the road in his own fashion. He knew there was no immediate harm in my knowing that search warrants were being prepared. Any moron familiar with law enforcement would expect that. But not every newspaper reporter could expect a favor like this, and if I screwed it up, he would shut me out of his chambers forever.

"Has the coroner made any identifications?" the judge asked.

"On one of the guys. I don't know the condition of the other two victims."

"That might get you started in the right direction, Skip. Listen, I've got to settle this piss-ant case in a few minutes. Drop by and see me really soon. You know, Skip, I really like your tie. You sure dress better than your colleagues."

Without hesitation, I undid my Marine Corps tie with the Iwo Jima flag raising icon, and handed it to him.

"I've got a bunch of 'em, judge." I lied, but I felt so good giving him something that meant so much to me. I was feeling better about myself.

I headed off to the county coroner's office in Perris, about a 20-minute drive from downtown Riverside. I always made it a point as a police reporter to hang out with deputy coroners and make friends with local morticians as a means for gaining an upper-hand on identifying victims of violent deaths before my competition. Now as a courts writer, I needed more sources.

"Hey, I'm Skip from the Riverside paper. How ya' doin?" I showed the secretary my press identification. "How's business?"

She had heard that line too many times before, and just handed me the official coroner's log, which served as a public record of any case under review. It was a three-ringed binder that contained tersely written reports on suicides, unattended natural deaths, traffic fatalities and homicides.

"Help yourself," she said, picking up a ringing phone. "You know," she said, after transferring the caller, "you—Is it Flip?—can check this online from the comforts of your office like everybody else in your profession."

"I just need the latest info."

I thumbed through the log in chronological order, finding the death of Chester LeRoy Desmond close to the top of the pile of papers. I did find an address in Hesperia that had been added over night that did not initially appear on the original log entry. I also found the name of the deputy coroner who investigated the case.

Next to Desmond's log entry was another fresh notation. And, it was not online yet. My hunch to drop by was correct.

It was for a 27-year-old. Hesperia man who was shot at the same address in Rubidoux as Desmond. He had died that night at the county hospital. The two men's cases at first glance did not appear to be related, except for the Rubidoux address and the same time of the shooting. The same deputy coroner was handling both cases. This victim's name was being withheld per instructions of Riverside County Sheriff's Department.

"How come you are withholding this victim's name?" I asked the unfriendly receptionist.

"What does it say on the log?"

"It says per instructions of the sheriff."

"Well, Flip, it sounds like you answered your own question."

"How come you're being so mean to me this morning?"

The woman sized me up before answering.

"How long have you worked at that sorry rag of a paper?"

"Not long."

"Look Flip, call the PIO and keep checking the log. That's all I can say."

Okay, be that way, but I'm still going to be polite, lady.

The PIO was a sergeant I remembered at the Rubidoux shooting incident, and he motioned for me to sit down in his cramped office decorated with a couple sheriff's recruiting posters and plenty of plaques from civic groups thanking the department for providing services at various events.

"Que pasa?" said Sgt. Leo Peters.

"Hi, I'm Skip. You probably remember my name for all the times I've called your office the past couple days."

"Yeah, Skip, we know you."

"What do you have so far?"

"Well, I've got the one dead guy's name, Chester, something like that, but not the other guy."

Peters said the second man's identity was being withheld pending some crucial steps in the investigation.

"But there was a third victim. What about him?"

"We're withholding his name, too."

"So we have two dead guys or three dead guys?"

"Just two," the sergeant said.

"Well, what happened out there? What kind of beef ended with three gunshot victims?"

"We still aren't really sure, but we're close," Peters said.

"So are you doing background checks on all three?"

"You bet we are."

"Which of the three men lived at the shooting scene? Chester?"

"No."

"Dude number two?"

"No."

"Dude number three?"

"As far as we know."

"Are you going to search the other two victims' homes?"

"That's just a routine part of any criminal investigation. We search any residence where there has been a violent act," Peters said.

"How many shots were fired?"

"A lot. I don't know specifically yet."

"How did the two dead guys get to Rubidoux? Did you find any car or truck or scooter that they may have abandoned near the scene?"

I could sense the sergeant went on alert when I mentioned "scooter."

"We found an abandoned vehicle we believe was used by the two victims."

"What do the next of kin say about all this?"

"Obviously, they were pretty broken up about it," Peters said.

"What do you think could have been the motive?" I was fishing.

"A woman?"

"Nah."

"Drugs?"

"Not sure, but we're exploring that."

"What about a motorycle gang war?"

"Why do you think that, Skip? Who told you that?"

"Nobody told me anything, except the neighbors say there are a lot of really bad dudes on choppers that come around that house from time to time."

"We don't know what the motive is."

"But do you have some good guesses?"

"Skip, mi amigo, lighten up man," Peters said. "We're getting close, and you'll be the first on my list to call when I have a new development. I gotta' go now. CBS wants me to give them a live telephone update in five minutes."

"Sergeant, what are you going to tell them that you haven't told me so far?"

"You got more than I'm going to tell them. Trust me," Peters said, treating me like he was my close, close buddy.

I left feeling the story was moving forward and pounded out an article that the metro editor wanted to keep short, taking up no more than 10 column inches. Afterwards, I sat down next to Ed who just began his shift.

"Ed, this case is really weird."

"Skip, I don't have time to go over this right now. Send me an electronic memo of everything you did today, and I'll call you tonight with some ideas about what you can do next."

Ed was right. Think two or three steps ahead. I told Stuart that I was going to drop by the Rubidoux shooting scene and talk to the neighbors again.

"Skip, take our news assistant Juan with you. Your Spanish is nada, no muy bueno, muy shitto."

"Roger that."

We spent several hours knocking on doors. Juan's fluency helped immensely. Neighbors confirmed the biker angle, but really had little to add that I didn't already suspect about the case. The victim who lived at the duplex was not home much, one neighbor said. And it was curious that the couple who lived in the adjacent unit was moved out by the county and put into a nicer place a mile away, the guy told me. Everybody in the neighborhood was jealous. It was pretty strange, one said.

Nobody was at the duplex where the shooting occurred, although the carport had been sealed with a huge tarp to keep out the lookie loos. Juan and I walked around the perimeter, and figured two people were trying to break into the rear carport door from the looks of the splintered frame and bullet holes.

The blood where somebody had fallen wounded at the rear of the carport had been washed away, but I could tell what had happened.

"It looks like an ambush from the rear," I told Juan.

We were leaving when I thought to check the old aluminum mailbox at the street. Inside the box were handfuls of junk mail, all addressed to "Resident."

I had to remember to check the county recorder's office the next day to see who was listed as owner of the property. I needed to get an early start.

No sooner had I got home, the phone rang and then my cell phone. Which phone should I answer first?

Stuart was calling on my house phone.

"Hang on, Stu. My cellphone is ringing."

It was another editor. That editor wanted to know why my story was not exactly 10 inches. Instead of screaming, I politely said it would be okay to trim the extra paragraph at the bottom of the story.

Now Stuart: "Did you check out the dead guy's house in Hesperia? Maybe talk to his family?"

"No I didn't have time to get around to that." They wanted me to work 24 hours a day, but none of it on overtime.

"Shit Skip. That's a major hole in your story. I'm going to let you have two hours overtime to drive up there and get a comment from the family."

"Stu, It's an hour's drive one way."

"I can only afford to give you two hours. The clock's running. Call me when you get there and get somebody."

I grabbed Ginger and took her with me, something she loved to do. The dog curled up on the passenger seat to nap. Despite my GPS and map, I still got lost. It was dark by the time I found the general area.

The house was a disaster. Litter was strewn all over the front yard. One window was covered by cardboard. The dump needed a good sandblasting and two coats of paint. Ginger was barking so furiously that I took her and knocked on the front door that looked like people kicked instead of knocked.

Chester's grieving widow answered the door holding a can of Coors Light and a lit unfiltered Camel. "Who the fuck are you? Cops again?" She seemed really pissed until she spotted Ginger, who was cowering in fear in my arms.

"Oh, you little cutie," she said in baby talk, grabbing the terrified dog in her arms and clutching her to two very large breasts unrestrained by any bra.

"Mrs. Desmond? I'm Skip Easley from the Riverside newspaper, and I wanted to talk to you about your late husband."

She was petting Ginger with the Camel dangling from her lips. "He's dead. What else do you want to know?"

"Well, who do you think killed him?"

"How the fuck should I know? He's hardly here no more. Got all his buddies he hangs with. Probably pissed off the wrong fucker this time. Put his teenie pecker where it don't belong."

"Well, do you know who he may have been going to see and who else may have gone with him? There were two others shot, one of them is dead."

"Mister! What's your-name? You don't know shit about those boys. I suggest you cool your jets and head back down the hill."

I needed a good quote to insert in the story or Stuart wouldn't pay my overtime.

"Was he a good husband and father?"

The woman thought for a moment to find the right words to convey her love. "He was a good lay, but lousy in every other regard. Put that in yer fuckin' paper."

She gently handed back Ginger and slammed the door shut. I was turning to leave, nearly twisting my ankle on a beer can I didn't see in the dark, when the woman opened the door again.

"Tell those fucking cops down the street to leave me alone!" She slammed the door even harder this time.

Stuart was amazed that I interviewed the wife. He even complimented me.

"Give me a couple grafs," he said.

"Okay, here goes. The grieving widow, who lives on the outskirts of Hesperia, said she had no idea what her husband was doing in Rubidoux the night of the shootings. She also did not know the other two shooting victims, one of whom died late last night.

"The woman said Desmond had been a good, loving husband. The couple has two young sons. She declined to discuss any more details of the shooting."

Stuart was happy as he typed the two short paragraphs. "What about a quote, Skip?"

"Okay. Here's a good one. 'He was a good lay, but not a good, loving husband."

Stuart dutifully typed the quote, then cursed. "Skip we cannot use this quote!"

"Can't you clean it up?"

"Skip I can't mess with a direct quote. If she said this, we have to use it just as you quoted her. Hold on."

I could overhear Stuart asking the metro editor if he could use this questionable quote. I then could hear the metro editor asking the managing editor the same question.

"What did they say?"

"We're going with it," Stuart said. "And I'll probably be fired tomorrow."

Stuart told me he had the research library to do a special computer background check on the dead man's history, and how long he had resided in Hesperia. The computer check found several stories about Desmond's checkered driving habits, one a few years back that detailed a police chase. Stuart said the old news story contained a laundry list of Desmond's convictions: all petty crimes.

CHAPTER EIGHTEEN

I needed to get out of town. See the sights as I thought about what to do with this story. I conned the editors into letting me conduct a routine recon patrol into enemy territory.

I decided to save gasoline and ride the Metrolink into LA on the company nickel. I was getting all these wild ideas about how to flush out sources. And the paper was agreeable to letting me try anything to move my story along.

Riding Metrolink to the U.S. Courthouse in downtown LA was a welcome diversion. Metrolink, which was connecting the greater LA with its countless suburbs, was a throwback to the heyday of the old Red Line which coursed much of Southern California until the car culture became imbedded into Southern Californians' minds and was replaced by an artery of highways and four-lane surface streets.

It would be another blister of a day. The smog was heavy and obscured the San Bernardino and San Gabriel Mountain ranges to the north. The train let me off at Union Station near the courthouse

I told my editors that I was going to visit every courtroom in hopes of finding one in which some grand jury might be meeting to consider federal charges against any of the characters involved in the Brea and Rubidoux shootings.

It didn't turn out the way I thought it would. All I got were annoyed looks from attorneys and court security whenever I opened the door and interrupted some court case.

After an hour of this, I figured my genius plan was a total bust. I found a bench on the third floor and read a discarded newspaper while I tried to figure out what to do for the rest of the day.

Exactly at noon, a courtroom door in front of me opened and men in expensive blue and black suits and red ties poured out and headed for the elevators like kids running to the cafeteria for lunch. A middle-aged guy in a sports coat and tie, holding a pen and reporter's notepad, was interviewing two attorneys as they slowly walked out of the courtroom.

I watched and tried to overhear what was going on. Maybe it was related to what I was here for, but I doubted it. Grand juries meet in private. No reporters allowed. The reporter finished and sat down next to me, going over his notes and scribbling a few lines and underlining a few points as he flipped through pages of notes.

He pulled out his cellphone and speed-dialed somebody, spending a few minutes updating the person on the other end. When he finished, he turned to me and noticed I was watching him.

"Big story?" I asked. Just trying to be friendly.

"Nah, just a pre-trial hearing, nothing special. What are you here for?" he asked.

"I'm Skip, courts writer for the Riverside paper," extending my hand to the guy. "Grant, from The Times. J. Lamar Grant."

"I didn't know there was anything going on today that might interest you guys in Riverside."

"I heard that a grand jury might be hearing some testimony on a case I'm interested in." I don't know if I should have said that to a competitor, but I did.

"I don't know of any grand jury hearings under way," said Grant. "They are always held in secret so you can't really tell when they are going. What case?"

I know he was sizing me up as a hick. I was earning only a fifth of what he was pulling down at one of the nation's most prestigious publications.

"It's a federal beef, obviously it's a federal case or I wouldn't be here." Whoops, stupid slip. "Murder, attempted murder. Man, I can't give you my story!"

"Skip, give me your card. Let me check around, but I know there are no murder trials going on, and I'm almost positive I don't know of any grand jury testimony under way. I'd be happy to call you and let you know what I found out."

"That's cool," I told him as we exchanged business cards. What a nice guy, I thought. Most of these dudes are so righteous they think the rest of the journalism industry is made up of hicks and idiots.

"I've gotta' get a bite to eat, and get back here for the afternoon testimony," Grant said.

"Yeah, I've gotta' eat and catch the 3:40 p.m. Metro back to Riverside"

I left the courthouse and headed down to historic Los Angeles, marveling at the quaintness of this slice of old Mexico in the heart of a modern megalopolis. I browsed through the historic old town and cramped Olvera Street, looking for a cheap place to buy a taco or big burrito.

CHAPTER NINETEEN

Grant was not having a peaceful lunch, and he was not letting his sources enjoy their noon break either. He hot-footed it back to his newspaper and began working the phone to find out something about a grand jury hearing testimony on a murder out in the Inland Empire.

Every attorney, prosecutor, public defender, court reporter, clerk and even one semi-retired judge Grant talked to were in the dark over any grand jury testimony. Grant still wasn't satisfied.

Grant was seated in the outer office of U.S. Attorney Frost, and was ready to sit there until hell froze over. He was, of course, from The Times, and no important public official could ever afford to ignore any reporter from that influential newspaper.

Warren Frost, probably the most important lawman in the state of California, if not the Southwest, would not see Grant until he was satisfied that he had his people research everything that Grant might be inquiring about. Frost had heard through the food chain from his prosecutors that Grant was inquiring about some grand jury. That was the first Frost had ever heard of a grand jury hearing any testimony this week. Certainly, not about any murder or attempted murder.

"'C'mon in, Grant," Frost smiled and ushered the reporter into his vast office. "Ice water? Cold drink? Anything?"

"No, thanks Warren," replied Grant, who had been waiting more than an hour in the outer office. He was used to his sources calling him Grant instead over fumbling with "J. Lamar." The attorney was hanging up his sports coat as if he had just returned from a meeting somewhere. Actually, he had spent considerable time working the phones in his shirtsleeves, and just put on the sports coat for Grant as a ruse to cover his advanced preparations for this interview.

"What's going on?" the attorney began.

"Warren, that's what I'm asking you."

They were smiling at each other. Just like old fraternity brothers.

"What do you need?"

"Look, Warren, I hear a federal grand jury is considering testimony on a murder case out in the Inland Empire. All I want to know is if this is true, and if you can point me in the right direction."

"Grant, my friend. You know I can't do that. Officially. Are we 'off the record?'"

"Warren, yeah, for the moment, just for background, but I've got to work this until I'm satisfied there's no story."

"Grant," the attorney began slowly. "I know of no grand jury investigating any murder in the Inland Empire."

"What about connections to the I.E.?"

"I don't know about that. Not that I've heard."

"What about your assistant attorney, Ms. Gonzalez, I think. Wasn't her husband shot and killed recently? Any connection there?"

"Isn't Brea P.D. investigating that?" Frost asked. "Isn't that a state crime? We're helping the locals because we owe Angela, poor thing."

Frost saw that Grant did not look satisfied with his answer. "Where are you hearing this? I'm curious as hell."

"I ran into a Riverside reporter in the courthouse and he was nosing around like he didn't know his way to the men's room."

"Got a name?"

Grant fished Skip's card from his shirt pocket and handed it to the man. Frost glanced at the name, wrote it down along with the phone number on a yellow legal pad, and handed it back.

"Never heard of him," Frost said. "You know those guys out there. This character is just fishing in desperate waters."

"Well, I'm fishing, too, Warren."

"Can't help you, Grant," and Frost stood, signaling the interview was over. "This was all 'off the record,' right?"

"Right. But you've got to promise me you will call if anything develops."

"You bet I will," Frost said, knowing this reporter was definitely the first one he would call or that would be the end of his career in LA. He showed the reporter to the door. The attorney was anxious for Grant to leave so he could start making some calls again. Goddamned prostrate, he moaned, heading to his private bathroom to urinate. That fucking, stupid name sounded very familiar.

Grant was not entirely satisfied, but he had taken this tip as far he could and came up empty. He had covered his ass. However, he felt good about the efficient way he worked the phone and his sources. He was upset that he had missed the afternoon testimony of the pre-trial case he was tracking. That stupid, fucking Riverside hick had messed up his afternoon.

The federal food chain was chewing on a number of asses up and down the federal legal establishment. The question was no longer whether grand jury testimony was being leaked, which was an offense, but who was talking to this Riverside reporter named Skip, also a breach of policy

Frost was ready to launch an investigation to the bottom of this. Assistant U.S. Attorney Duncan, who headed up the special task force on cracking the prison gang conspiracy, got an earful from Frost, who now wanted an immediate update on the investigation

"You know this reporter named Skip? You been talking to him?" McLaughlin's supervisor was blunt and vengeful. He scolded the deputy for letting his team put him on the hot seat with the federal prosecutors.

"Nah, I only know the guy from saying hi to him once outside court in Riverside last month. He's a pesky SOB, though."

"Let's get some results," the supervisor told Frank, dismissing him like a corporal.

McLaughlin couldn't wait to touch base with Sgt. Heacock back in Riverside.

"How's your deputy?"

"He's coming around. Can't talk still. Scribbling weird notes about actress Salma Hayek coming to his hospital room to pin a Medal of Valor on him. Spelled it Selma Kayah, but the nurse figured it out. Bitched that he can't find the medal, and insists we launch a full-court search for it. He's really serious about the Salma thing! Do you know anybody in Hollywood we could call to have her come out and do that? Be a real boost to his morale."

"You gotta' be kidding me! You think I run with Salma Hayek's people?"

"Well, Frank. You do work the area."

"Heacock! Get serious, man! We've got alligators nibbling at our nuts and you're asking me about Salma Hayek?"

"Well, I just thought it would be a nice touch for the poor guy."

McLaughlin wanted to know more about what Crawford had scribbled in his notepad

"He said, I mean he kinda' wrote, that two guys, one of them this fucker Mongo, shot him after he got a tip from one of his biker buddies that he was being targeted for the hit. He won't say who tipped him."

"That's progress," McLaughlin said . . . "I mean, he's coming around. His memory. But we need that name of his C.I. Keep somebody feeding him notepaper. For chrissakes, get him a picture of Salma. I've got something I gotta tell you about our friendly newspaper reporter Skip Easley, but not on a cellphone. I'll hook up with you in a couple of hours."

"Shit! Shit! Shit!" Heacock said.

They met at a Denny's, and Heacock couldn't wait to share more bad news.

"The sheriff, he's under a shitload of pressure, and is going to release the I.D.s of the victims," Heacock began. "Terry, too. You know, one of our own, undercover detective, nearly slain during the course of a dangerous investigation. That kinda' thing."

"When is he going to do this?" McLaughlin asked. He expected this would happen sooner or later.

"I dunno, but soon. He left it to me to withhold just enough details so that our case is not compromised. I haven't had time to figure it out yet."

"Has the sheriff contacted the feds or anybody on my side?"

"Not yet. He wants me to pave the way," Heacock said.

McLaughlin exhaled a long, drawn sigh and rubbed his eyes. "This is a huge cluster fuck."

"To make matters even worser," Heacock complained, "we've got this goddamned reporter Skip nosing around and fixin' to come up with his Pulitzer story. We gotta neutralize him, make him happy."

McLaughlin had an idea . . . "Why don't you feed Skip the I.D. on Crawford and the unclassified stuff about this investigation?"

"It might cool things down a bit."

The next step was to head to the hospital and interview Crawford. Maybe his memory had improved.

Lying on the hospital bed that had been raised so he could watch television, Crawford with his bandaged head and body looked much worse than his doctors were diagnosing. He would talk again after an undetermined number of oral surgeries. The wound on his side was healing. Doctors said it would be months before he could ever return to duty.

Both lawmen touched his shoulder in a gesture of deep affection for a fellow officer who had nearly been killed by two idiots.

"'Member anything, kid?" Heacock asked his man.

'Uhhhmmmnnnnooooosssss."

Heacock and McLaughlin looked at each other confused. Heacock found the legal pad and pen on the side table and held it for Crawford.

Heacock started raising his voice as if the poor man were deaf. "Write it here."

There were intravenous tubes that hampered Crawford's writing, but he wrote slowly and in big letters.

SALMA

"Mother of Mercy!" McLaughlin groaned.

Heacock grabbed the pad as if to write a note, then realized that Crawford wasn't deaf. Well, maybe he still had a ringing in his ears from the gunfire.

"Terry, we're working on Salma for you."

Crawford nodded excitedly.

"But you hafta' help us find out who shot you!"

Crawford nodded again. He grabbed the pad and wrote: "Mongo. Another guy."

"We know that." Heacock was getting impatient, fearing this was not going anywhere.

"Nasi.". Crawford scribbled and underlined it three times. "Contrac hit." Heacock could forgive Crawford's misspellings.

"How do you know that?" McLaughlin asked "Where did you hear that?"

Crawford wrote "Ernie" on the pad.

"Who's Ernie?"

"Read my reports," Crawford wrote, flipping a page. "CI No. 2".

"OK, I remember now," Heacock told Crawford. "The bikers you were hanging out with in Rubidoux?"

Crawford nodded.

Now, they were getting somewhere.

Crawford wrote "Be careful" and "protect CI" on the pad. He then wrote: "Change is bad ass. He ordered hit."

CHAPTER TWENTY

Heacock and McLaughlin, trying to coordinate an ever-expanding investigation, now had to coordinate a press release. Heacock wondered how many people would it take to make this happen, as he looked at his captain, the public information officer and three detectives all sitting in his office.

"How can we put the best spin on one of our finest being gunned down by the most vile, fucked up pieces of shit in the entire fucking universe?" Heacock asked.

Everybody sat in silence for several moments until the public information office, a veteran sergeant who was tired of working the boonies on the graveyard shift, made a stunning and brilliant suggestion, one that Heacock and McLaughlin already considered.

"Let's call that fucker Skip," he said.

"Okay, what do we tell Skip?" Heacock began, taking a huge bite from a big glazed doughnut that he had eyed since he purchased the dozen just before the meeting. His fingers were sticky and he had sugar glaze on his mouth, too big a chore for one little napkin.

"Well," the PIO Leo Peters offered, "we give Skip a press release that says our guy is recovering well from a gunshot wound inflicted by these two bad guys."

"The first thing he's gonna' ask is why you waited so long to announce this?" McLaughlin said. "What are you gonna' tell him? What are you gonna' say about the other two dead dudes? What are you gonna' say about the investigation?"

"Just remember," McLaughlin said. "You can't drift from the truth. You can withhold some things, but you can't say something that's gonna' be challenged or criticized down the road."

Heacock had another problem. "OK, we give Skip this story identifying Terry and some details of the shooting. We're in deep kimchee with all the other reporters who are going to say why didn't you send out a blanket press release to everybody. They are gonna' scream that we're playing favorites."

"Okay," Sgt. Peters offered. "We leak this through somebody else, and when Skip calls we just confirm it. Does our guy have a mom or girlfriend we can use?"

"Boy, that's just cold," said one detective. "Yeah," another agreed. "That's bullshit. He's one of our own. We owe our guy."

"Okay," Heacock said, turning to his captain for some advice. "What do we do?"

Sgt. Peters had an idea. "Okay, I call up Skip, give him a release that says our guy is in intensive care with wounds and the two guys who shot him are dead. They are bad dudes suspected in the shooting of the Brea lawyer. Right?"

"Yeah, that's good," Heacock said. "Give me a rough draft and let's work on the wording."

The press release was written, proofed, sent up the chain of command, re-written and then re-written a second time. It was nearly noon when the release was finished and waiting for Skip to knock on the Peters' door.

CHAPTER TWENTY-ONE

Change was having a bad case of the hungries, but was too afraid to venture too far from the bar for a hamburger and fries in case the cops were watching for him. This was a major cluster fuck and Change knew he was responsible. He'd hired Mongo to whack the attorney to scare his wife, and he'd sent Mongo and Ace to whack Gunner—just in case Gunner was ratting them off.,

Change was no military tactician. This was no war on terror with all the CIA tricks and gimmicks. Shit was beginning to drip down on his balding head. Just thinking about that image, Change instinctively raised his eyes toward the ceiling as if to avoid another drip.

Change decided his best course of action would be to do nothing. Protect his turf. Do nothing and just wait for the shit to stop dripping.

"Skip, my man. Good to see you." Sgt. Leo Peters, the PIO, was almost too friendly to me. I should have been more cautious, but I was desperate for a break in this story. My editors were pushing me hard, and Ed was trying to keep the dogs at bay while constantly boosting my lagging confidence.

"Just checking in to see if anything has developed, you know, in the shootings."

"Funny, you should ask. Great timing." Peters handed me a press release.

"This is going out pretty soon, but since you are the first to come in, I'll let the local press have first crack," said Peters.

I read the release quickly. "Who else is getting this?"

"You get it first. Somebody else comes through my door, he gets it, too."

"Man, this is just huge. I have some questions." I got the feeling this was too easy and convenient, but I wasn't going to pass up a big story, especially with Stuart breathing down my neck.

"I can't tell you much more than what is in the release."

"I need more than this. Does the deputy have any family?"

"I hear Terry has got a brother," Peters told me.

"What's his name? How can I get in touch with him?"

The sergeant called his secretary and got the number.

"I owe you, Leo."

"We aim to serve!"

I was waiting for the number from the secretary when she offered to call him for me. "He's a former cop, and I don't think I'm allowed to give you his phone number."

I waited and tried to figure out what I'd ask him. "He says he'll talk to you now," the secretary told me.

"Hi, I'm Skip Easley from the paper. I understand it was your brother who was shot in this incident in Rubidoux?"

"Yeah." He didn't sound too friendly.

"Can you tell me a little about your brother and what you know?"

"I can't tell you much. There's so much that's under investigation that I am not at liberty to discuss."

"That's cool, I understand," I told him. "Tell me when was the last time you talked to your brother?"

I needed some good quotes or this story wasn't going to make Page One.

"Terry was an exceptionally dedicated cop. He risked his life as an undercover detective for a long time. You know, he knew he could be killed at any moment from the really bad, vicious people he was investigating. My family is so damned proud of Terry, and I hope he makes a full recovery from this ambush."

What did he mean by "ambush?"

I was asking him more questions, but he begged off and hung up. I forgot to ask him his first name. I think the PIO called him Jeff. Boy, that was a blunder I worried wouldn't bite me in the ass. He did give me a cellphone number and said he'd talk to me later. I'd ask his first name then. The cellphone number was probably bullshit.

"Leo, I need to talk to your detective in the hospital. And what's his brother's first name?"

"Skip, my friend, the guy's been shot in the jaw. He ain't talking to nobody. He writes us notes. Part of the reason we had to delay this release is that Terry was unconscious for so long, then he couldn't talk. He still cannot talk. He's writing notes! Jeff is his brother."

This was good stuff.

"What kind of notes is he sending to you guys?"

"Get this, my man. He was so screwed up mentally there for a time he thought Salma Hayek had come into his hospital room and personally awarded him a Medal of Valor. He's going ape-shit—don't use that word, dude—he's going nuts because he cannot find his medal. Can you believe that shit?"

"That's just too precious," I said. "You gotta get him a medal, though."

"Off the record, we're trying to get him a medal pretty soon. You know, help him recover mentally."

I had to get more time from Leo before he gave this story to my competition.

"Gimme a break, Leo. Let me have this scoop. I really need it, man. If I get scooped on this my editors are gonna' fire me."

"Can't promise, Scoop. I will promise you this. I won't answer my phone for a few hours."

I had to get my editors on the phone immediately. Maybe we could advance the story on the paper's website.

"What's up Skip?" Stuart said, finally picking up his line after a dozen rings.

"The wounded man in the Rubidoux shooting was an undercover sheriff's officer!"

"Wow! Good job, Skip. I told you to call the sheriff. I knew you stirred up a hornet's nest."

Fuck me! Now Stuart wants to take credit for this story. Bet he wants to share a byline, too.

The editors were so excited that they got me going a dozen different directions at once. I was ready to implode once I got back to the newsroom.

Ed came to my rescue and took over before I went berserk and trashed the newsroom.

He nearly was sitting on my lap as we worked over each sentence and I answered every question that came to his mind.

"Do you know how old this Terry Crawford is?" Ed asked. I didn't, but I could find out from the PIO.

I could see my story unfolding with the drama that made me love this fucked up profession.

Ed was reading over my shoulder as I typed the part about Salma Hayek and Crawford's dream of his Medal of Valor.

"Nice touch, Skip."

Ed and I were the focus of attention in the newsroom. Me, the new guy from Seattle, had scored a big scoop. I knew the newsroom would Be filled with jealous reporters. The knives would be out when everybody read my story and they would be nitpicking me for errors.

I was exhausted and Ed was shaking hands with editors. I was mentally numb.

"Skip, the boss wants you to get an interview with the wounded cop. They also want a photo. Can you find any cops who knew him? The boss wants a nice profile of a cop in peril, who laid his life on the line, who stayed incommunicado with his family and friends for so long while he was undercover."

That would take me all day, maybe two, to land that story.

"Ed, we've got a huge story out there, and writing fluffy features isn't going to help us."

"I know Skip, but you've got to give them something really good, and you've gotta' continue delivering good stories if you want to stay on top of this project," Ed told me. "You know Skip, there's not a single reporter in this newsroom that I know of who could deliver this project except you."

For the first time since I set foot in this newsroom, I felt appreciated. Maybe Ed was bullshitting me, but it made me focus on what I needed to do.

"Get me a better story, Skip, and I give this feature to somebody else."

I saw an editor coming toward my desk.

"That was really a sweet touch with Salma Hayek," he said. "It gives this story such emotion, such depth, such gusto." I actually saw his eyes water up.

I checked my e-mail before going home, and there was another message from jjdancer: "Hi Skip. I'm reading your exclusive online right now. You are so awesome. Don't forget you are just scratching the tip of the iceberg. Is that a mixed metaphor? You are the writer, not me. You really should try to reach Angela. If you want, I'll help. Love J."

If I could get an exclusive from Angela about the killing of her husband's murderer, I would have another Page One bombshell and forget the sweet feature on that cop.

"JJ: Call me NOW, e-mail me NOW. Get me Angela NOW!!! All my best, Skip." Was that urgent enough? I learned something from this story. I had to do my interviews face-to-face, not rely on the phone calls. And I needed to be on top of my sources like flies on shit.

CHAPTER TWENTY-TWO

Change read the newspaper story as he drank his morning cup of coffee, slowly going over each word for some nuance that might tell him what the cops were really up to.

The story was not very specific about naming the two dead bikers as the actual killers of the dead attorney, but Change knew the implications were fairly clear over tying the aborted hit on the cop to the other shooting. He wiped his bald head, picked his nose, scratched his itch that was spreading over his abdomen, and nervously grabbed another powdered doughnut from the box on his kitchen table. He munched the doughnut, and decided to finish off the box.

This was not a good turn of events, and Change knew he was going to hear some grief from his superiors. He recognized the name of the reporter on the story as the same guy who had been covering other stories since the attorney's shooting. He read the story a second time, then tore the story from the paper to save just in case he needed to keep pace with the escalating mess that was developing. So his suspicion about Gunner was correct. Nothing but a damned cop, Change thought.

Change thought about every conversation he had with Gunner. Was there anything he had told the fucking cop that could come back to bite him in the butt? It was very possible that Change's little empire was about to crumble. He thought about shutting down his bar and disappearing for a few weeks. He was beginning to worry that he could be under surveillance.

As the day passed, Change was surprised that he had not heard from his superiors or his rag-tag bunch of enforcers in Hesperia. Maybe they didn't know about the newspaper story. Maybe they didn't care. His bar was curiously slow with only a few regulars coming in for his luncheon special of a foot-long hotdog, bag of chips and beer for $2.99.

Just as he was beginning to relax, two men who were obviously cops entered his bar and walked directly toward him.

The men identified themselves as sheriff's detectives and showed him pictures of the two dead hitmen. "These guys ever come in here?"

Change figured they already knew the answer. "Maybe."

"You recognize them?" the one detective said as the other surveyed the bar where a handful of guys drank and talked and watched television. This was a crowd with a lot of time on their hands. Few had regular jobs, and most preferred loafing to physical labor.

"I dunno, maybe," Change answered casually. "I seen them pictures in the paper this morning. I dunno no names, tho."

"You seen this guy?" the other detective said, pulling a picture of Gunner from his pocket,

"Yeah, that's Gunner. He comes in a lot. Nice guy."

"He hasn't been in here in some time, has he?" the detective asked.

"I dunno," Change was poised for the next question. "I guess it's been a while. I ain't here 24 hours a day, you know?"

"Thanks, dude," the two detectives said, turning to leave. Change was surprised that they didn't have more questions.

"One more thing," one detective said. Here it comes, Change thought, the old trick question. He was surprised, however. "Two hot dogs and chips to go."

"Sure thing," Change said. He felt them watching his every move as he prepared the buns and fished out the hot dogs from the roaster. "You want the beer, too?" he laughed. The cops laughed at the lame joke and left him a $5 bill. He was pissed that they had shorted him a buck.

"Keep the change, Change," said one cop.

"Cool." But that recognition of his nickname was a signal. Now, Change was getting a super headache.

Outside the bar, the two detectives wolfed down their dogs and laughed about sticking it to Change. One flipped open his cellphone and called Sgt. Heacock about the development.

"Want us to stick around here, see what happens?"

"Yeah," Heacock said after pausing to think about the development. "See what happens. You got any other leads to check on over the phone while you wait?" Heacock was a supervisor who didn't like his people to waste any idle moment.

Change's current state of mind, which was near berserk, had gotten the best of him. He got one of his regulars to tend his bar and took off in his sedan to make a phone call. The old Dodge Caravan the detectives were using was completely overlooked by Change who constantly checked in his mirror to see if he were being followed.

"Dude," Change greeted his contact, Tommie. "Gotta problemo and we need to chat." He was told to meet at the same In-N-Out in the High Desert as before. "That's good 'cause I'm hungry and no more hotdogs today. There in 45 minutes."

By the time Change drove to Interstate 215 and headed toward San Bernardino, the detectives knew they were heading out of their jurisdiction. Heacock told them to continue the tail, and alerted the feds about their lead and what was developing.

McLaughlin thought this was the perfect opportunity to call for some air support. He got permission to enlist a U.S. Marshal Beechcraft out of Burbank for the pursuit. It would take at least an hour for the rendezvous, but the feds' aircraft had all the latest surveillance equipment that might help them locate and identify whoever Change was going to see. Too bad, the detectives did not have time to plant a GPS locator on Change's vehicle.

Change was waiting for his contact in the parking lot of the In-N-Out when the Caravan pulled into a nearby parking lot. McLaughlin and Heacock each heard the detectives' transmission about a beat up 1956 Ford pickup pulling into a spot near Change. This vehicle,

McLaughlin thought, sounded familiar to him, maybe the one had he spotted tailing him a while back.

Change and his contact did not go inside the restaurant but conducted their business quickly and departed. Except Change suddenly changed his mind, and went inside to order two Double-Doubles and fries. The pair of detectives was told to follow the Ford pickup. It soon became too dangerous to continue the tail as the road the pickup followed became more remote as it moved out of town. The detectives turned over their surveillance to the circling aircraft that had just joined the hunt.

The aircraft's team soon radioed the license number on the truck, which McLaughlin began tapping into national databases on his laptop.

The truck came back registered to Sandra Smith, a 51-year-old woman with no record and apparently residing in a duplex in Hemet, not far from the Metropolitan Water District's giant reservoir at Diamond Valley Lake. The address did not match any existing dwellings on an upscale cul-de-sac, according to their computerized residential locators. Although frustrating, the detectives were veterans of many bum leads, but this was a development that gave them a subtle signal they were homing in on somebody of intense interest.

The pickup headed toward a location where continued aerial surveillance was easy, but difficult to coordinate with air traffic controllers as the truck traveled down the Cajon Pass and eastbound on Interstate 10 toward Palm Springs. McLaughlin was worried the plane might need to refuel if the pursuit continued for hours and hours. An hour later, the truck turned toward Desert Hot Springs, a town that had seen better days since it was an oasis for sun-lovers. The truck parked on the front yard of a big rambler on what looked like a five-acre parcel, facing a dirt road that was not on the cops' road maps. There were several out-buildings near the house that the air surveillance team photographed and e-mailed back to McLaughlin, who was downloading the files on his laptop as quickly as they were sent. The team recorded the coordinates so that McLaughlin and his team could do some research on property deeds, and then track them through their databases. It was general knowledge among detectives that methamphetamine dealers loved to use these very remote locations to cook their batches of illicit drugs.

McLaughlin decided to send a team down the road in front of the suspect's house, and toss out a miniature camera hidden inside a crumpled beer can near the driveway so that they could keep an eye on the front yard. That would have to be done late at night so the suspect could not get suspicious about any strange vehicles or people coming to his neighborhood.

If McLaughlin could not find a friendly neighbor of the suspect, they would have to try some other innovative way to get a surveillance team near the suspect's house.

This was going to take some time and some intense planning to launch the surveillance mission. These cops had tried many different ruses over the years. Sometimes they worked; sometimes they didn't.

McLaughlin was positive they were closing in on their target. It made him uneasy knowing that the pickup driver had gained some inside information that pinpointed the general location of the safe house. Somebody had tipped off the bad guys, he thought.

McLaughlin and Heacock linked up at the sheriff's precinct to plan how they could take a closer look at the dude in the pickup. A young female detective, Sue Dominguez, who was brought in to help the expanding investigation, came up with a creative idea.

"Get a Latino yard-cleaning crew to knock on the door and solicit some clean-up yard work."

This was perfect, the detectives agreed.

"We're going to have these suckers trembla en su pantalones," the woman laughed.

"Huh?" all the detectives chorused.

"You know, trembling in their pants."

"Que bueno, que bueno!" Her choice remark made her an instant hit with the team. Heacock decided she would be perfect to serve as the lead on the yard crew's stakeout. She could pretend to be the only one of the yard workers who spoke English.

"Shall I dress down or go like this?"

"Short skirt! Tight sweater!"

"Okay, let's launch this tomorrow morning. Everybody meet here at 0600," Heacock said.

Everybody was nervous about too many people knowing what was up.

More convinced than ever, McLaughlin believed there was a leak somewhere that affected his detail and was endangering Janelle and Angela. Nobody believed in coincidences. He headed back to the safe house to double-check the security. The two women seemed in a great mood, and that brightened his own.

"Hey girls, how ya' been?"

"Frankie, my darling," Janelle cooed. "My knight in shining armor, my savior from this fucked up boring life I lead."

McLaughlin affectionately squeezed her arm and walked toward Angela, who looked relaxed and comfortable in shorts and tank top. McLaughlin gave her a consoling hug, but was worried over his poor grooming and locker-room smell from working in the grueling summer heat all day.

Angela wanted to talk. "I've got to get back to my job, Frank. I can't stand sitting around here any longer. I'm going nuts here. Why can't I leave? Nobody's going to touch me now."

"Angela, and you, too, Janelle. I'm afraid things are gettin' tense. We may have to move you two to another house or split you up. I was telling Manny that we now know one of the people we're looking at was just down the block some time back. This place may be compromised. We'll stick it out for the time being, but I may need to double the security here."

"Frank, Janelle's got a great idea we want to bounce off of you," Angela in a not-so-subtle sexy tone intended to fend off any objections.

"What's up?"

"You know the reporter Skip?"

That name was not one that Frank enjoyed hearing.

"I think we can use him and the power of the press to move this case along a bit faster," Angela said. "Janelle can help."

"Girls, girls," McLaughlin protested. "You don't understand how critical this shit has become. We're in a shit-load of trouble if we screw up what we're working on this very moment. I shit you not. I can't emphasize that we are at a make or break point."

"C'mon Frankie," Janelle said. "Just listen to our plan. It's mostly Angela's idea."

The women told the deputy that they wanted to let Skip interview Angela about her situation, and let that be a means for keeping the pressure on the bad guys with another series of news stories. Let Skip interview Crawford, too, Angela said. Give Skip just enough information to keep the story in the public's eye.

"I'd have to clear this with everybody, and who knows how long that would take. I would bet my last nickel they will say definitely nada, nada and muy nada," McLaughlin said.

"What if you say you never knew about it?" Janelle asked. "What are they gonna' do, lock us up in a safe house?"

"What are you going to tell him?" McLaughlin felt himself being manipulated by these two very persuasive women. And he was so hot and tired and he just didn't feel like arguing.

Angela told McLaughlin that she could tell Skip that she is still mourning the loss of her husband, felt somewhat safer with the killing of the suspected assassin, and was confident that the case would be solved very quickly

His head was throbbing with a massive headache. Maybe his judgment was impaired, but he just looked at them numbly and shrugged his shoulders in a show of surrender.

The stakeout was on his mind. He relented to the women against his better judgment, shaking his head in resignation and walking off to take a shower.

"Okay, okay," he shouted to them from the hallway. "Don't tell me too many details. Fuck it! Tell me nothin.' Just don't compromise what we're doing or let this reporter know anything about this safe house. Clear?"

The women were excited to be doing something other than waiting for Frank to visit them. They went to the patio and began plotting their sales pitch for Skip. The first thing Janelle suggested was to contact Skip by e-mail and ensure that he would communicate quickly and agree to their terms.

For once, Janelle got a quick e-mailed answer from Skip.

Janelle and Angela teamed up to write Skip an e-mail with Angela's statements about her response to Dan's murder. Remembering Skip's stalling on the Tacoma dancer story, Janelle wanted a solemn promise that he would do the story. And she threatened to give it to CNN if Skip didn't swear he would publish the story.

Janelle's message was returned immediately with Skip begging that Angela call him on his cellphone.

CHAPTER TWENTY-THREE

All this negotiating with "JJ" and Angela was driving me nuts. I couldn't even relax at home. I didn't have a personal life any more. I had these two good-looking women anxious to talk to me, except they were in cyberspace. I sat staring at the screen, waiting for something to happen.

My cellphone's ring startled me.

"Skip, it's Angela." She was all business. That was disappointing. But it was my cue to be just as professional as she was.

I took notes, interrupting her only occasionally to clarify a few points, and was satisfied that I had most of what I needed for the story.

"Skip, Dan's murder is definitely related to Terry Crawford's case. This is very scary to Janelle and me. We need you to keep the pressure on. We need your story."

Thanks for the pressure, Angela. That's all I need now.

"How's JJ? Can I talk to her?"

Did she say "Janelle?"

"That would be awkward, Skip. I've borrowed a cellphone here to make this call. I'm breaking a lot of rules talking to you, but I'm willing to risk it. This story is too important. She's very happy you are working on this story for us."

"I'd like to apologize to JJ or Janelle or whatever her name is."

Another voice, one that I faintly remembered, came on the line.

"Skip. It's Janelle. That's my real name. Honest."

My voice suddenly got scratchy as I tried to be nonchalant. "That's good to know. I do like that jjdancer business, though. Look, Janelle, thanks for your help. I love your e-mails and I'm so sorry I screwed up your story back in Tacoma. I got fired over it."

She was being sweet to me this time. "That's ancient history, Skip. I can't talk long, but I'd like to see you again when all this is over. I've got your number."

I really wanted to see her again. And I hoped we could talk on the phone. It gave me all the incentive I needed to knock this story out as fast as possible. I had to push harder.

CHAPTER TWENTY-FOUR

"Your team all in position?" McLaughlin asked Heacock. They had found a safe place about a mile from the location where the pickup was last seen in front of the house south of Desert Hot Springs.

"Roger that."

Heacock had dispatched his team at 3 a.m. to find a spot at the rear of the suspect's home and hide in the sage while waiting for any action inside. He did not want any chance of them being spotted as they got into position. The detail pretending to be gardeners was waiting for the signal to start its operation.

Earlier before day-break, McLaughlin had one of his deputy marshals creep up to near the front driveway of the suspect's house and place the miniature camera hidden inside a crumpled beer can.

His team radioed that the camera was in place, but that McLaughlin should be wary about contacting any of the suspect's neighbors. Frank decided not to approach the neighbors in the house where the dirt road suddenly ended about 500 yards from the suspect's house.

McLaughlin and Heacock inspected the sheriff's team and their rag-tag Chevy pickup truck and trailer that contained all the tools of the "mow and blow" trade that comprised the industrious yard maintenance industry.

Despite donning raggedly clothes, the so-called day laborers didn't quite look like the lean, industrious and fast-working Latinos who normally do the heavy work for these landscaping businesses.

McLaughlin tried to download the video feed from the soda can from his laptop.

"Aw, crap," McLaughlin said, turning the laptop so Heacock could see what he was looking at. "I don't know what we're looking at, but it ain't the front fuckin' door."

Somebody had kicked the can out of place that morning. The lawn maintenance team was told the canned camera was not a very good option, and to eyeball the neighborhood closely as they went house to house looking for work

Deputy Sue Dominguez, the sole female of the four-person detail, was chosen to be the lead person who knocked on the doors of each house, soliciting for help. Her crew tried to look the scruffy role of day laborers by not shaving that morning, sporting straw hats, faded t-shirts and worn-out blue jeans. They looked too well-fed and tall to be immigrant workers.

Dominguez decided to use her best lilting Spanglish, unbuttoned the first two buttons of her blue work shirt, and knocked on the first door of a rambler with red tile roof on the pot-holed street that was more dirt than asphalt.

"Buenos dias," she greeted the guy who opened the door. "Habla Espanol?"

"Nada baby," the middle-aged guy answered with a smile.

"You need us to cleeen yer yard? Really cheeep?"

The guy started laughing so hard he began coughing.

"No money, honey."

"Okay, gracias"

"This place is a shit-hole, but I ain't gotta dime to pay for no work," he said. The detective surveyed the mostly weed-strewn yard—the only green visible—and decided to try again.

"Lotta' trash here," she laughed.

"I got more shit to haul off than you can fit in your pickup. No money, honey." He waved and closed the door. Probably had a batch of meth cooking in the kitchen, Dominguez thought.

Next house was down about 50 yards and across the roadway, not far from the target house. Nobody was home, or if they were, they were not answering.

They pulled the pickup to a spot in front of the target house and all eyes scanned the dirt for the miniature camera inside the can. Dominguez went to the door of the rambler sitting amid a pile of construction debris, an old couch, bags of crushed beer cans and bottles. A beat-up Chevy in gray primer, cheap chrome wheels and tires that looked like they were worn out re-treads, was parked in the driveway on a short concrete pad. The suspect's '56 Ford pickup was gone.

"Buenos dias," she told a balding guy with stringy salt and pepper hair and a week's worth of stubble on his face. He did not answer until looking up and down the street, and eyeing the yard crew standing by their pickup.

"Whattaya want?"

"We need work. Cleeen yer yard. Haul trash. Very cheeeep," she answered sweetly.

"How much?"

"Twenty an hour," she answered.

"I got no cash. You take a check?"

"If eetz goood to cash," she said.

"Lemme think. Hold on." He closed the door.

Within minutes, a heavily tattooed skinny guy wearing no shirt opened the door, momentarily startling the detective. He looked her up and down, stared at the crew and closed the door again without a word.

The first man came out the door, carrying some old flip-flops that he dropped on the ground and adroitly stepped into. "County been around telling me to clean this place up, but I ain't got no time. You got lawn bags?" She nodded affirmatively. "C'mon and I'll show ya' what I want dumped."

He walked her around the front and backyard, pointing out old tires, cans and debris he wanted to remove. Dominguez spotted the Ford pickup parked in the back, almost adjacent to a sliding glass door of the house.

"I got a half acre and you could spend five months and still not clean this shit up," the man told her. "I'll give you an extra tip if you do a good job. Bad job, muy malo, senora, and no peso. Comprende?"

Dominguez nodded and pretended she was overwhelmed by his generosity. The man disappeared into the house, but continued to watch them from his front window. Dominguez shared the news that they actually were going to do some hard manual labor on this gig.

"If he's gonna give us a check, we can use it to help ID these guys," one detective said quietly. "Let's see if we can re-position the camera," a second one added.

"Remember," Dominguez said. "They're watching us. We're just here to observe and take notes. No problemo, eh?"

The four of them divided up the front and back, carrying some burlap bags that would carry more than the typical plastic yard bags. They were careful not to wear gloves so as to not arouse suspicion that they were anything but hard-working immigrants fresh from an illicit border crossing.

The crew was actually working up a sweat as the morning sun began roasting the desert with 88-degree heat—and getting hotter by the moment. They even whacked some of the huge weeds in front, making a big pile of trash to eventually toss into the pickup's trailer.

McLaughlin and Heacock, a mile away, watched them from a small video surveillance camera that had been positioned to the side of the pickup. "Do you think we got close-ups of those two dudes?"

McLaughlin was nervous and glued to the laptop. "I dunno. We're screwin' the goose if we didn't."

For two hours, the four workers picked up trash, bagged it in huge burlap tarps and tossed them into the pickup and trailer. They were able to secretly re-position the miniature camera beneath sagebrush behind the house, and were preparing to leave.

Dominguez, her sweat dampening her shirt around her breasts and back, went to the front door to get their money.

"Dos horas. Forty dollars," she smiled at the first man who had promised a check.

"Lemme see what you did." He walked with her around the front and back, inspecting the place as if it were a Laguna Beach estate overlooking the Pacific. "What's that?" he pointed at an old Baby Ruth wrapper.

Ah, dios," Dominguez responded, stooping to pick up the wrapper and catching the guy looking down her half-opened shirt. What a creep, she thought. But giving him a peek at her breasts might be enough to sweeten the deal.

They walked in front of the house where the man pulled out a folded check from his old shirt breast pocket. "Gracias, muchas gracias."

Dominguez opened the check, saw it was written for $50, and then thanked the man. Her crew was standing by the pickup drinking from old Gatorade jugs filled with lukewarm water. They doffed their straw hats and bowed to the man standing near his front door.

"Let's go over what we've got," Heacock said after gathering the re-con team a safe distance from the target house.

McLaughlin and his investigators quickly came up with property records of the house and a possible lead on the owner, whose age matched that of the first man who answered the door.

"Guy's name is Charlie West, d.o.b. 5/23/56. Record for methamphetamine, child endangerment, theft of auto parts and forged checks. Did a few years in the joint. Delinquent in his property taxes, filed for bankruptcy twice and is so far behind in spousal support his three ex-wives have given up," McLaughlin reported, reading from his laptop screen.

"Guy's a loser big-time," Heacock said. "Is this the kinda' guy who hooks up with a bunch of bikers?"

Just then, the hidden team called that the suspect was leaving in his tricked up Ford, lowered with over-sized tires and chrome wheels that sounded like an anxious Harley-Davidson. "Which way?" Heacock asked. "Can't tell. Heading toward front of house. That road dead-ends, so they gotta' be coming your way."

The surveillance team could not get organized fast enough to track the Ford pickup.

However, they had taken a small step forward in their investigation. At least, they had eyeballed the two men, possibly gotten pictures, and canvassed the neighborhood.

The house was recorded in the name of Charlie's elderly mom, who lived in Corona. He was a loser as soon as he dropped out of high school. According to a probation report, Charlie had gotten his high school sweetie pregnant and found a job changing oil at a fast-service auto lube shop where he had a habit of showing up late for work and leaving early. His mom kept bailing him out financially, paying the rent of his studio apartment and buying groceries for the hapless couple.

Life never improved for Charlie. He lived with four other women over the next 15 years, fathering another six children. His last wife, with whom he fathered two mentally disabled sons addled by the drugs that their parents had used, currently was serving 10 years in state prison for manufacturing and selling methamphetamine.

To nobody's surprise, the check that old Charlie had written was completely worthless. He had bounced four other checks from his account that month, and the bank was ready to close out his account and notify the local police. The check was more than bankable for the cops, however.

CHAPTER TWENTY-FIVE

I was on a roll when I delivered the story about Angela's plight. Another Page One story for Mr. Skip Easley, who may not have to worry about his probation. I was feeling more confident at this paper and other reporters were friendlier. I liked being the center of attention again, just like I was in Seattle. I felt like I was the paper's go-to guy, somebody the editors could depend on to deliver the big one.

The story had a soft lede for the first paragraph, but I liked it.

She spends most of her days waiting by the phone at a secret location, hoping to hear some good news that may unravel why her husband was slain earlier this month by suspected gangsters.

It is no longer safe for her to work as a federal prosecutor in Riverside and Los Angeles federal courts. She fears she may end up just as a number of other victims in a widening federal and local investigation into an underworld of assassins and assorted criminals.

Angela Gonzales, a veteran prosecutor, is in hiding as lawmen search for accomplices in the murder of her husband Dan that could expand to other as yet unsolved murders, assaults and assorted crimes.

My story provided much more detail on the shootings in Brea and Rubidoux, and the murder of the topless dancer in Tacoma that I earlier covered and then flubbed. I even talked to my old Tacoma detective friend and got a quote that the case is moving along.

The story came out pretty much as I wrote it, much to my surprise. For a change, my editors weren't fucking with me. Ed called me at home and urged me to keep pushing. I needed his constant reassurance, and he seemed to be there when I needed a push, and then he was always there to heap on the praise.

I got some nice e-mails from Janelle and Angela, and my cop sources didn't seem to complain too much. I know they were trying to protect Angela as much as possible.

I spotted this one e-mail. This one was brief. "Nice job sucker. Get ready to duck."

Was that a threat? Bring it on, Bubba. I killed out the message and decided to make my rounds at the courthouse and bask in the limelight of my blockbuster story.

CHAPTER TWENTY-SIX

Change read Skip's story while consuming a half dozen freshly baked blueberry muffins that he mixed from a box. He was glad that he didn't bake bran muffins that he originally planned for breakfast.

Change was groaning with alarm as he read each line. "Ohhhhhhhhhhmygod. This is bad . . . ." The horrible rash had now spread around his belly button. He was in agony, both mentally and physically.

He turned on his favorite National Public Radio station and sure enough, the story had been picked up. "The heat is on, according to federal law enforcement officials," the news reader announced.

Change disregarded strict protocol and called his enforcer in Desert Hot Springs and his superior.

"You hear?"

"What?" It was a voice he heard only on urgent issues.

"The news."

"I don't listen to no news."

"Get a paper or listen to the radio."

"I don't give a shit."

"You will when you read this."

Change read most of the story to him.

"Call that sucker and tell him to write no more 'bout that. What's his name? Where does he work? Let's give him a little howdy. Get rid of him."

Change liked to make money while watching his enforcers do their dirty work from a safe distance. He was a sidelines kind of guy, but his superiors were forcing him to the frontlines. He preferred keeping his hands as clean as possible. They were beginning to get a little soiled.

After he sent the threatening e-mail to Skip, Change walked from his living quarters into his bar in hopes of eventually finding a few scraggly patrons in need of some freelance work. His nimrod enforcer up in the desert was not his first choice for this job. Change needed to enlist somebody to do some dirty work, but one so unlikely that the cops wouldn't come back to him for a visit.

A Friday afternoon, the bar was beginning to get busy and would be hopping that night. He figured he could twist some arms of some of the heavy drinkers in need of some cash for the weekend. A friend of Change's at DMV, who was hopelessly deep in debt, ran Skip's name (only one Easley in Riverside) and came up with an address for $500.

Somebody was screaming for another beer. "How ya' doin' buddy?" Change remembered this guy was fresh out of county jail for a slew of speeding tickets.

"Tony the Tiger," the half-drunk patron introduced himself to Change with a smile that revealed a missing front tooth. His other front tooth would rot away soon. "Been busy."

"C'mere," Change said, waving Tony to the side. "Ya' need some cash?"

"Always, dude."

"Take this guy out and come back and see me," he said, handing a faxed copy of Skip's driver's license and photo i.d. "Wait till early evening when he gets home. He drives an old cherry lookin' Camaro."

"Dude," Tony said, slapping Change on the back. "Tony's ya' daddy."

Change made the mistake of filling Tony's beer glass again and again. Tony looked okay to Change, but a busy bartender on a Friday can be excused for making an occasional miscalculation on sobriety.

Change called a cab for Tony, thinking the numb-nut loser would go home and sober up before heading out on his assignment. Tony the Tiger had other ideas. Get the job done fast, that was the most important message he learned from a father who knew how to booze.

Tony the Tiger, who Change would learn later had earned his moniker from observers who saw Tony at his drunken worst, took the cab directly to the address that Change had given him. He had not sobered up by the time the cab reached an apartment complex not far from the University of California, Riverside, campus.

Tony had no clue where he was headed and a fading image of what he was supposed to do. The cab driver kept looking at him from the rear-view mirror, and wondered whether this fare, which looked as though he would throw up on his back seat, would ever pay him for the $40 that was fast accumulating on the meter.

"Here we are," the driver announced.

"You shitin' me? This ain't it, is it? Tony asked the cabbie. Mentally, Tony was not at his prime for this gig. "This ain't even a decent dump."

That pronouncement had no meaning to the cabbie who was used to the incoherency of some of his clientele bent on getting from one bar to some other destination where they could sleep off a good buzz.

"This is it, my friend," the cabbie assured his fare.

"Hold on a minute," Tony the Tiger slurred. "Wait. I'LL BEEEE BOCK." Tony liked to mimic the governor's "Terminator" line as much as possible.

"Not long, my friend," the cabbie replied. "I have other fares to take care of. I'm a busy man, my friend."

Tony struggled for another sentence and could only find one word for the cabbie. "Back."

Tony just stood there looking at the side end of the modest apartment complex, then spotted the covered parking area in the rear. He told his feet to move and not to stumble.

In the world of coincidences, Tony's helter-skelter meeting with Skip on his way home from a tough day at the newspaper has to rank as the one of the most unlikely happenings ever to occur in Riverside. Tony could not have planned it any better if he were truly sober.

Tony, barely able to stand erect, showed up just as Skip rumbled into the parking area in his Camaro, which Tony somehow correctly assumed was the target's car. Tony just assumed this was the guy he was supposed to whack and that the gods had placed him before his eyes.

Moving toward the parking area, Tony walked up behind the Camaro and reached into his boot and pulled out a .22 caliber revolver.

"Yoooooou Skip Measley?"

The first three shots went in the general direction for which they were intended. Tony the Tiger was not a proficient killer. Tony's blurry vision was not clearing as he squeezed the trigger again. When he emptied the revolver, Tony just squeezed off another six empty rounds and looked profoundly confused when he heard no BANG after he pulled the trigger.

CHAPTER TWENTY-SEVEN

"You fuck, you shot my car!" I was screaming and profoundly annoyed. My mind was not focused for this sudden interruption. I was day-dreaming about what Janelle might look like without any clothes. One second I'm seeing her boobs and another I'm hearing what sound like gunshots.

I've been shot at before, except I was prepared for it and ready to duck. Some idiot takes a pot shot at me and breaks my car window and I didn't know whether to fall flat on the pavement or chase the mother-fucker.

This guy took off running down the parking lot toward the street and I took off after him. Where was my M-16? And then it hit me: What the fuck was I thinking?

"You fucking asshole! You shot my car!" I stopped running when I remembered he called out my name just before he squeezed off all those rounds. The shots sounded like a small caliber, but they could still kill me.

I slinked up toward the street, in full combat mode—without any clue what to do—and heard a car door slam. I saw a taxicab speed away. Here I was, a combat veteran of a very brief Gulf War hiding behind a bush at the corner of my apartment building. I felt like a failure for not doing something more heroic, like tackling the bastard and holding him for the cops.

I walked back to my wounded car. Windshields can be replaced, although my insurance deductible would set me back five hundred bucks. It was just a reflex when I looked at the front of my shirt too see if there were any bloodstains.

An apartment tenant ran out barefoot and assured me that he had called the police. "Don't worry man. I got a description," the guy told him. "Tall, weird, drunk white guy," he said triumphantly.

Wonderful. That matches the description of my dad. My mind became a fog. Maybe wanted to rip me off. My heart still pounding, I sat on the lawn and waited for the cops to arrive

I knew Friday nights in Riverside are not as heavy with action as in East LA, but the Riverside police shift is typically busy. It was an hour after the shooting until the officer finished the basic information. I heard him call his supervisor on his cellphone about the status of the shooting and drove off to the next call.

"Victim is a journalist for The Press. All shots missed. Suspect seen running for the street and got into a taxi. No other description than white man, 20s or 30s."

I could tell the cop on the other end was asking for my name

"Skip Easley," the officer radioed back looking at me. I waited for a response over the phone, like That award-winning journalist.

"He says he's a courts writer."

"Nothing on Channel 2? 10-4, roger that."

The officer turned to me.

"We're keeping radio traffic to a minimum on this. Why? I dunno."

I calmed down by the time the cop's lieutenant showed up, interrupting my dinner of jelly beans and a Diet Coke. Ginger, who always ate better than I, was so happy from all the attention of each officer coming into the apartment. Ginger, don't you know your master almost got killed? I was annoyed that my only buddy wasn't more sensitive to my situation.

"I'm Lieutenant Ferguson. You Easley?"

"Yes, sir."

"What do you make of this?" Ferguson asked me.

"Fuck if I know. Sorry I don't know, sir."

"Anything to do with your work?" Ferguson went over to my coffee table and picked up the paper with my Page One story of Angela. I was saving it for my scrapbook.

"Maybe some dumb-shit guy who just wanted to rob me." I had a gut feeling I was wrong, but I just needed the lieutenant's feedback that maybe this was some random act.

The lieutenant held onto Ginger tightly as she licked his cheeks and squeaked with joy. "Stay here until we're done."

It was nearly midnight when two plainclothes cops arrived, not bothering to knock on the front door and just barging in. I was in my recliner, holding Ginger and watching television as another uniformed officer sat at my kitchen table monitoring the radio and writing out all his shift reports.

I didn't recognize either Heacock or McLaughlin, but I knew the names. It dawned on me that McLaughlin—without his nice suit and tie—was the deputy marshal I met from the federal courthouse.

"You told this officer that you got a threatening e-mail earlier," Heacock said, without any comforting words after the brief introductions. "This true?"

"Yeah, but I didn't think anything about it. It comes with the territory, ya know?" I was mentally filing all the information that I could use for a story on this incident, in case the paper was interested in my future health. I wondered if the paper would pay me overtime for this.

"Do you still have the e-mail?"

"Nah, I killed it out. Sorry, but it never occurred to me . . ."

"You're in a heapa' trouble," Heacock said. "You dig it?"

Dig it? What 1960s rock group did he play for? "I'm cool, man," I answered, maybe too glibly.

"You understand what just happened to you?" McLaughlin said.

"It's coming to me."

"We've got a pretty clear picture of some heavy dudes trying to whack you, Skip. We can report this piss-ant shooting and you can make a big fucking deal out of it in the newspaper and be a hero, or we can nail this fucking shooter to the cross real soon," Heacock told me

McLaughlin took over. "We can also use this in the investigation that you so righteously reported today, and fucked up, incidentally, and maybe bring some real heavy dudes to justice, like ASAP. Understand that, Skip?"

They were working me. I needed some sleep, but they had my full attention.

"Are you with us, Skip?" Heacock was going to be the hammer on this full-court press on my conscience.

What did they want? There's always a catch.

"You hurt? Just your old car was shot up. No harm, no foul. Keep this to yourself and we'll dial you into this investigation as shit happens. We can make some real book on this little pissant thing," Heacock told me.

"Old car? That's a valuable classic! I've poured a ton of money into it. How am I gonna' drive to work?"

"No problemo, compadre."

They wanted to offer me protection and a safe place to live temporarily. They even wanted me to stay away from work. Forget that shit. Easy for them to say. I was trying to figure out how I could drive to work with a giant gunshot in the back window without some cop pulling me over as a suspicious person. "Okay, if I'm helping you, what's in it for me? Whatcha' going to give me in return for keeping this just between me and you?"

"When we break this case, we call you first," McLaughlin added.

I should have asked how long that might take.

CHAPTER TWENTY-EIGHT

How would my obituary read? Very few career highlights, no tearful tributes from close friends or lovers, and my goddamned newspaper could care less if I got killed. Hell, my mom still thinks I'm working in Seattle. The only thing that really mattered—my little Pomeranian—would be homeless. If they dug up my service records, they might find my Purple Heart was a generous pat on the back from my lieutenant. I was with three other Marines when we were peppered from shrapnel after one of the guys tossed a grenade toward a metal shed where Saddam's thugs were hiding. The grenade bounced like a rubber ball off the roof and onto a stone wall in front of us, exploding just as we all screamed: "Shit!"

I had a beautiful, coveted Purple Heart for a couple of shrapnel wounds in my butt. They call that Friendly Fire, but that wasn't my take on it at the time.

I had to get over all this self pity, so I got a pot of coffee going and went out to get the morning newspaper, hoping the carrier had tossed it onto my doormat that states "Don't Bug Me Anymore." I found a brief story about my attempted murder.

"An assailant fired multiple shots at a Riverside resident getting out of his car, narrowly missing the victim. The gunman escaped on foot." That's it. Nothing more. A story right above it about some kids throwing rocks at cars was twice as long.

I needed to talk to somebody. I wanted to run my normal two miles, but the cops told me not to leave the apartment. I flipped from one sports television channel to another and finally got bored. I almost didn't answer my cellphone.

"This is Skip, can I help you?"

"Eeppp! Eeets Trrreee Crrrerrferrd."

"What? Who is this?"

"Ah-eee gat shaatt. The caap. 'Meemer meeee?"

"I can't understand you, man. Say again, please."

"Sshkkeeepp. Eeets Trrreeee. Gat shaat en da maauth. Rooobidoooo. Memmer?"

It was like a bad light suddenly flickered on. "Deputy Terry Crawford?"

"Ehhh, Skkeeeppp!"

"I'm fuckin' A-OK! You sound like, like, like you got shot in the mouth!" I was screaming into the phone.

"Ahhhh deeeed!"

The conversation became more coherent as I figured out how to translate the deputy's fractured language barrier. He said he got my phone number from Heacock and wanted to call and reassure me that the bad guys were going to get caught soon.

Terry was getting tired of talking. I figured he was as bored to death in the hospital as I was sitting in this apartment with little to do.

"Hey, man, I could write a story about your recovery, and I wouldn't disclose where you are being treated. I could tell people that you are doing okay and that you are confident the bad guys behind the shooting will be caught. I could write a bit about what you remember from the shooting, and all that. And that you're still waiting for Salma Hayek to pin your Medal of Valor on you. All that shit is big news, man."

"Yeeee-haaaa! Saama!"

"You bet, Salma would read this and rush to your bedside, man."

I couldn't make out Terry's exact response, but he seemed pretty excitedly about seeing Salma.

Terry needed to rest from time to time as he answered each question. I had to repeat some of it back to Terry and ask if it was correct.

"Fooknn A!" Terry added a lot of drama to the ambush that had already been covered pretty thoroughly.

I asked about his future, and whether he felt he could return to police work. He told me he was sad that his undercover work probably was finished. If he regained his health, he said he hoped to return to investigating crimes again. He told me his doctors felt he would speak normally again after lots more surgeries. He was beginning to hate doctors.

A nurse came on the line.

"Deputy Crawford's getting very tired and I want him to rest his jaw. He's done enough talking, don't you think?" The nurse was friendly but firm.

"Nurse! Nurse!" I was frantic she was going to hang up.

"Can I talk to you for just one second. Would you be so kind as to take a digital photo of Frank in bed and email it to me? You have your cellphone camera, right?"

"I've got one 'cept it's not here," she said.

"Look, it's incredibly important that Terry get his story told, and a picture of him all bandaged up and in bed would be huge, really huge."

"I don't want to break any hospital rules."

I pleaded as if I were begging for a goodnight kiss on Senior Prom Night. "I don't think there are any hospital rules banning photos of patients, are there?"

"There probably are," the nurse said. "I need this job and don't want to get fired. Look, I've got a lot of work to do with other patients and I can't promise anything. I've gotta go."

"Just take a picture of Terry for his scrapbook, and tell anybody who asks that I told you that I was making a scrapbook for him. E-mail me the photo and nobody will be wiser. I promise you I never reveal my sources."

"Give me your e-mail real fast, bud, and we've never had this conversation, okay? No promises, either."

"Gotcha."

I saved Terry's call-back number on my cellphone, although chances were excellent I would never hear from him again. Except to complain about my story was just the hallucination of a stressed-out reporter.

Something hit me about this story. I really wanted to do my very best because I felt like Terry and I connected like comrades in arms. He deserved all the public adoration from any little feature that I wrote. I felt a sense of duty, something I hadn't felt in 10 or more years. I was a journalist who had a commitment to serve the public. This wasn't just a story to pad my resume or my over-sized ego. Terry deserved it.

The story was beginning to take shape so I could march into work Monday morning and announce my latest scoop.

I was so bored I constantly surfed the Internet and checked my e-mail, hoping to hear from Janelle. "Hey, Skip. Heard somebody took a shot at you. You have to stay safe for me and Angela. We need you in one piece. We hope you are doing okay and let me know ASAP you are okay. Love J."

Janelle wasn't the best writer, but I got her message very clearly. Somebody else cared about me, too.

CHAPTER TWENTY-NINE

Police interviewed the cab driver that took Tony the Tiger to and from his assignment to kill Skip. He was less helpful when told that he may be called to personally identify the shooter once he was captured.

"This is dangerous work, my friend," the cabbie said. "Are you going to protect me and put me in witness protection?" The officer, tired of working no-brainer cases, just stared at the man in disbelief.

The city police were anxious to hand the case over to Heacock's special task force, and promised to help, if ever called. Heacock turned it over to the two detectives who had earlier visited Change's bar in Rubidoux.

Heacock and McLaughlin were energized that Change appeared to be such an important piece in this investigation, but unsure how hard to push the man's panic buttons. There was a chance that Change could be one of the major players. And the guy in Hesperia with the Ford pickup was another key player they were keeping tabs on, but still had not yet identified.

"Ya know," McLaughlin said, "this bartender dude is going to get suspicious when he sees Skip ain't dead."

Heacock's two detectives went back to the Rubidoux bar just as business was picking up late Saturday afternoon. They walked in and sat at the bar, ordering Diet Cokes and worked through a bowl of peanuts. The rough crowd instantly knew the two men were cops. The holstered .38s on their belts could have been a good hint, too.

They had been sitting at the bar when the man they were looking for walked in from the back.

"Dude," one detective began. Change hated that word coming from a cop. Anybody else could call him dude except a cop. It was like calling him a mother-fucker or worse. Change thought he might punch one of them if they called him dude one more time.

"What your name?" he said.

"Everybody calls me Change."

"Whatcher momma call you?" the detective pressed. His partner just sat there with a smile, crunching peanut shells and popping nuts into his mouth.

"My liquor license," Change said, taking down his license from the wall behind the cash register.

The license was issued to Lindsay T. Bartholomew. "What's the T stand for?"

"Tough."

"Lindsay, let's be nice now," the second detective said. "Our records say the T stands for Thomas. Aren't you proud of your name?"

Change, who hated his first, middle and last names, kept control of his temper and yanked the license back from the first detective.

"Lindsay, do you remember a patron last night who took a cab into Riverside about 5 p.m.? Kinda' wasted. Real ugly sonfabitch. Mid-thirties. T-shirt, jeans, scraggly beard."

"Dude," it was Change's turn to insult the detectives. "That sounds like my whole Friday night crowd."

They unfolded an artist's sketch of the suspect and spread it on the bar. "He came back here in about an hour. Took the same fucking cab, can you believe it?"

"Look around, dude," Change said, emphasizing the word dude. "All my customers look like that. This sketch looks more like Charles Manson or Richard Ramirez, though."

As they left the bar, both turned to Change. "Thanks Lindsay T. Bartholomew. If you see this character, you better tell him he needs some practice on the firing range. Six shots. Six misses."

Changed called over to one of his bartenders washing dishes and cleaning off tables and chairs as the cops left.

"You seen Tony?"

"He drank a whole shit load last night, and supposin' he's sleepin' it off today,"

"Have somebody pick 'em up and bring 'em here. Comprende?" He handed his worker a $20 bill and turned away.

Even at 300-plus pounds, Change moved fast when he needed to as he was told that Tony was waiting behind the bar. Change carried an old baseball bat and swung it back and forth as he moved toward the rear exit.

"Tony! Where ya' been, man? I ain't seen no obituary for that reporter you killed. You did kill him, dint cha?"

"Shit, dude, I did a line of meth and I'm sooooo wasted and feel real shitty. I shot em but he got away. Ya' understand, dude. I'm hurtin.'"

Change grabbed him by the T-shirt and picked him up with a flourish that had Tony bouncing on his toes. With his other hand, Change struck him in the stomach with the bat, causing Tony to vomit a stinky pile of intestinal residue on the ground near where Change was standing.

"That's gross, Tony!" Change yelled. Change swung the bat around again and whacked Tony on the back of the head. The two guys Change sent to find Tony picked up the unconscious man.

"You each get $500 if you wrap this garbage up and take him out to the desert and bury him. I don't wanna read about some body being found by hikers. Comprende?"

"What 'de do, Change?" one of the two asked.

"He fucked up mighty royal, dude.'"

They picked up the barely alive Tony the Tiger and tossed him in the back of the pickup as Change watched.

"Jeez, you fuckin' idiots! At least cover him up or tie him up or wrap him! It's prolly a 60-mile drive. Please don't fuck this up, or you join Tony."

The El Camino headed up a road off Interstate 10 near Whitewater in the barren shelf known as the Banning Pass, about 20 miles west of Palm Springs. The road barely had patches of asphalt circling deep dirt holes. The pickup churned through the holes with Tony bouncing in the back like a ping-pong ball. If Tony wasn't dead by now, he surely would die from a severe concussion of beating his head on the truck bed.

More than a little spooked by the terrain near Morongo Indian reservation land, the two deliverymen found a spot that appeared in the moonlight to be suitable for burial. Plenty of rocks were available that probably had rattlesnakes sleeping beneath them. Now, Tony would be buried like any of the pathetic snakes hiding on the desert floor.

"Bye Tony."

CHAPTER THIRTY

I was getting anxious to pop this story on the heroic deputy and decided to call Ed for some advice on Sunday, just so I could be prepared the next morning when I went into the newsroom. Getting the photo from the nurse was a wonderful break. I didn't think she'd send one.

"You have a photo?" Ed was more excited than me.

"Give me an hour and I'll be over at your apartment. I'll even bring fresh bagels."

Ed wanted to read what I had roughed out and called Stuart at home. Stu's first question, Ed said, was whether anybody authorized my overtime pay to work this story over the weekend.

"Fuck it! Let's just forget I ever called Deputy Crawford!"

Ed ignored the tirade. "Let's see what you got." He sat down at my computer and scrolled quickly through the story, correcting a few typos he found along the way. I smelled Ed's exotic after-shave and nervously waited for his reaction to my story.

"You don't have any other voices in the story except this deputy, do you?"

"No, I've just got the deputy's story, and a lot of background from my previous stories on the shooting." I was defensive and disappointed with his initial reaction.

"Skip, we need that stuff or we can't run this story. You've got the foundation and framework. You just need the roof, the siding and the front and back doors."

171

Ed looked at his watch. It was nearly noon. "See if you can reach anybody in the next hour. I know it's a Sunday. Try the sheriff's spokesman. Call the FBI. See if you can talk to Crawford's brother."

"What if I can't get anybody?" I wasn't expecting this extra work, and really needed a Sunday afternoon nap.

"You want me to turn the story over to the weekend cop reporter? She's got all the phone numbers and contacts. But then you share a byline with her. You want that?"

"It's my story, Ed, and I don't like sharing."

"You have an hour. You got all your phone numbers here at home?"

I went looking for the pile of business cards, packed by a rubber band, that I carried home for situations just like this.

I got four law enforcement sources on weekend duty who knew enough about the case to say something fit for print, but not entirely earth-shaking. That was OK. The less they said or knew the better it was for me. I didn't have to work that hard by adding a bunch of "No Comments."

Crawford's brother finally answered his page and called. It wasn't much, but it was enough to please Ed.

Only then did Ed call the executive editor golfing in San Diego, and told him about the new development. "It's a really great yarn, Milt."

Ed finally smiled at me. "Skip, old friend, you did a tremendous job on this. Nobody can match what you accomplished in such short order. Look at it this way, you got to do it your way and worked at home. I don't know how you tracked down Crawford at the hospital, but I'll get all the details tomorrow."

"Ed, I'm sorry you had to give up your day off. You go to church?"

"Skip, the paper is my church. I do enough praying to keep all the nuns smiling when I finish a story like yours. Listen, bud, you got to keep your spirits up. You're on top of the world now, and you are going to be a hero in the newsroom tomorrow morning."

"Thanks Ed. I was beginning to wonder whether you thought the story was worth the effort."

Ed e-mailed my story to the newspaper and trudged off for another day of work.

CHAPTER THIRTY-ONE
WOUNDED DEPUTY RECOUNTS AMBUSH

Undercover officer tells of fending off two would-be assassins

Sgt. Heacock could see the headline when he picked up the paper on his driveway just as he was leaving for work. He was only interested in how the Dodgers and Angels did that night.

From the kitchen, his wife heard his cursing in triplicate. She ran to the garage door and found him groaning as he leaned against his car scanning the story. He knew Skip might write a story, but not this fast. His superiors would not be happy.

"What's wrong sweetheart?"

Heacock's reply sounded like a Nazarine testifying in tongues. Worried, she grabbed the paper from him and began reading about Crawford.

"Sweetie, this is a terrific story about Terry. I don't know what you're complaining about."

Heacock looked at his wife, still in her bathrobe. "You think so?" She had a way of calming him down.

"Terry deserves all the credit in the world, God knows."

"Maybe, you're right, babe. I can't control everything, God knows that."

When he got to the precinct, he was surprised that his team felt the same way as his wife. Deputies were overjoyed that Terry was getting some credit. They felt the department was downplaying Terry's shooting.

"Maybe we outta' stir the shit pot even more," McLaughlin suggested over the phone after reading the story.

"Like how?" Heacock, stretched back in his office chair with hands behind his head, was on the same brain wave but not quite as quick as the deputy.

"Make the bad guys think we know more than we do."

"How?"

"Skip Easley. He loves a good story. Let's give him another big scoop."

"I like it. What would make the bad guys squirm?"

"What if old Mongo was still alive?"

"What if Mongo gave a death-bed confession?" McLaughlin suggested to a dozen cops and lawyers listening in on a hastily arranged conference call to discuss any new developments.

"It's bound to make our bad guys nervous. Won't hurt to see what happens."

"Let's do it," one voice on the speaker phone advised.

A four-page death bed confession was created, but McLaughlin tore off the first three pages.

"This is the meat of it right here."

"Now, what do we do with it?" McLaughlin provided a momentary solution.

"Lemme take this back to the safe house this afternoon. I gotta' idea that might work."

Manny and his team had taken Angela and Janelle to San Diego where they walked along the beach on Coronado Island. These closely supervised excursions were necessary to keep the women from going insane.

McLaughlin, who always looked dog-tired nowadays, changed into his swimsuit and dove into the pool. For the first time, he used one of the upstairs bathrooms shared by the women. He left his clothes crumpled on the bathroom floor, and left the one-page document on the bathroom counter next to the sink cluttered with skin care products that looked like Janelle's.

Janelle, who had been enjoying the pool and patio after the San Diego excursion, announced that she wanted to take a shower and change clothes before dinner. Frank, hoping she would read the document he had left for her, watched the woman climb from the pool in her white bikini, water dripping from a body that appeared that she was sticking with her daily exercise routine.

At first, Janelle was pissed that Frank had used her bathroom and cluttered the floor with his sweaty shirt and jeans. Men were so messy, she thought: That's why she never considered marriage or living with a guy. He probably left the toilet seat up, too. After slipping out of her bikini, Janelle picked up Frank's clothes and tossed them into the hall. The paper on the counter caught her eye.

Standing there naked, Janelle scanned the page that obviously was part of a police report. She read it more closely, realizing that it involved the wounded undercover officer. She was about to talk to Frank about the contents when she realized that she might have unintentionally read something that was classified.

So the cops know more about the criminal enterprise than Frank has so far admitted. Janelle considered putting the page into Frank's jeans. Still naked, Janelle went to the little office nook between her and Angela's bedrooms and copied the page on the official government combination printer-copier set up for Angela. She put a copy in her room, and took the original back to the pile of Franks' clothes and stuffed it into his back pocket.

Her shower took longer than usual as she thought about this development. Angela was torturing her by not letting her call Skip on the cellphone that Angela was granted exclusive use by her office.

Maybe Skip would be interested in this development, if he didn't know about it already, she thought. Before she went to bed, she would e-mail Skip at his personal PC and get his reaction. She wondered whether she should confide in Angela. Angela was getting pretty bossy and might want to manage things in a more bureaucratic fashion. Angela tended to take over the details when they discussed some of the back-door strategies they were considering to help Skip.

Janelle bounded down the stairs to join Manny in the kitchen, feeling sexy and in a mood for a party. Some days she just craved the stage and spotlight where she could dance for hours.

Frank came in from the patio.

"Frankie, you left all your shit in MY bathroom," Janelle scolded.

"Manny was using the downstairs bathroom, and I couldn't wait. Sorry, lady."

McLaughlin later saw the folded paper in his back pocket of his discarded jeans. The question now was how soon would Janelle act.

As they ate dinner, Janelle asked Frank the status of any new developments. Frank decided to bait the hook even more.

Frank cursed Skip for breaking the story on Crawford.

"What do you expect, Frank?" Angela chimed in. "Any journalist would have done the same."

"Is Skip okay?" Janelle sounded worried.

"I don't think he cares about getting whacked, if you ask me. I tell you this. He's just a fucking jarhead who keeps charging forward. Gotta' hand him that."

They talked about the progress of the investigation, and the women pleaded with McLaughlin to speed things up. They wanted to resume their lives. They were tired of the confinement, although their security detail was loosening some of the normal restrictions, mostly because of manpower restrictions. Angela was in constant touch with her office and seemed frustrated doing much of her work via her laptop computer and phone. Janelle was doing some routine paperwork for Angela, and keeping a daily journal of her experiences in hopes of some day writing a book, dreaming that she could make a television appearance on Oprah Winfrey's show.

She began writing a detailed e-mail to Skip who was now becoming the most important person in her turbulent life.

Her e-mail was more personal this time. She told Skip that she was shocked and concerned upon hearing that he was shot at by some criminal.

"Skip, I really hope we can see each other very soon. I would like to get to know you better. We have so much in common, and I feel very close to you now, but it's so strange that we only spent a few minutes with each other those many months ago. Stay safe, Love, J."

Janelle needed to see Skip. Without much thought or preparation, Janelle found McLaughlin working on his laptop in the kitchen. It was unusual that he had not yet left that morning. He normally did all his paperwork and computer details in the evening.

"Frankie, whatcha' still doin' here? You're usually outta here at the crack of dawn."

"I'm real behind in my reports and stuff. What's up?"

"Frankie, dear Frankie. I need a favor."

"Don't ask."

"I really, really, gotta' see Skip. I'm so worried about him. I've gotta see for myself that he's OK."

"Janelle, you know the rules. That's just not going to happen."

"Frankie, you make the rules. You could take Angela and me on a ride and we could just hook up with Skip for a brief visit. You could be our guardian angel and nothin' would happen. Tell, your bosses that we've gone stir crazy. We went nuts. Anything. I gotta' see Skip. I think I'm going nuts for him. I miss him so bad."

"Well," McLaughlin was going to drag this out as long as possible. "Look, Angela has been wanting to visit the gravesite of her husband. You could tag along. I don't want Skip near Angela. That clear? I can't afford another story from Skip that recounts a face-to-face meeting. My ass would be in a huge sling. Understand?

"Be ready to go in an hour. No e-mails, nothin.' I'll call Skip. Understand?"

She was stunned. She never thought the deputy would agree to a personal meeting. Turning to go to her room, Janelle sprinted up the stairs to change clothes. McLaughlin called after her: "Tell Angela I want to see her."

What should she wear? How should she act? Would they have a private moment so she could pass on the police report to Skip? She was in a daze as she changed into some shorts and a crop top, then decided she should wear a skirt or a sundress. Her hair was a messy tangle of curls that she had neglected for the past two months. She worked on her hair, put on some eye shadow and liner, and fretted over the color of lip gloss to match the pink sundress held up by the smallest of straps on her tanned shoulders. Too much cleavage showing? Maybe not enough. This was almost like going on a blind date.

She was ready. But where could she stash the piece of paper for Skip? The slinky sundress was designed to reveal her bosoms, hips and graceful legs, not an indelicately placed piece of paper stuffed down the front of her dress. She could place it in her panties. No, that would be embarrassing to retrieve in front of Skip. She found a small clutch purse and jammed it with her lip-gloss and other makeup.

McLaughlin laughed to himself as he saw Janelle come down the stairs in record time. Of all the women he had known, this was the first time one of them had actually been ready on schedule. Angela soon followed, dressed far more conservatively in white slacks and black top.

"Wait here," he ordered. McLaughlin flipped open his cellular phone and dialed Skip's cell phone.

"This is Deputy Marshal Frank McLaughlin. Meet me in 45 minutes at Riverside National Cemetery."

Janelle could hear Skip's voice discussing some problem or conflict.

"Break it and meet me in 45 minutes. This is very confidential. And don't be late.

Meet me at the National Medal of Honor Memorial."

CHAPTER THIRTY-TWO

"Skip?"

I was expecting a pissed off deputy marshal, but this was that familiar voice calling.

She walked over the big military service emblems on the walkway leading to the memorial and I could see the silhouette of her body barely obscured by a nearly sheer pink sundress.

No need for a rain parka this time. Was it Salma Hayek or was I day-dreaming?

"Janelle?"

She walked to the memorial to the nation's most decorated combat heroes at the center of an expansive walkway. I got up from the bench where Ginger and I were waiting at the edge of a reflection pool. We were surrounded by black granite walls inscribed with the names of nearly 3,500 heroes dating back to the Civil War, each categorized by the war in which most had died in combat.

"Who's this?" Janelle leaned over to pick up Ginger whose appointment with the dog groomer I was forced to postpone because of McLaughlin's unexpected call.

"This is Ginger, my little buddy."

It was an awkward moment because I could only stare at Janelle, particularly when she bent over to pick up the dog and revealed a cleavage that got me thinking about a very lasting relationship. That possibility was clearer when Janelle gave me a bear hug as she held my little dog. Then she kissed me lightly on the cheek.

"I don't know if I deserved that," I told her.

Ginger was licking Janelle's face as if she had known the woman her entire life.

"Ginger has found a real close friend," I said.

We sat on the granite bench, and I didn't know whether to start talking about work or inquire about whether she had time for a quick dash to a nearby motel. "I'm, I'm so sorry about screwing up that meeting we had in Gig Harbor. I'm such a friggin' goofball."

"Yes you were," she replied righteously, holding the squirming dog's face next to her own. "I don't know how much time we have, Skip. I don't know where to begin."

"Gawd, it's so good to see you. I can't imagine what you've been through."

"You either."

I asked her about the last few months and whether she missed dancing, how Angela was coping, and what she saw in the future. We talked for an hour as Ginger found a snug place to doze in Janelle's lap. I had to tell all about my firing, and how my fortunes had improved at the Riverside paper.

"I miss my friends, skiing, hiking and climbing, but I'm beginning to like this place. My only friend is Ginger." I forgot about Ed. But that would need some explaining. I instinctively reached to pet the dog, and touched Janelle's hand as she was grooming the pooch.

"Skip, I hope we have time to get together after all this. But I hafta' give you something that might help you with your stories."

She reached for her pink clutch purse and pulled out a folded sheet of paper, handing it to me without comment.

"That's interesting. Where'd you get this?"

"Can't say."

She could see that was a problem for me.

"Here we go again, Skip. I've giving you some good stuff and you're telling me once more that you can't use it. I thought you learned your lesson."

"You're right. I'm sorry, Janelle. I'll make this work. Just help me with more. I need more pieces."

I saw McLaughlin appear at the opening of the monument, hold up five fingers and walk off.

"Skip I've gotta' go real soon and I don't want to. I need you to help me and Angela really, really bad. I don't want you to get yourself whacked, though. Be careful!"

She was hugging Ginger so close to her face and seemed reluctant to let her go that I said it before thinking: "I want to keep you, Ginger."

Ginger was terrific company, but she was lonely when I was gone for such long spells at work. Ginger would be good for Janelle and Angela. They needed her more than I did.

"Ginger, you wanna' come stay with me?"

"You hafta' get her groomed, though. I was just taking her to the groomer."

I gave her my dog and I got a big kiss on the mouth.

"I want another," I said, holding her tightly and kissing her again. Ginger was getting in the way of what I was hoping could be a nice make-out session on the bench.

"I gotta' go. We gotta' go," she said, putting Ginger on the ground. She stood there in front of me, a breeze blowing her short, skimpy sundress to reveal those dancer's legs. She gave me a long look before she twirled and walked off with my dog. "Stay here, Skip, for a few minutes."

I saw her walk to a car where McLaughlin and Angela were waiting and watching. I wanted to greet Angela. She saw my face and gave me a wave. I saw Janelle burst into tears as she climbed into the back seat.

I should be the one crying. Ginger walked off with a stranger and didn't seem to give a shit about my feelings.

Ed had just come into the newsroom to work the afternoon copy desk and dropped by my desk as he always did as I was studying the paper from Janelle.

"How ya' doin' Skip?"

"Cool, man. How ya' doin' Ed?"

"Just fine, just fine. Whatcha' working on?"

Better tell him now than later, I thought.

"A source leaked me this page from a police report."

Ed found a chair and plopped down as he began reading it. "Where did you get this?"

"From a source."

"I'll need to know who."

I could tell him a topless dancer who had just kissed me on the lips, one I seem to be falling in love with and who has my dog, just handed it to me without saying where she got it. I could be fired if the truth ever got out about this.

Ed read the paper slowly and leaned back in his chair when finished. He just sat there and twirled his bifocals by one stem as he thought about the contents. "When did you get this?"

"Couple hours ago."

"Do you know who wrote it?"

"Nope."

"Do you know what's in the rest of the report?"

"No, but it looks like some kind of update or follow-up report on the ambush of the undercover officer Terry Crawford."

"Any date on it?"

"No, but it reads like it was written within the last week or so."

Ed was being missed at the copy desk, and Stuart soon joined us and wanted to know what was going on.

"I think we have something very important that Skip found."

"Let's go," the editor said, leading us into his office and closing the door.

"Tell me how you got all this, Skip."

I told them I got an e-mail from a source. "We met at the Riverside National Cemetery."

"Why the friggin' cemetery?" Then Stuart mused. "Probably 'cause it's quiet." He seemed to be content with his own answer.

I didn't realize what a shit-fest this piece of paper caused me. One meeting after another. I was getting more nervous with each session. Five key editors, plus Ed and me, went over the report and discussed all the ramifications. They discussed what I could produce in terms of denials from law enforcement. If this purloined page from a police report came from documents that were filed in court, the paper could have some protection because the report was privileged information—covered by being a public document. I told the group I had no idea if this was privileged information.

"Do we really need this story?" said the editor in chief, Milton, the one who hired me and until now seemed to question the wisdom of his decision. "What do we lose if we don't use this?" Milton was a veteran of many leaked documents and an expert on public documents and First Amendment rights.

Ed was the only one who ventured a response. "We could ignore this, but risk getting scooped if somebody else leaked the memo or is getting ready to."

Milton—I didn't feel comfortable calling him Milt just yet—wanted to know whether the newspaper could face any legal fall-out if we printed the document. He called the paper's attorney and put her on the speaker phone.

"My advice," she concluded, "is to go slowly. Be absolutely sure this is genuine and part of the overall investigative report. And if it is not privileged, don't use it."

The editor turned to Ed for advice on how to proceed.

"Skip has already gone over all this with his source. We have what we have."

I was hoping Milton would kill the story and save me from having to answer tougher questions if this report ever was published.

"I don't think it's enough, Skip," the editor turned to me. Oh, thank God, I thought. "Work your source and nudge around a bit for 24 hours and let's meet tomorrow afternoon."

I didn't know how I could verify the report. I read the page again, and knew Janelle stole it from McLaughlin or one of the deputies guarding her. Maybe Angela had given it to Janelle to leak to me. If it came from the federal agents, it had to be true.

I made several copies of the page and hid the original in the pile of papers on my desk. I could start with Sgt. Heacock.

The sheriff's switchboard operator wanted to know why I had to see Heacock.

"I need some advice on where to get my windshield repaired." She repeated the message and hung up.

"He says to wait."

The sergeant came out in his green polo shirt with the sheriff's logo and motioned for me to follow him back to his office.

Howya' been, Skip?"

"Hey, man, just cool. How's Deputy Crawford?"

"Unofficially?" Heacock said over his shoulder as they walked.

"Yeah, of course."

"He's buggin' the shit out of me and the sheriff over when Salma Hayek is coming. He's still hallucinatin' 'bout that. I'm friggin' worried that he's now goin' to want to be on Oprah Winfrey. I don't know what to do 'bout that."

"Why don't ya' just call Salma's press agent. Jeez, get your PIO to do it. It's great PR for the department and for Salma."

Heacock picked up the phone and dialed the PIO Peters and repeated my suggestion. Hanging up the phone, Heacock turned to me with an expression that he was pleased to accomplish something. I handed him the report.

Picking up his reading glasses, the sergeant read the page as if it were for the first time. "Interesting. What do you want from me, Skip?"

"I want you to say that everything in the document is true."

"Skip, where did you get this?"

"Hey, man, you know I can't tell you. I'll die before a name passes my lips."

"Skip, you know I can't talk about any of this. We're at a very critical point in our investigation. Crawford, thank God, survived. We're working 24-7 to find the fuckers who did it."

"Sergeant, can I use that quote?"

"Err. What did I say?"

"We're working 24-7 to find the fuckers who did it."

"Can you use 'fuckers' in the paper?"

"No, but tell me what I can put in the paper."

"You're gonna' use this in the paper?" Heacock looked worried.

"I hafta' verify it first."

"Skip, I can't help you. My hands are tied."

"What can you say?"

"No comment."

I needed to know Mongo's time of death. That might pinpoint when this report was written. I copied the official report at the coroner's office.

I prowled the courthouse looking for familiar faces and maybe somebody who might have some insider information. One elevator was too crowded for me to enter, so I waited for another that followed. Inside was my favorite federal judge.

"Hey, Skip!" the judge told yelled. "Gotta' 40-pound halibut over the weekend in Baja."

"Your Honor, that's just too sweet."

I pulled out the report as we rode the elevator

The judge chatted about his fishing trip as he read the page. When we got to the lobby, the judge handed me the paper and slapped me hard on the back with a big smile.

Was that a validation of the information? I thought it was.

I spotted a sheriff's lieutenant who was such a gossip. The lieutenant, in his jogging shorts and a sleeveless muscle shirt, was out for his noon run through downtown. The lieutenant was running toward me, and was about to pass when I called out. Running in place as he stood, the lieutenant read the page.

"Holy, fucking Mother of Mercy!" the lieutenant said. "Where'd ya' get this?"

"Can't say, L.T." I liked to use military jargon when I chatted up with police officers.

"You can't use this, Skip!" I couldn't believe how excited he became. "This looks highly classified." And then he ran off.

Was this another confirmation? You bet.

"Got anything, Skip?" Ed interrupted an e-mail I was writing to Janelle.

"Not much, Ed. But I showed the page to a number of people in key law enforcement positions. I get the feeling that I stumbled across something pretty hot."

"Any chance that this paper could be in the hands of the competition?"

Any good journalist who wants his story published is going to tell his editor that he spotted the competition following him from source to source.

"No way of telling, Ed. No guarantees."

Ed was ready to go to war for me and asked me to follow him into Milton's office. He was exceeding his role as a copy editor, but was risking his job for me.

"Whatcha got?" the editor snapped at Ed.

"The bottom line, Milt, is that I think we have no choice but to find a way to get this information into the paper. It's just too competitive."

"I'll be the judge of that," the editor replied, almost trying to shoo us from his office. "You just tell me why we need this story. Who's your source, Skip?"

Milton's query startled me.

"I can't say, sir. This source's career is at stake if I name him or her. He or she wants this information out and he or she offered it to me. That person thinks the cops are doggin' on this investigation and he or she wants to light a fire under some of the brass."

It was a lie, and I felt my face numbing as I concocted this elaborate ruse. I had to stop before I got myself into more trouble. I was used to lying when it was convenient and the risks were not as great.

No mom, I didn't take the twenty bucks from your handbag. I never screwed our neighbor's daughter, mom. No sir, I never smoked marijuana, I told my Marine recruiter. Sure, boss, I worked all those hours I logged as overtime. I tried to reach that source, but he wouldn't return my phone calls. I was always a good liar.

This time I had to minimize my lie to protect Janelle, and keep my story alive. It was a righteous lie this time.

Milton wanted details. "Okay, Skip, what are you going to write?"

I told him the story would be fairly bare-bones with the lead paragraph something to the effect that law enforcement got a death-bed confession from the would-be assassin of an undercover officer, and that Mongo was pointing his finger at a clandestine network of criminals who wanted to eliminate an infiltrator who was about to expose them.

The editor mulled this over as the other editors jotted notes in silence.

"You know," Milton said, leaning back in his chair and beginning to smile. "A million years ago I stumbled across something that involved a huge pension rip-off of public safety employees. I just kept pulling the fucking string and the whole thing fell apart in front of my eyes."

"Okay, get outta' here and I want to see a top to the story in 15 minutes." By "top" he meant a rough draft of the first part of my story so that the editor could gauge its news value.

They all filed out with me in procession. "A minute Skip." Milton said. "Close the door."

The editor sat there for a moment and his eyes bored into me as I wondered if he wanted me to confess my duplicity.

"You're doing a good job, Skip. I called your old boss, Mike, this morning and told him that. Mike told me to tell you that he's still got a rusty pair of pliers handy. Now, get outta' here. You've got 13 minutes to give me something."

It was close to 6 p.m. when Ed and I polished the story and prepared it for the next day's issue. Frantic editors were awaiting final approval from Milton who I thought was staring at me from his office.

Milton, however, apparently was reading what I was writing and making suggestions to sharpen it and give it more context. I was getting each suggestion from line editors interrupting my work. Time was running out, although the paper's official deadline was midnight. Nobody wanted to work that late.

I was done and watched Milton walk slowly toward Stuart's desk. They talked near the coffee machine. Stuart walked up to me.

"Milt wants to hold the story for a day," he said apologetically. "He wants to sit on it and let it percolate. He wants to think about it, and have you make some more calls tomorrow. Don't tell anybody we're not running it. Just go home and have a drink and relax."

Ed was dejected, but I was relieved. Maybe something would break and I would have a better handle on that leaked report.

Milton seemed in a jovial mood as I walked past his office. Maybe he knew more about this than I thought. I could be set up for failure.

CHAPTER THIRTY-THREE
June 28, Chino, Calif.

WOULD-BE KILLER GIVES DEATH BED CONFESSION

Says hit was ordered by gang

Skip's story was must reading everywhere the paper landed, and even on the Internet. Heacock and McLaughlin were pleased with the story they planted, although it took an extra day to see it. The media bombarded the agencies with requests for interviews, but everybody kept their word to stick with the "no comment" responses.

Skip's story also fascinated one reader who had a lot of time on his hands. Located about 25 miles west of Riverside is the sprawling home for 6,200 inmates at the California Institution for Men at Chino. The 2,500-acre complex opened in 1941 as California's third state prison to absorb all the overcrowding from San Quentin and Folsom.

Known more simply as Chino, the prison in suburban western San Bernardino County handles all the in-processing of inmates from throughout Southern California's court systems where these men wait to be re-assigned to other state prisons. Sometimes the wait can seem like a lifetime for prisoners whose crimes run the gamut of the California Penal Code. Mainly, the prison houses low and medium-security inmates.

Dean Raley, 24, was waiting patiently for reassignment so he would serve a five- to eight-year term for his second auto theft conviction. He was Charlie's favorite nephew hoped to inherit the Desert Hot Springs house some day if Charlie ever overdosed on his own drugs.

A rail-thin 5-foot-7, Dean, a happy-go-lucky guy who was much smarter than Charlie, served as a messenger for his uncle and was perfectly willing to serve the same capacity in prison as another pawn in his uncle's expanding drug network. Dean didn't know much about his uncle's illicit business, but he understood that Charlie and his friends were trying to work with the super-secret Aryan Brotherhood. This was one of the most feared and ruthless prison gangs in the nation whose power reached out through the penal system and onto the streets of cities where the incarcerated power brokers needed to conduct their business.

Dean, Charlie, Change, and all the other San Bernardino and Riverside area mid-level crooks, were not nearly as smart as the "AB" but were aiming to be just as ambitious while careful not to over-step into the AB's turf. To operate with the AB's blessing, the local group must pay a tax or a percentage of its illicit profits. Dean's job was to pass "kites" or encrypted messages to AB friends in the county jails, Chino, Corcoran, Folsom, San Quentin and Pelican Bay. A conduit of intelligence, Dean found his future assured by helping out other allied prison gang members with tidbits of information. In return, Dean earned status and safety.

The newspaper story Dean read in the prison library where he spent free time studying for his GED became a huge priority as his day unfolded. It was critical that he send a kite up the chain of command. He prepared a note "Mongo talked" that he intended to pass to a "brother" in the exercise yard that afternoon.

There were a score or more "brothers" who could pass the kite along until it reached the boss man who now resided in Folsom, near Sacramento. It might take several days, but there was always some prison bus leaving with a load of inmates being transferred to the various prison outposts in the vast state prison population.

Dean wadded up the kite and tucked it in a partially unstitched fold of his blue prison shirt where the buttons were sewn. During the hour-long exercise, Dean sauntered over to where a group of white shot-callers were gathered and palmed the kite into the outstretched hand of one inmate known to have connections with the AB. "Airmail for the Duke at Folsom."

Dean's mission was complete, but he had committed the news story to memory just in case additional information was requested in subsequent kites.

The kite made its way through the clandestine network of minions that traded favors with the white prison gangs. At Folsom, the kite—artfully inserted in a dental bridge—found its destination the next afternoon in the hands of Marion "Duke" Murphy, 56, a lifer who was serving time for murder in San Bernardino that he committed more than 12 years ago. Murphy and his buddies would now have to repay many favors for the kite arrived in record time—not as fast as an e-mail, but certainly safer.

Murphy, who sported an Iron Cross tattoo on the back of his neck and W P tattoo on the sides of his neck, was used to getting kites from his network and nonchalantly read the note before he swallowed it. It would be another hour before he could find a way to respond to the kite. Murphy, a very cautious man who longed to be a major kingpin in prison, knew he would have to use communication networks beyond his own small network. He needed to find somebody who was scheduled to see a visitor. His request passed along his cellblock until one inmate signaled he was waiting to see his girlfriend.

Murphy worked out a shorthand message that was relayed to the waiting inmate, who knew he risked disciplinary action if caught by the guards or a shiv in the neck from his cellmate if he failed on this mission. The verbal message was coded. CUT LOSSES. PLAN B.

The anonymous man who answered the phone was impatient with the young woman who felt she had to identify herself, her boyfriend, the prison, where she was staying and when she would be driving home to Fresno.

"Lady," the voice interrupted her. "This ain't no counseling office. What the fuck do you got?"

"Freddie told me to tell you that the Duke says you should cut your losses and go to Plan B," she said.

"THANK you, for chrissakes, lady. I'll send a little gift bag tomorrow for your troubles. Freddie will get a nice thank you card, too."

The Duke obviously was pretty pissed over this situation, the go-between thought. An AB associate, who kept a mental accounting docket of all the organization's contacts and business deals, reached Duke's younger brother, Jake.

Jake was working in El Centro, overseeing the manufacture and transportation of cross-border loads of marijuana, methamphetamine and cocaine, as well as coordinating a lucrative trade in stolen cars sent across the border into Mexico. For Jake, the news about Mongo might as well have occurred on the planet Mars. Jake had no clue that everything he had ordered Change to do was causing his brother such concern. Jake didn't know much about his brother's link to the AB, but he made sure he had a tidy bundle of hundred-dollar bills for the AB to pick up at the first of each month.

Jake snapped shut his cell phone and turned up the air conditioner in his brand new Toyota Tundra parked at a Denny's restaurant on the outskirts of the small farming community, where any casual observer would wonder how in the world anything could grow in this climate. Hotter than a tin roof in Kuwait, El Centro is a vast farmland that sustains much of the Southwest's produce markets and employs Hispanics fresh from their border crossings in nearby Mexico.

The agreed upon Plan B that Jake and his brother had devised over a year ago was the basic cut-your-losses move to wipe out any of the mid-level players that might incriminate the two brothers and their expanding network. The mid-tier level or any individual could be quickly replaced without endangering the brothers or their enterprise. If they weren't careful, Jake knew he could be the next one whacked for being any liability to the AB. The Inland Empire connection had become a very critical part of the enterprise that was spreading nationwide in the crankshafts of non-descript cars.

As Jake waited for a drug courier to carry his load of marijuana—one that he needed to verify had successfully been flown to a dirt strip on the Mexican side—Jake contemplated his predicament and decided that he needed to make the three-hour drive back to the Inland Empire as soon as his business was finished.

His drug shipment was off-loaded and sent to a pre-arranged cache. That's where seven Mexicans in the dead of night carrying heavy backpacks began lugging it into the U.S near Calexico. Any sign of the cops, the Mexicans would bury the backpacks and wait for further instructions. When he got word of the border crossing, Jake began making his way to the Riverside area.

It was late when Jake pulled into the parking lot of Change's bar in Rubidoux. He wondered how Change ever made a dime with all the losers that hung out there.

Jake, wearing a simple white T-shirt with a breast pocket for his cigarettes and nicely styled Levis and Tony Lama cowboy boots, casually walked into the bar that smelled of cheap beer.

The side door behind the bar opened and Change entered and immediately went to the cash register to check the receipts. Change nodded at Jake, then grabbed a clean pitcher and filled it with beer as he picked up a freshly washed beer mug and sauntered toward Jake's table.

Change just plopped into a chair and dejectedly poured himself a glass before he said a word. "Glad you're here, dude."

Jake filled his glass from the fresh pitcher. "I'm hearing that we're in a real shit fit," Jake told him. "I'm all ears."

"I don't know where to begin, Jake. I don't even know if this place is safe to talk anymore. I've had cops here askin' questions, and got people watchin' the place," Change said.

"That ain't good," Jake answered, getting more and more pissed as he listened to Change, who he always thought was rock solid and trustworthy. "Jist tell me the damage."

"The cops, you understand, know about my crew in Hesperia. I dunno, you know, you know," Change was struggling to find the right phrasing to say that he was in the middle of a massive meltdown. Jake could see that the situation was, to put it bluntly, fairly dire.

"Look dude," Jake stared at him as he spoke slowly. "I don't need no problems now or never. I got people to answer to and problems make these people very pissed off. Just tell me what I'm looking to expect."

Change's face told Jake that he was scared. "Understand, I been tending to business as best I could. You know, I been watching the store for you like a good Christian. I'm more fucked than you, you know." Change was whining and making excuses that angered the impatient Jake.

"C'mon fucker, just speak," Jake told him.

"It didn't work the way I figured," Change admitted. "Member? I told ya we was having some problems, man."

Jake remembered regular chats with Change, but admitted that he was more interested in his own dealings on the border.

"This has been in the fucking news?" Jake's voice was contained rage. He said it slowly, emphasizing each word in such shocked dismay that Change started getting really nervous. Jake was used to his operation flying like a Stealth bomber over Venezuela on Hugo Chavez Day.

Change gulped down his beer and poured another. "Yup. This fucking same reporter won't give up. I wait every fucking day for another fucking story in that fucking newspaper that won't let the fuck up." He told about the aborted ambush on the reporter.

"This ain't no good, Change. How we gonna fix this shit?"

"I dunno, you know. You know, we all should head to Mexico, you know. Just fuck it, dude. I can't do no more time in the joint. I got investments, man"

Yes, Jake thought, it was time for Plan B. "Yup, it's time to move on. Shut it down," Jake finally said with obvious sadness and regret.

Change nodded in agreement, thinking about a new life in Mexico, sipping Coronas and eating lots of crab and lobster.

"Pack a bag and your computer. Don't leave nothin' to fuck us up, Dude. We'll go get your crew. I got people waiting to get us across the border."

Within 30 minutes, Change emerged from his office with a blue backpack, his briefcase with the laptop, and again went to the cash register to clean out another $100, although he had stashed more than $25,000 in his briefcase.

"Let's go," Jake said.

They drove to the Coachella Desert, outside of Desert Hot Springs, to Charlie's house, satisfied cops were not following them. Change called his crew to meet them at Charlie's. Jake was getting more details of what was transpiring, and Change was happy to share what he knew about the news reporter who seemed to show an unusual interest in their operation.

Charlie was anxiously waiting, drinking a bottle of Budweiser, when Jake and Change arrived. The handful of enforcers that Change contracted within the thinning ranks of the biker club had not yet arrived, however. Jake and Change walked into the house as Charlie offered them both a bottle of Bud, and invited them to sit down, although there was only one small couch in the house that would be better served with a well-aimed Cruise missile. The place stank of chemicals. Charlie seemed oblivious to the health hazards he was breathing, and to Jake's astonishment, struck a match to light a cigarette.

"Charlie, we gotta' clear outta here," Change announced as he settled down in the so-called living room, stacked with plastic garbage bags and cardboard boxes, probably containing chemicals. Jake preferred to stand, not wanting to ruin his nice Levis.

Charlie seemed stunned to think he might have to clear out of his home and surveyed his household as if it were jammed with valuable antiques. "When?"

"Like now, man," Change said. "Pack a bag and Jake's gonna' take us to Mexico."

This was too much for a tweaker to comprehend all at once and Charlie seemed frozen in mid-air. His face was as blank as the features on a Nordstrom mannequin.

"I'll help ya," Jake said. That seemed to relieve Charlie of some of his anxiety, and he led Jake back into one of three bedrooms that contained a mattress stuffed in the corner, along with a dresser chosen from the Salvation Army. Charlie happily picked out his cleanest underwear and socks to take to Mexico.

Charlie bent over to pick up a plastic garbage bag in which to stuff his T-shirts and underwear. The click of Jake's switchblade knife opened only inches from Charlie's neck. It was an extremely sharp blade that neatly and accurately severed the carotid artery. Charlie fell onto the mattress with only a soft choking sound before he died.

"Hey, Charlie," Change was yelling as he walked down the hallway, "pack some meth so we can sell it down there. Might as well set up shop as soon as possible."

Hearing Chance clomp down the hall, Jake positioned himself near the bedroom doorway. Chance peered into the bedroom and spotted Charlie's bleeding body slumped on the bed. For a man accustomed to a violent world, Chance took a second too long to react and froze in disbelief that Jake would do such a thing as kill some poor junkie like Charlie. Jake took advantage of that precious second and lunged at the hefty man, sinking the blade into his throat in an upward thrust that caught the man right below his chin. Jake tore the blade through Change's neck and stabbed him again on the left side as he fell into the bedroom. Change was choking to death when Jake stepped over his prone body and backed into the hallway.

As an afterthought, Jake went through the man's jeans for the wad of cash and his wallet before it got soaked in blood. He also lifted Change's cellphone, which suddenly began to ring.

"Hey," Jake answered.

"Who's this," the voice asked.

"Jake. Change is taking a crap."

"Typical. We're on our way. Be there in a few minutes."

"That's cool."

Until that moment, Jake had not yet considered how to deal with Change's crew of idiots. Dealing with more than two, maybe as many as five skilled brawlers required more than a switchblade knife.

Jake hurriedly went to the Tundra outside the front door and found his pump-action .12 gauge shotgun and his AR-15 assault rifle. He was loading both as he hurried back into the house, thinking he heard the noise of motorcycles or vehicles coming down the long, dirt roadway.

Jake waited for them in the hallway as they took their time parking, cursing at each other and sharing a joint as they waited to go inside together.

Jake had no idea how many he faced. They pounded on the door for some reason, and then barged into the house, joking and jiving.

"Change?" one yelled. "You still on the shitter? What the fuck is this all about? I was just getting' laid when you called. You owe me, big time, dude!"

Jake heard what he thought was the last to stomp into the house and gather in the living room. Walking down the hall with the AR-15 waist-high, Jake sprayed the five men with an entire clip loaded with the maximum 30 rounds. The noise inside the house was deafening. Acrid smoke from the gunfire was heavy and the agony of dying men on the floor began as soon as the reverberation of the automatic fire had subsided.

Jake thought he was going deaf from the noise. These were the first people he ever killed, although he had ordered a handful of killings. It was all business, he told himself.

Picking up Change's briefcase with all the money, Jake walked out and didn't bother to pick up his shell casings. He knew forensics experts would be hard-pressed to link him to the murders. The slaughter did ruin his nice Levis and T-shirt. He figured he could clean up once he got away from the scene and found a safe spot in the desert.

Jake closed the door, leaving bloody boot prints on the soiled carpet and front porch steps. He removed his blood-splattered T-shirt and used it to open the door of his pickup.

Jake was lucky because Charlie's neighbors were too scared to investigate any noisy gunfire they heard. Gunfire from Charlie's house was not that uncommon, however.

Another ring on Change's cell phone jolted him as he drove from the scene. At first, he thought the ringing came from his own phone, but saw the dead man's phone on the truck seat next to him light up as it rang.

"Yeah?" Jake answered.

"Is that you, Jake?"

The voice was familiar, a loose end that Jake carelessly thought he dealt with at the house.

"Yeah."

"I was late, dude. I just left Charlie's and guess what I found?"

The voice had a chilling tone that caused Jake's pulse to quicken and saw him break into a cold sweat on his forehead.

"I'll be seeing you soon, Jake. I'll find your fuckin' ass and cut you up in tiny pieces."

CHAPTER THIRTY-FOUR
July 3, Desert Hot Springs

The 911 call to the dispatcher came from a pay phone in Desert Hot Springs. "Lotta bodies you need to see," and gave Charlie's address. Two Riverside County sheriff's deputies dispatched to the scene opened Charlie's front door, then backed out to wait for supervisors, detectives and the coroner's office.

Charlie's address triggered an alert notice on the law enforcement database used by cops to obtain background information about the owner or occupant of the residence. Within the hour, Sgt. Heacock was awakened at home and given the news about the rampage.

"Joe, wake up. We've got more trouble at the Desert Hot Springs house. Mass murder or mass suicide. It ain't Jonestown because nobody found Kool-Aid."

By the time every agency showed up at Charlie's, the dirt road looked like a law enforcement open invitation to take target practice on a Colombian cartel drug house.

Neighbors had brought out lawn chairs and any available beer to watch the events happening at Charlie's—a guy few knew and even fewer had ever seen. But everybody seemed to have something to say about Charlie to the cops. Poor Charlie. Anonymous most of his life; a celebrity in death. The radio chatter between dispatchers and cops on the scene piqued the interest of a freelance photographer who followed the directions he heard given on the police scanner and pulled up to a roadblock a half mile from Charlie's house.

"Whadaya got?" he asked a deputy guarding a roadblock.

"Hey, Freddie, you're earning your lunch money tonight," the deputy laughed. "Can't go no farther, though."

"You think it's worth me sticking around, Jimmie?"

"Trust me, Freddie," the deputy replied. "Get a dozen donuts, a Thermos of coffee, and stick around. Can't say no more."

In the next hour, carloads of police passed in and out of the roadblock. Finally, a detective Freddie knew motioned for him to get in his cruiser and took him to the bloody crime scene.

"You got five minutes to shoot and scoot, Freddie," the detective said. "You deserve the scoop, but I can't let you stay out here any longer."

Freddie used his Canon digital camera and a video camera to record the scene. Five minutes of work and he'd collect enough to pay off more than his credit cards.

"I gotta' ask you some questions, detective," Freddie said.

"Ask away."

"How many dead?"

"Seven."

"Men and women? Any kids."

"No kids. Just men."

"All gunshot?"

"Some had other wounds. Can't say all. But some were shot."

"That's a lotta bodies. Murder-suicide?"

"It's a homicide. Too big for us locals to handle. We have outside help."

"Any suspects?"

"Can't say. There's a lot of work to do. We could be here for a long time."

"Neighbors hear anything?"

"Just shots."

"Who lives here?"

"Can't tell you now, but we believe he was one of the victims. Gotta go. No time for any more questions."

Freddie snapped his photo. "That's for your scrapbook, detective."

The detective pulled out a card and told him to where to mail it.

As official "guests" at the crime scene, Heacock and McLaughlin were escorted through the house by the lead detective and recognized the faces of Charlie and Change, and were clear that this was a pre-emptive strike on their investigation.

"Frank," Heacock said. "I guess I never thought our leaked story to Skip would lead to this."

"Me neither, man."

CHAPTER THIRTY-FIVE

As soon as I flipped on the television to watch the morning news, I figured it was going to be a busy day.

"Seven murdered in Coachella Desert. Details in just a minute." I waited for the commercials to end before I saw the video of the murder scene. Where the hell was Coachella.

I was the new guy and I was warned that I was on-call for any police action over the holiday weekend. The newspaper wanted me to head out to the scene immediately.

Lord, this was going to be a long, long day, I thought. I found the remote site north of Interstate 10 by spotting the circling helicopters. I parked at the tail end of a line of cars crowding the steep shoulder of a pot-holed, two-lane road whose centerline markings had faded in the sun years before. I walked toward the police barrier in front of a dirt road, and held up my press I.D. for the officer.

"The PIO is the person you need to talk to," one deputy snapped.

"Sure is hot out here." I was just trying to be friendly. The deputy just glared at me as I walked to the command post. The door was locked. Just my luck.

I could hear voices inside the mobile home, so I waited patiently outside and smoked a cigarette. The door opened and out poured seven or eight reporters and photographers.

"Hi, I just got here," I told a guy in civilian clothes who looked like a cop.

"Who are you?" I gave him my card and he told me that he had already given a briefing and didn't have time to talk to me.

"Can't you just spare a few minutes to bring me up to speed?" I was learning to be more aggressive. "I don't know what the hell's going on up here."

"Skip. Join the crowd, amigo. We don't know what the hell's going on either."

At least Paul Dinwiddie, the assistant PIO for the Coachella Valley and 25-year veteran of the sheriff's department, was in a jovial mood—something about a mass murder that makes cops and reporters switch on the defense mechanisms.

He told me what he told the other reporters, but with more detail because we shared the same sense of gallows humor.

"Who called 911—I assume it was 911?" I asked. Dinwiddie paused before answering. I bet the other reporters didn't ask that question.

"We don't know who. Might be a connection there."

"Did any neighbors just peek inside the house, and then maybe call?"

"Skip, I just don't know."

I thanked the PIO and was walking out of the mobile van when I saw a Riverside County-issued flatbed truck loaded with three or more motorcycles coming from the murder scene.

"Paul, come here and look at this," I shouted to Dinwiddie. "What's that all about?"

I could tell Paul was trying to come up with some explanation. "I think some of the victims owned those bikes."

"Were these your average Harley dudes who are doctors, lawyers and titans of business or just your average bad asses?" Paul shook his head and smiled. "I don't know what to tell you."

Thank you, God, for keeping me focused on this strange story. I had to talk to Heacock.

The newspaper was screaming for me to start writing my story after an editor saw CNN's Wolf Blitzer get excited and announce "Massacre in the Desert."

Heacock was not returning my phone calls, and all I could do was write about all the violent acts that seem to be happening on my watch. My editors wanted confirmation that everything was linked, but nobody would confirm that.

I was ready for a fist-fight if the editor deleted any reference to the Brea and Rubidoux incidents. Nobody challenged me, but insisted that I keep trying to get that connection confirmed. I promised them I would, but the easiest way would be to confirm it with Janelle.

CHAPTER THIRTY-SIX

Jake checked into a fleabag motel in Indio and made sure his vehicle showed no signs of his bloody handiwork. He piled his blood-splattered clothes and boots in a heap on the motel room floor. He cleaned the shotgun and AR-15, carefully lubricating and oiling the parts with loving attention, as he watched CNN's occasional updates on the killings.

Jake knew the Fourth of July in this largely Hispanic town in the Coachella Valley would be just as muted as it usually is in El Centro. The illegal immigrants from Mexico could give a righteous damn about Independence Day, although they appreciated any opportunity to celebrate and party.

Change's cell phone rang again, and Jake wondered when the battery would eventually wear down.

"Jake?"

"Yeah, Tommie."

"I want some money or I go to the cops."

"How much?"

"All you got."

"I got a buck fifty in my left pocket. That enough?"

"It's a start. Let's meet."

"Charlie's house again?"

Tommie couldn't help but laugh. "How 'bout In-N-Out?"

"I could use a double-double," Jake laughed, too.

"Drive-through in Barstow."

"Fifteen minutes fast enough." Jake had no interest in giving Tommie any clues on his whereabouts.

"Lemma know when you're gettin' close."

Jake began packing his gear to leave. He paid for two nights, but this chore might change his itinerary for the next few days. There was no question that he had to kill Tommie as quickly as he had dispatched poor old Charlie. Taking the back entrance through Joshua Tree National Monument, Jake might reach the drive-in within two or three hours. Jake made sure his motel room was spotless, nothing carelessly left that could prompt the housekeeper to call police. He wrapped his blood-soaked clothes and boots in a large bath towel and found a dumpster tucked behind the motel.

Jake headed east on Interstate 10 and made the steep incline through the rugged hills before he took the cutoff to the national park. The park ranger at the gate was friendly and wanted to tell him about all the desert flora and fauna he would be seeing. Jake was probably the only tourist to come through in several hours. He was impatient to move on, but reluctant to be too rude and arouse suspicion.

Jake called his people in El Centro to see how his cross-border operation was faring as he drove through the desert.

"Donde esta, amigo," his contact, Javier, greeted him.

"Indio, amigo," Jake told him. "Como esta nuestro negotio?" Jake wanted to know how the business was going. "Quando es approximo paquet?" When was the next package of meth arriving?

"Bueno, mi amigo," Javier told Jake. "Uno, dos dias." Maybe one or two days.

Jake told him to keep him posted and prepare the network for moving the product northward as they always did. That would involve secreting the drugs into the crankshafts of some slick cars and moving the drugs to their next destinations.

"No problemo, amigo."

"Muchas gracias, Javier."

Jake savored the moment of dealing drugs via a cell phone, so different from only a few years ago when his shoestring network was more hands-on and dangerous.

Within two hours, Jake was nearing the outskirts of Barstow on Highway 40, approaching from the east in the late afternoon. Jake dialed the last incoming phone number left by Tommie on Change's phone, hoping the phone had enough battery power to complete the call.

"I'm lost, dude," Jake told Tommie. The noise of the freight train and blast from its air horn was convincing to Tommie.

"Where you at?"

"East of town on Highway 40."

"I'll head that way, dude."

That was easier than Jake thought it would be. He actually was east of Newberry Springs, still about 30 minutes away from Barstow if he drove at 80 mph. Finding a good spot for the meeting, Jake waited until he spotted the black primered '56 Ford pickup heading eastward and passing him. Stupid guy, Jake thought. Still driving his favorite ride despite the possibility that the cops knew all about his truck.

Jake quickly took his AR-15 from its black leather gun carrier and left the Tundra passenger door unlocked as well as unlatching the hood of the Tundra, then carefully walked into the sparse scrub and sage about 50 yards from the turn-out clearing. He worried about coming across a desert rattler, and the brush was not as thick for cover as he had hoped. He began hearing noises that sounded like deadly snakes beneath every bush he passed. Jake hunkered down behind some brush, somewhat confident that he was obscured from the highway.

Tommie's pickup pulled up and parked a safe distance to the rear of the Tundra. Tommie sat in the truck for a few minutes before venturing out and slowly approaching the Tundra from the rear. A caravan of three huge tractor-trailer rigs roared past, kicking up dust that engulfed Tommie who shielded his eyes for a second. Tommie tried to open the driver's door, which was locked. Jake could see Tommie peering into the truck. Just as Jake thought, Tommie walked around the front of the truck, looked at the unlatched hood, scanned the horizon looking for Jake, and moved to the passenger door. This was a moment that Jake was waiting for but he could not help but feel nervous and afraid. The slaughter he inflicted in Desert Hot Springs had happened to fast that Jake had little time to contemplate becoming a mass killer until after it occurred. This was strangely different for Jake than killing all those guys.

Jake's breathing and heart rate were increasing as he followed Tommie's movements. He feared he would miss this shot and his concentration was being rattled by the thought of some snake curling up his pant-leg as he flattened himself into the rocky, bone-dry soil. The usual desert breezes were blowing from the east with an occasional gust. Jake feared the wind might cause him to miss Tommie if he did not compensate for that factor.

Tommie, slowly opening the passenger door as it if were connected to a time bomb, quickly jumped into the passenger seat, and surprised Jake with three quick shots he fired into the terrain where Jake was hiding.

One shot kicked up a rock and dirt only five feet away. Tommie apparently knew he was going to be ambushed, and figured the approximate spot where Jake was hiding. Tommie was too cocky to miss his chance to grab the leather pouch that contained a stack of $100 bills lying on the passenger seat. His plan was scoot into the driver's seat and take off in Jake's pickup with his money.

Jake, his left eye stinging slightly from a bead of sweat dripping down from his forehead, was not ready for Tommie's bold move to hide inside his truck. He had no choice but to gently squeeze the trigger, aiming at the passenger door, and fearing the 50-yard distance might be beyond his ability as a shooter. Tommie, lying on the seat, felt the lucky shot strike his behind, almost a clean shot up his rectum, and the burning sensation of the high-velocity bullet traveling up through his bowels and into his chest.

Jake was startled by the rifle's recoil and the reverberating sound it made that seemed like a Howitzer cannon in the wide-open terrain. The shot probably was heard by hundreds of motorists and residents,

Jake feared, as he rushed toward his vehicle, carefully opening the bullet-damaged door and spotting the wounded Tommie face down on the seat. Jake, thankful that Tommie wasn't bleeding too much in his pickup, felt better about his marksmanship and was proud of himself over his clean shot. Tommie was losing consciousness as Jake leaned over him.

Tommie's glassy eyes were blinking open and shut as if in pain, and Jake wondered whether Tommie recognized him. An eastbound semi-tractor trailer rig passing on the other side of the highway sounded its air horn as it passed.

Jake pulled Tommie by his leather belt as the man moaned in shock. Jake maneuvered the dead weight so that Tommie fell onto the ground. He then pulled him toward the brush where he had just hidden.

Despite the wound, Jake saw that Tommie was still alive and bleeding profusely

"Tommie, you fucked up bad, dude."

Tommie's eyes were moistening and his lips moving silently as blood oozed between his teeth and out his mouth. Jake rolled the man into the brush. He went through his pockets. The cellphone and wallet and the truck's keys now went into Jake's pockets. He heard another semi truck approaching from the east before sticking his buck knife into Tommie's throat.

Jake now needed to get rid of Tommie's pickup. Highway 40 is surprisingly busy with truckers and tourists headed to and from the Colorado River and Arizona. It's not bumper to bumper traffic, but there can be a steady stream of vehicles in both directions. When it is 113 degrees out in the desert, only the most assured motorist or a naïve one will stop to aid somebody as tough looking as Jake appeared to those passing by.

Satisfied that Tommie was dead, Jake moved to his Tundra and found that his rifle shot had traveled completely through the passenger door, leaving a big hole in the door panel that now needed to be patched. Luckily, the bullet did not travel through Tommie's body and exit in the driver's door.

Composing himself and wiping the sweat from his forehead with his T-shirt sleeve, Jake headed toward the Tommie's pickup, which looked more battered the closer Jake got to it. He climbed in and turned over the big block engine and gunned it several times, then drove it into the open terrain for several hundred yards. He was kicking up dust that could be seen for miles as he bumped over rocks and ridges that looked so flat from a distance but rutted by the harsh elements. Jake spotted a 10-foot deep ravine carved by the occasional fierce thundershowers that sweep through the high desert, changing sandy dry channels into rushing rivers of swift-moving muddy water.

He got out and pushed the truck a few more feet before it rolled over into the ravine. Only a passing helicopter or small aircraft would ever spot the pickup.

By the time he returned to his own pickup, Jake was ready to pass out from thirst and the exertion.

As he drove slowly into the town, Jake turned his radio to an all-news station to catch up on the Hesperia murder investigation. It took awhile before he got the update he sought.

"One of the journalists covering the case believes this homicide has more sinister implications," the announcer reported. "Skip Easley, a veteran reporter with the Riverside Press, had this to say. 'I believe these murders are linked to the murder of a Brea attorney and the attempted murder of a Riverside County undercover detective.'"

That reporter's name seemed to ring a bell to Jake, who then remembered hearing the long, drawn out diatribe from Change as they were driving up to Desert Hot Springs. Skip Easley continued to give his theory on what was transpiring, and it came pretty much close to the truth.

"Guess I'm going to Riverside," Jake mumbled to himself. "Happy Fucking Fourth."

PART III

CHAPTER THIRTY-SEVEN
July 5, Riverside

I was in the office by 7 a.m., and was ready to hit the streets by the time the first editor walked into the newsroom. It had been a very soul-searching night. Ed said Milton and Stuart weren't happy with my last story. They thought I was relying too much on the usual sources, and the cops were threatening to cut off the paper from any more cooperation from the story. The editors wanted to bring fresh blood onto the story to help me. I just don't think they trusted me—yet. They kept giving me these shitty little notes about my crappy writing. What do they want? Let them find somebody who can chase this story like I have done.

I was ready to give up. I was fantasizing every moment about making love to Janelle, and I only had one big juicy kiss to spark my fantasies. But could Janelle love a guy who dropped another story?

I thought about letting down Ed if I bailed on the story. Giving up would really disappoint him after he fought off the fucking dogs on my behalf. I decided to push on, but work smarter.

Like they loved to say in the military, I had to get my boots on the ground. I had to work the streets and stay out of the office as much as possible. I needed to stay out of sight of the editors.

I headed off to the Riverside County coroner's office to see whether autopsies had been completed on the seven dead men and when they would release their names. The deputy coroner on call was surprisingly friendly, but had nothing to add that would help at this point.

"Mr. Easley," he said as he shook my hand, "this is a very popular story, it seems. I'm expecting to get a call any minute from Katie Couric. Or maybe an interview on the Today show."

"Don't hold your breath," I joked back.

"No, I'm serious."

I looked at the guy who had the eyes of somebody who had seen some really bad shit, but had no authority to talk about it. He kept looking toward the front door as if television crews would be arriving any minute to set up for his cameo interview.

"Before you give the scoop to Katie, when do you anticipate having anything on the I.D.s?"

"I can't release any names because we're having trouble identifying one of the victims. As soon as we get dental records and fingerprints—maybe by tomorrow."

That was an important development, and I knew it would mean a lot of work fleshing out all the backgrounds of the victims. So many victims needed to be checked out; so many families contacted; so many court records to comb over. I was relieved that I didn't need to worry about the coroner's angle now. Maybe I could pass that off to another reporter so I could continue slogging ahead.

While I was out of the office, I thought I could zip up to the crime scene in Desert Hot Springs before the day got even hotter.

I parked outside the victim's old house and stepped on and around scores of cigarette butts tossed into the roadway. It had been a long night for the cops. I walked around the house posted with an official no trespassing sign and tried to peek into windows. I couldn't see much.

"You're not supposed to be here! Can't you see the no trespassing sign? Get out now or I'm callin' the cops!"

I walked up to the man in jeans and a dirty T-shirt that sported the Hooters chain. "I'm a newspaper reporter."

"I don't give a shit if you're Walter Cronkite. Get the fuck outta' here."

I pulled out my notepad and tried to be friendly. "Hey, man I'm just trying to do my job. I need to know who lived here."

"You're all fuckin' vultures! Cops tole me to keep an eye on the place. I don't know shit. Fuckin' tweaker lived here for a few months and the whole fuckin' neighborhood went to hell."

What a revelation. Looking at the nearby houses decorated with overflowing garbage cans, I tried to envision what the neighborhood might have looked like before a tweaker moved in.

"Bet that was a real downer to the neighborhood."

"Fookin' A!"

"You live here?"

"Fookin' A!" The man pointed to a desert brown stucco house with a torn screen door.

"You hear anything that night?"

"Look man, I'm not talkin' to you! Cops tole me to keep my mouth shut!" I wondered if he was deaf because he kept shouting even though we were only two feet apart.

"I bet you want this horrible crime solved, don't you?"

"Dude, I don't care if the cops solve it! Let the fuckers rot in hell! Good riddance!"

"I take it you didn't like the people who lived there?" I had to keep him talking.

"They was scum! Scary types, man! One dude here a lot was ole' Charlie."

"Mind if I get your name?"

"Friendly Eugene Carmichael." The man lowered his voice for the first time, almost to a conspiratorial tone. I was curious about his nickname, but decided not to ask.

"Mind if I use your comments in the newspaper?"

"Keep my name outta the paper!" His voice was at a shout again. "I don't want no problems!"

"Cool, but I can still use your comments without your name?"

"I guess, but I don't want no problem."

As I drove back to Riverside, I speed-dialed Terry Crawford, whom I had not called in a few days since the nice profile. I guessed that he was still hospitalized.

"Terry, my man, it's Skip!"

Terry Crawford's speech was better.

"Miss the Fourth of July. Sheeet. Nobody brough me a hotdog."

I made small talk for a few minutes, then asked if he were still obsessed with Salma Hayek.

"Don't go there, Skip!"

"Look, Terry, you heard about all the shit happening up in Desert Hot Springs?"

"Have to be a fucking Martian to not have heard, Skip." Terry's pronunciation of M was still a bit distorted but I was so excited that the cop was feeling and speaking better. I filled him in on the latest details, most of which Terry said he heard from Sgt. Heacock.

"Terry, some neighbor up here just told me the house was owned or rented by some dude named Charlie. That ring a bell?"

"Lots of Charlies out there, Skip."

"This guy's a tweaker."

"Look, Skip, you're moving in the right direction. There's a biker bar in Rubidoux. I'll get in trouble if I tell you the name. Bartender was involved in all this shit. Check it out."

"Okay if I keep calling you, Terry?"

"Great to hear from you, Skip."

"Salma is en route to see ya'!"

If I stepped on it, I might check out the only biker bar that fit the description from the police and court reports I'd seen. It was not far from where Terry was ambushed. I was on the clock and ready to go home for a beer.

There were a few motorcycles parked outside the front door, and two vehicles parked in the back. One was a dusty Camry. It looked like it had been there for a few days.

As I approached the front door, I had this image of myself as a gunslinger in the Old West, opening the door to confront some bad guys.

"Cops are not welcome so you can take your fucking business somewheres else."

I continued walking toward the bartender and held up my hands in a show of mock surrender. "I'm no cop, man. Just a newspaper reporter, man."

"What's yer name, dude?"

"Skip Easley."

Jesus, I thought the place was going to riot. I had no idea my byline had such an affect on people.

"Look, I'm trying to investigate the murders of seven men up in Desert Hot Springs the other day." I said.

"I thought that was the cops' job," the bartender replied.

"Yeah, it is, but they aren't telling me squat. And that's why I'm here, man."

"We don't know shit," the bartender said. "We get our news from you, so get the fuck outta here."

"Let me get rid of this dude." This Latino guy with his black hair braided into a rat-tail came at me.

He grabbed me by the elbow and began pushing me outside, yelling to his buddies "Watch this."

Then he told me in a whisper: "Dude, don't say another word.".

The man pushed me toward my car as his buddies watched from the bar. "Are you stupid, man? Word is, you know, that you're the next dead guy on the list."

I was bracing for a beating from his guy who looked like he could rip off my left ear. "Huh? What list?"

"You are real stupid, dude!"

I leaned against his car and pulled out a Marlboro and began lighting it. The man pulled it from my mouth and began smoking, so I lit another.

"Dude, I don't know, you know, how to tell you this, you know, but you stepped into a pile of shit walking into the wrong place. These dudes are scared shitless they be the next dead ones, you know. Leave this shit to the cops, you know. Them cops know the story, man, you know."

I didn't know what to say.

"Look dude, I'm gonna' punch you in the gut and leave. Meet me in 30 minutes at the Santa Ana River."

With that, he drew back and punched me in the stomach, pulling his swing just as his fist hit my gut. I doubled over and fell to the dirt. He may have pulled his punch, but it still hurt.

I found a dirt road on the southeastern side of the bridge over the dinky river that looked like it might lead to the river bottom that was lush with weeds and bamboo stream.

The man was waiting for me, sitting on his motorcycle and looking pretty much like a dangerous dude who could kill me.

"Hard time finding this place." He didn't seem to mind that I was late.

"You know, that cop, you know, that guy that was ambushed?"

"Yeah," I said. "Terry Crawford. I know him. In fact, I just talked to him, man."

"Yeah?" The guy was actually smiling at me. I relaxed a bit. "How's the dude doin'?"

"He sounded pretty good, actually."

"That's cool, you know, 'cause I know him. Called him Gunner."

He said his name was Ernie Salas, and that he wanted to change his life and become more respectable. Yeah, right, and I could see him with a white shirt and tie at Sears selling chainsaws. He said he warned Terry that afternoon before the ambush and how everything in his life had been turned upside down ever since.

"Fuck this shit, people killin' people. Tired of this shit, dude. Mas problemos, es muy malo."

I didn't know much Spanish, but I got the point.

"Listen, amigo, I'm gonna' tell you sum-ting I'll kill you if ever you snitch me out, man. Comprende? Understand, dude?"

I nodded.

"You know, I tole some cops about all this, man. I tole them to warn you that you are dead meat, man. They know shit. And now I'm gonna' tell you, but I kill you if it comes back to me. Unnerstand?"

I nodded.

Ernie, for some reason, felt I could use the information to help him get rid of the pressure he was feeling from law enforcement.

"Pretty soon, dude, I'm outta business, you know?" Ernie said, shaking his head in genuine sorrow.

I nodded, resisting any attempt to lift my notepad from my back pocket. "Well, what can I do? Tell me who's behind all this?"

Ernie looked at me in disbelief. "If I fuckin' knew, man, I'd take care of business. Fucking kill them bastards."

Ernie told me chances were good that the man who killed the people in Desert Hot Springs would be out gunning for me. "He don't miss, dude."

"Describe him for me."

"Middle-aged, nice Tony Lama boots and $200 Levis. Long hair. Don't shave much. Kind of dude who throws his power around, you know?"

He told me about Change and how this dude came and got him, and old Change was never seen alive again.

"You like bikes, dude?"

"Nah, man, never rode one in my life, except the pedal kind."

"You wanna go ridin' lemme know," Ernie said, turning to straddle his motorcycle.

"Tell me how I can contact you if I need you again?"

Ernie opened his wallet that was connected to a chain attached to his jeans' belt loop, extracted a business card and handed it to me. "Call Ernie For Good Times." It had his cell phone number.

I had to call the office to tell Stuart about what check I'd found out. He was busy, but the news assistant said everybody was curious about where I'd been most of the day. She told me I better get back to the office.

As I drove around looking for a parking space at the paper, I spotted two Riverside police cars parked near the paper's loading dock where bundled papers were tossed into waiting trucks.

I didn't give much thought to the patrol cars until I flashed my I.D. to the paper's security guard.

"Hey, Skip," he said.

"What's going on at the loading dock?"

"You haven't heard?"

So why the fuck would I ask?

"Skip, you better get your ass up to the newsroom. You've got some problems."

It was as if the entire room turned its collective attention to my entrance. An assistant metro editor walked up to me and told me to go to the editor's office.

"Am I getting fired?"

"I don't think so, Skip, but we've got some problems. The editors are discussing the situation now and you better get in there."

I headed down the wall of glassed editors' offices. I could see nine or 10 people inside Milton's office.

"Skip, glad you could finally make it," Milton greeted me with a sarcastic chuckle. "Boy are you causing us some trouble."

I was amazed that an assistant editor got up from his chair and motioned for me to sit down next to Ed.

"Skip, have you heard what's been happening here while you were so conveniently gone?" Milton began.

"No, sir."

"You got in early this morning, didn't you?"

"Yes, sir."

"Well, our security's day shift discovered a message for you and the newspaper that was spray-painted on one of our trucks this morning. Damned security guys completely missed whoever did it. But that's my problem to deal with later on."

"What was the message, sir?"

The editor tossed a glossy 8-by-10-inch photo of the side of one of the trucks. In black paint, the message: "Fuck press. Easy die."

I couldn't resist joking. "Obviously, not from one of our staff writers."

Milton shook his head. "Believe me, I considered one or two suspects on the staff."

"What do the cops say?"

"It's related to your stories and investigation. I guess you're doing something right, although I didn't think so yesterday." The editor paused, then added: "Skip, I got personal phone calls from the police chief and Sheriff telling me that I have to back off the story, let them handle the investigation, and pull you off the assignment. They want to put you in a safe place until they get the guy who did this. Can you handle that?"

"Oh, man." I was squirming in my chair, trying to find the right words to protest. "Look," I began, "you can't do that. I've worked so hard on this story. I'm making some real progress now. I've got a description of the killer and I'm getting close."

The editor studied me for a full minute.

"Skip, you need help on this. You can't do this solo," Milton said. "If those suckers think we're going to back off this story, they have their heads up their ass. Skip, I don't want you killed. I prefer to kill you myself if we lose this story. Ed, you and Skip give me an update on what we've got and what we need."

I gave a rambling rundown on what he had been doing since covering the Desert Hot Springs shooting and what I had been doing.

"Have you left out something?" Milton asked.

"What?"

"The police chief said you had been threatened last week before the Desert Hot Springs situation."

I was stunned that the police chief had told him about the ambush in my parking garage. Heacock and McLaughlin had promised me that that was classified and wouldn't be reported if I cooperated.

"I don't know what he's talking about," I answered. "I get a lot of nasty e-mails that I just ignore and delete." Maybe I wasn't lying very well. I knew the consequences of being caught negotiating deals with law enforcement without prior approval from my editors.

"I think the cops are trying to muzzle us but I want Skip to report any more threats directly to me. I'll deal with all this. That understood?" Everybody in the room nodded their approval like bobble heads at a circus arcade.

"All right now, what are we going to do? I want something in the paper tomorrow morning. Skip, you're out of this one. I don't want your byline in print just yet," Milton ordered.

I was disappointed, but not too much. I needed a breather from the story and a chance to pursue some of my new leads. I did as I was told and headed home where I worried some assassin might be waiting.

My place smelled badly of cigarettes. I had to stop smoking inside the apartment. It was bad for Ginger, I thought, and then I remembered her and Janelle.

"Dear Skip," Janelle's e-mail began. "Worried about you and really want to see you. Frank won't let me rendezvous with you again until it's safe. Angela is doing good. Ginger is the best company I've ever had in my entire life—except for you. Tell me what you've been up to. I've been swimming 20 laps in the pool every day. Topless!!! Wish you were here! Love, J."

Topless? I tried to visualize that as I typed out a response. I told her how much I missed her—and, of course, Ginger. I sent the e-mail just as my cell phone rang.

"Skip?"

"It's me."

"Sgt. Heacock here."

"Hey, man, hear about my latest threat?"

"Yeah, I've been dealing with a shit storm from the brass over here. Everybody wants to let the bad guy kill you, but I'm trying to hold off the lynch mob."

"I'll bet."

"Look, we're really concerned and I want you to back off until we identify and locate this guy."

"The paper is going full speed ahead, sarge. I can't control that. They are letting me work the story, but keeping my name out of the paper for now. Anything you can do to help me resolve this thing would be most appreciated."

"Look, Skip. We're not 'CSI' so I can't tell you how long it will take to process the Desert Hot Springs crime scene to see if there's any workable evidence. We believe it was a lone shooter, but we're not proof positive."

"Can you give me anything on the record?"

Heacock was ignoring me. "Do you need somebody to babysit you?" he asked. "Got a handgun? I can loan you one if you don't."

"I have my old .22 revolver, but no bullets."

"Come by the precinct tomorrow and I'll sneak you my extra .38 snub-nosed revolver."

"Cool. Probably like 10-ish."

CHAPTER THIRTY-EIGHT

"They want to move Janelle to another location and prep her for testifying in some AB case," McLaughlin told Heacock as soon as he entered the sergeant's office.

The investigation into Janelle's deposition was now part of a much larger case and prosecutors wanted her to be a key witness to show the reach of the AB into other criminal enterprises.

"Wonderful," Heacock said. "Where does that leave us? I've got bodies all over the place"

"It's complicated."

The federal indictment of 40 leaders and members of the Aryan Brotherhood, McLaughlin explained, and the sworn depositions of key witnesses, including some AB members, was already in the federal courts.

"Janelle may not be needed for any testimony in the federal case, but then again, she might be crucial," the deputy said.

McLaughlin said Angela had gained some stature for breaking Janelle in the deposition, and now she was assigned to start debriefing all federal agents, including him.

"Angela is hell-bent on us cracking this case. I thought there were conflicts of interest rules," the deputy complained.

"Does Janelle know about her new status?" Heacock said.

"Not yet. You wanna' tell her for me?"

Keeping Skip preoccupied with Janelle was essential at this point, Heacock said. They decided to keep the news from Janelle, and plod along with the status quo as long as possible.

"What are we gonna' do about Skip?"

Heacock felt a pang of loyalty to Skip, as he would any crime victim, and wanted to insulate Skip from any physical harm. At the same time, he needed the journalist to help them corner a suspect about whom they were slowly gathering more leads. Forensics was optimistic.

"We need to trap this sucker," Heacock mumbled. "Like real quick. We need a plan to push this squirrel into a corner where we can stomp on the sucker flat."

They sat and muddled through various ideas, sipping black coffee from Styrofoam cups as Heacock's coffeemaker perked another fresh pot. It would be another long day of phone calls, waiting and more waiting. Supervisors were never happy with the speed of any investigation.

"Heacock," he said as he picked up the phone. His face and eyes froze for a moment. He could hardly breathe at the news. As he listened, he grabbed a notepad and jotted down information, taking a second to look up at McLaughlin and nod his head. Heacock listened and asked a few questions that made no sense to the marshal or reporter.

"We'll be out there as soon as we can. Thanks for the news."

He hung up the phone, and smiled at the deputy marshal.

"Thank God!"

CHAPTER THIRTY-NINE

I needed to pick up Heacock's .38 handgun and see if they had any developments. I told the sergeant I'd be by in the morning, but I got busy with other stuff. I checked in with Heacock's secretary.

"He and that marshal stormed out of here like a rocket," she told me.

I felt screwed. Serves me right for taking my eye off the ball. "Can you get in touch with Heacock for me?"

"Honey, he's flying in an airplane somewheres."

I was ready to collapse on the floor in frustration.

Deputy Sue Domenguez came to my rescue. "Skip, I've got to talk to him anyway. What do ya' need?"

"I guess I need an update. What's going on?"

"Skip, you need to be somewhere else right now. Let me get the sergeant's authorization to tell you what's happening."

She came back in a few minutes and handed me a copy of a map. "You may be late, but get there—right now."

I tried to reach my editor. It took six rings before the news assistant answered. All the news editors were in a meeting and couldn't be bothered for another 15 minutes.

"Skip, I can't keep you from going," Ed told me, "but you know the boss is not going to let you write the story, whatever it is. We have to keep your byline off the pages. Just go do what you have to do. Keep me posted and call when you get there. We may need to send another reporter and a photographer."

"That's cool. I'm gone like a cool breeze."

I headed up the Cajon Pass along Interstate 15 and noticed my temperature gauge was rising as I throttled past 90 mph up the steep grade.

Despite the usual heavy traffic, I was passing Daggett on Highway 40 and making great time.

But then traffic was slowing in the eastbound lanes and my blood pressure was topping out from the pressure of the developing story, whatever it was. Had they found the killer? Long lines of tractor-trailer rigs were backing up in the outside lane, while the inside lane inched ahead toward Arizona. Finally in the distance, I could see flashing blue lights on the westbound side of the highway. Maybe that was the crime scene.

I pulled behind a parked tractor-trailer rig on the side of road. At least 10 marked police cruisers, a paramedic's truck and a coroner's vehicle jammed the area. It looked like I might be the only reporter on scene, but I didn't want to bet.

As I walked toward the cops, I could see a police helicopter sitting in the field about 200 yards from the police.

"Get Sgt. Heacock and Deputy Marshal McLaughlin. They know I'm coming," I told a cop who was guarding the crime scene.

"The Riverside County guys? They're over there," he said, pointing to a location about a quarter mile away. A heavy tow truck was parked nearby. This was a pretty casual crime scene or maybe my reputation as an ace police reporter preceded me.

The area looked like it was the scene of volcanic eruptions a million years ago. I spotted the two cops who turned as I approached.

"What took you so long, Skip?" Heacock joked.

"You could have given me a ride on your chopper. What's going on?"

"C'mon and look," McLaughlin answered. Both cops looked happy and relieved for some reason.

We peered over the edge of the ravine and I saw a '56 Ford pickup. "The driver is over there," McLaughlin said, pointing to another group of cops near the roadside turnout.

The killer was not as careful as he thought. When he was disposing of the Ford pickup, a passing trucker en route to Flagstaff spotted somebody pushing the vehicle into the desert and vowed to check it out when he made his return run.

The trucker, who was returning with an empty trailer box, intended to retrieve the junker pickup and sell it once he restored it, Heacock told me.

"He called us when he smelled a corpse and found the body," Heacock said.

"The trail is getting hotter," Heacock told me. "But this is not the whole story. There's more. And," Heacock drew out the punch line, "it gets better. A lot better."

An Indio deputy sheriff's routine report of suspicious activity caught the eye of an investigator who immediately saw a possible connection to the Desert Hot Springs shooting, he told me.

"We got a bloody pair of boots from a dumpster behind an Indio motel," Heacock said. "Some homeless space cadet. No way he passes up black lizard boots when all he owns are flip flops Said some suspicious gringo in a gray Toyota pickup".

"Any forensics?" I asked.

"Working it now as we speak."

McLaughlin, for once, offered me a tidbit. "Forensics says these Goodyear tire impressions are from a Toyota pickup."

"Looks just like them that we found in Desert Hot Springs," Heacock added.

"Skip, we're finally making some headway," Heacock said. "Here's what I want you to report. What I think will be OK to release to the public."

I ignored the sergeant's reportorial advice, but dutifully took down the notes of the developments from Heacock's much less detailed description of the crime scene. It was enough for me to report that key evidence had been discovered at two remote locations that may lead to the arrest of the killer. And, I could report that the killer had added another body to his list of victims.

Maybe this was enough to move the story ahead for another day and keep the editors off my back and save my job.

I called Ed with the latest developments, leaving out all the inside information. I wanted to see this killer captured, but I was conflicted about being overly helpful to the cops while keeping my integrity as a responsible and ethical journalist. Yes, I had ethics.

"What else do you have?" Ed asked. "This is good, but we need you to set the scene. Describe what's going on out there. Talk to cops. Talk to motorists. Give me some color."

I was leaning against my car smoking a cigarette after dictating my story to a veteran reporter who wasn't too happy to be jerked into this caper.

"Hey, dude, can I bum a cigarette?"

The question roused me from my sour mood and I looked up to see a burly, bearded man with a huge potbelly protruding over his blue jeans. He wore red suspenders to keep the pants from falling down to his knees.

"You a cop?"

"Nah, reporter."

"Sumpin 'bout that dude who killed that other dude in the bushes."

"You saw that?"

"I seen this dude pushing that '56 Ford into the desert."

I could have kissed the man on the lips.

"Fuck me silly! No shit!"

Here was the trucker who thought he was going to claim a junker and ended up discovering the latest grisly murder scene.

"Mind if I use your name and tell your story?" I was damned sure not going to let this trucker drive off without adding his description to the story.

"Shit, dude. I ain't goin' nowheres no time soon. Cops tole me to stick around, so might as well tell you what I tole them. I'm losing money sitting here, but maybe somebody will buy my story in the National Enquirer."

The desert was dark now, the shadows of the jagged peaks illuminated by a full moon and the glow from a billion stars that spread 360 degrees around him. The stars were so fascinating that I was forced to concentrate on my footsteps as I made my way toward a cluster of detectives. That was where they found the body.

Shot through the ass by a high-caliber bullet. I thought his soul would be mortified to see medical examiners probing his rectum in search of a bullet. All these dead bikers were sitting around a campfire in Biker Hell comparing their wounds. This sucker would have to admit his ass was a bullseye.

CHAPTER FORTY
July 6, Riverside

I could see the banner headline as soon as I opened my apartment door.

Leads In Desert Point to Mass Killer

I was so anxious to see my story that I jumped out of bed as soon as I heard the news carrier drop the paper on my doormat. When I picked it up, still groggy from the previous long day, my second in the high desert area, I was certain it would be the lead story of the day.

The story byline was tucked beneath the fold, which I did not see immediately.

"Those fuckers screwed me!"

By Donald Williams
Senior Staff Writer

It was my story, maybe not as I dictated it, but all of the information was from my reporting. I wasn't credited for one fucking verb or noun. Don Williams was one of the best whose specialty was long, complicated projects. A favorite among editors, Don always was left alone to work his magic until editors needed some help on a breaking story like the one that I dictated. My nugget of information about the lucky trucker was played prominently, up high in the story. I read the detail and could almost imagine the guy talking to me again.

The paper even had my digital photograph of the crime scene, which was credited as a "Staff Photo."

I felt more ambushed than a WalMart checker working alone on payday.

The editor had warned me a few days earlier that my byline needed to be left off the paper for my own safety. But this was an injustice. The killer was probably in Anchorage or Tijuana by now. There was no way the killer would come after me now.

This turn of events pissed me off so much that I decided to show up late for work. I decided to run a few miles to work off my bad attitude. Two miles for Skip; one for the Corps! Semper fi, dude.

Dripping wet and doffing my soaked T-shirt after the quick run, I felt better and vowed to cut down on smoking.

Late for work and still in a sour mood, I needed to calm down a bit more before I could walk into the newsroom. I checked my e-mail for any message from Janelle and found two: the latest more frantic than the first which was posted the day before when I was so frantically busy.

Janelle's fractured message from 7 a.m. that day: "Where are you? I NEEEED to talk to you NOW!" I replied to Janelle's last message by telling her what I went through in reporting the latest developments and the paper's big screw job of not giving me a byline on the story.

"I'm calling you NOW!" was her short reply. My cell phone rang and I wasn't pissed any more.

"Skip, I need to talk real bad."

She had heard, not from McLaughlin but another deputy, that the feds were going to take her out of the safe house and prepare her for crucial testimony in some federal trials. She wanted to meet me and see if we could discuss some details about her staying with me until all this mess was settled.

"If you don't want me to be with you, just tell me!"

"Hey, sweetie, that's just perfect. Except there's still somebody out there who still wants to kill me. I'm worried about you being here. Let me talk to McLaughlin."

"I'm sure they will get the killer before they release me," Janelle said. "Let me talk to Frank and see if he'll take me to your place tonight so we can talk."

Yeah, we can talk for a few minutes, and then let's get acquainted. "Great idea! You sure cheered me up. I gotta' go to work. Let's meet after 5. Frank will let us know where we can meet that's safe."

I showered and was at the paper within an hour, walking in and expecting the editors to flog me for being late. I sat down and sifted through the papers and notes strewn from weeks of assignments and interviews.

"Look, man, sorry about the byline. Not my idea, friend." It was Don Williams, the author and expert re-write man. I swiveled my chair and saw the tall, lanky reporter with a fashionable light blue shirt and Scottish plaid tie knotted tightly at his neck.

"I know, I know. I worked so hard on that story."

"Skip, I want you to hear it from me first. The editors want me to work the story as the lead reporter from now on. I've made some calls already and we can talk later."

It was as if nobody wanted to approach me to discuss the story. I sat at my desk and read e-mails that had backed up for two days. Most were how I could improve my sex life and enlarge my penis. I was particularly interested in one drug that warned of the danger of a four-hour erection. I'd check that out later if Janelle and I got it on. Another e-mail had an urgent message in the header. I opened it, thinking it was from a source.

Dear Mr. Skipp: Let me introduce myself. I am a humble public servant for the city of Lagos in the rich and religious nation of Nigeria, which you know is in the great Continent of Africa, the birthplace of civilization. I am in need of your assistance in tracking down a culprit of the most heinous fraud in the history of our prosperous nation. Please let me know that I can count my many blessings on you aiding me to find the nefarious Mr. Abu Mohammad who has robbed my city of tens of millions of U.S. dollars $$$ and must be stopped immediately before he financially ruins me and my countrymen. Please send me a money order for the amount of $500 and I will be able to launch my nation's investigation and re-pay you ten-fold once we collect Mr. Mohammad's stolen fortune.

Your humble Servant. Ambassador Nigel Washington

He even had the address and phone number, just in case I wanted to call for more information.

I hit REPLY on Nigel's solicitation.

Dear Ambassador Washington. Thank you for your courteous note requesting help. If you send me Mr. Mohammad's last known address, along for a check for $10,000, I will be happy to track down the wicked crook and slit his throat from ear to ear and return your stolen treasure along with his two severed thumbs.

Best regards, Mr. Skipp

I logged off and looked around for Ed. I needed some counseling and any marching orders for the rest of the day. It was already 2 p.m., and I really wanted to go home and get ready for Janelle. Ed was editing some stories budgeted for the weekend.

"There's the star reporter!"

"Don't bullshit me Ed."

"Skip, you know the drill. The big boss doesn't want your byline in the paper until the cops get this killer. Everybody was very happy with what you did. Why don't you knock off a couple hours from the OT you collected yesterday and go home early. You deserve it!"

"Thanks, Ed, I think that's exactly what I'm gonna do. I'm pretty tired."

I went back to my desk and made a few notes on what I needed to do the next day, and got up to leave. One by one, reporters and editors in the newsroom began cursing as their stories and e-mails disappeared from their computer screens. Some screens just froze and wouldn't operate.

"What the fuck happened?" the editor in chief screamed as he stormed out of his office. "Call technical support immediately!"

Technical support already knew the paper's computer system had just crashed. Somebody screamed all 1,500 computer terminals in the building had suddenly turned to black screens. It was time for me to leave. Everybody was blaming this latest meltdown on the computer nerds. I suspected Nigel was up to some mischief. This cracked me up so much I had to get out of there before I confessed to old Milt.

I just hoped the elevator worked as I waited to flee the bedlam. Editors were screaming at reporters to try to save all the words on their screen by writing them down in longhand. Reporters were throwing pencils at their frozen screens, swearing viciously and threatening to quit. The mutiny was building as the elevator doors opened and I stepped inside, descending to a lobby that appeared quite normal.

"Have a good day, Skip," the guard told me.

For the first time in months, I looked forward to going home, such as it was. We only had two brief meetings, and one back in February was not particularly satisfying. The relationship over the past few months had grown from Janelle's curiosity over my new job into a complicated arrangement via hundreds of e-mails that gradually slipped into a romance between two people who needed each other.

Clutching an armload of groceries that contained a $12.99 bottle of Merlot, I opened my stifling apartment and turned on the air conditioner. I changed into some shorts and a freshly laundered polo shirt. It was close to 5 p.m., and I had nothing to do but wait for Frank to call me where we could meet.

A little of Eric Clapton's "Layla" on the stereo, a little Merlot and a lot of Janelle would make for a perfect evening. But it was unlikely that Frank would allow us to meet at my place.

Finally, Frank told me to go to the Mission Inn. It was Riverside's historic hotel that had been renovated and made into a posh destination for people like Janelle and me. Frank gave me the room number, and it seemed like I was there within five minutes. There she was at front door, waiting for me to come off the elevator.

I didn't know whom to kiss first. Frank or Janelle. Frank left us with a smile, the room key and a bottle of Merlot.

"How long can you stay?"

"As long as you'll let me." She gave me a full look at her short white skirt and vibrant floral blouse with three very open buttons.

"You've got a great tan, lady!"

I wanted to unbutton the two remaining buttons, but I didn't want to appear to be overly anxious or a complete jerk. No stupid Skip mistakes with this was lady like I've made in the past. We caught up on all the events since our last rendezvous at the national cemetery that seemed like months ago. Then we sat on the couch and made out like teenagers at a drive-in.

Thank God Janelle didn't have any tattoos. I took my time looking for them. She found my Purple Heart wounds. It was like an Ian Fleming novel. She was Pussy Galore and I was James Bond. Well, I thought I was.

The moment—I repeat it was just too brief a moment—turned out just as I fantasized, and I needed to catch my breath before I asked for another. She smelled great. She wanted me on top, then she wanted to be on top. We hugged and kissed, and I played with her breasts—mostly to satisfy my curiosity that they were all hers and not siliconized. They were real, baby.

And then I began wondering whether I disappointed this exotic woman who may have had scores of more satisfying and exciting lovers, for all I knew. She was asleep and soon I was dozing.

When she awoke, we enjoyed our time together for a few more hours before a deputy marshal came to take her back to the safe house until she could return, which I hope would include her suitcase.

CHAPTER FORTY-ONE

A telephone call interrupted Jake's attention to the latest porn flicks on his motel television not far from the Highway 60 and Interstate 215 interchange west of Grand Terrace.

Jake recognized the area code and phone number of Folsom State Prison on his cell phone as he prepared to answer. "Are you the brother of Marion Murphy?"

"Yeah." Jake became worried because this call didn't seem to be like all the other collect calls he usually got from his sibling.

"This is the medical administrator at the prison hospital and I'm sorry to tell you that your brother has suffered what we think is a major heart attack. He's asking for you and I suggest you visit him immediately."

"Uh, sure. I'll be there as quick as I can."

Perfect timing, bro, Jake muttered to himself. Fuck you very much. He was sitting in the motel lounge chair in his white briefs with a six-pack of Budweiser, and one unfinished stick of beef jerky. There was still so much to do here yet, and Jake was torn between ignoring his older brother and running to his bedside. It occurred to him that this might have been an urgent signal from Duke who could be faking the heart attack and just wanted Jake to personally brief him on all that had transpired.

Jake's concern was getting to an airport, probably Ontario International Airport, and stashing his pickup so that it wouldn't draw attention by roving security patrols. He didn't want to risk taking all the bundles of cash he was carrying, but he would need money for the airline ticket, a motel, meals and a rental car once he got to Folsom. What if he got stuck in Folsom and ran out of money?

Jake needed to buy some decent clothes—very conservative—and a carry-on suitcase that wouldn't arouse suspicion from the airport security screeners. There was no way he could leave tonight, so he spent the rest of the evening putting together a list of tasks and calling airlines for available flights the next afternoon. He booked a flight that would arrive just before 3 p.m., giving him time to drive to the prison and see his brother.

The next morning, he headed toward Ontario to go shopping before his flight. Crossing off each item on his list, Jake was a far more efficient shopper than he was as a killer. A buzz cut haircut and a close shave from the barber transformed Jake into an obscure, middle-aged redneck that could pass for a construction worker, as long as nobody looked at his soft hands that really had not seen much work, except for the trigger finger. Tossing two packets of underwear and a handful of white socks into his shopping cart, Jake found some baggy khaki shorts with a tie string in front, a pair of leather sandals, a couple of polo shirts, and a pair of Levi's that fit him too snugly despite a 42-inch waist. The XXL polo shirts drooped in the back and were hiked up in the front as they tried to cover his potbelly. What the hell, Jake thought, life on the road was a bitch when he had to live on hamburgers and fries and milkshakes and beer.

Jake found a nice black carry-on suitcase to stash all his new clothes. Finally, Jake was ready to head to the airport, unsure which parking lot to use and which terminal contained his airline. Jake hid his AR-15 and other weapons behind the seat, stuffed his old duffel bag with all his worn clothes and stepped into the stylish leather sandals that he immediately regretted buying. They made weird slapping noises when he walked. He looked pretty ridiculous—not his intent—but sufficient to portray some anonymous tourist on a hot summer day.

It was not until a few minutes before 5 p.m. that Jake arrived at the historic prison's entrance and checked in at the visitor's center. The granite fortress of a prison, which underwent construction in 1874 as a source of labor for the construction of Folsom Dam on the American River and opened for business four years later, was both impressive and startling to Jake. The little town of Folsom, so quaint and filled with tourists and clogged with commuters heading to million-dollar homes was so incongruous as home for a notorious prison filled with 4,200 inmates owing allegiance to every conceivable prison gang. Regular visitation hours were only Friday through Sunday, but Jake was assured earlier that officials would let him momentarily see his brother because of the medical emergency.

Jake parked his rental convertible Mustang in the prison's visitors parking area and walked toward the visitor's reception building. The gray granite walls of the prison and a tall watchtower increased his uneasiness. Inside the visitor's center, Jake was told to wait for authorization for a special hospital visit, which probably would be delayed until the next day.

Jake had never done a day of hard time in a prison, and only a few nights in a county jail on drunk driving charges. The experience of visiting this ancient monument to corporal punishment, which even had a small museum that sold souvenirs, was unnerving. This was where they used to hang condemned prisoners in the 1880s. With due respects to Johnny Cash, his song sugar-coated the place for Jake who was thinking about all the murders he just committed.

Jake was told that he needed to return at 9 a.m. the next morning and be ready to see his brother promptly at 10 a.m. Jake would be placed at the top of the waiting list of visitors, only if he passed a background check and had no criminal history. Somebody who had planned for months to visit his relative would be bumped so Jake could see his brother. Duke was being treated in the huge hospital ward where hundreds of inmates are daily treated for colds, hernias, backaches and stab wounds. Jake was assured that his brother's condition was stable. If he had doubted Duke's illness before, Jake was now convinced the request for his presence was genuine.

After showing up as scheduled and told to wait until noon, Jake watched inmates in blue jumpsuits working outside the prison walls, hauling trash or doing menial tasks that were anything but trivial to men who have little to do in their cells than to watch the clock. Jake wondered if his brother had a job like that.

Jake and the 23 other visitors were ordered to line up in front of the main entrance, each assigned an escort who would take them to the family visitation area inside the walls. Jake, who was amazed that he was not searched by guards, was under the impression that he would be taken to his brother's hospital bed.

Jake and the others waited in the visitor's room for the inmates to be brought to them. A guard motioned for Jake to follow him to the hallway where a hospital bed had been parked. A male nursing assistant, who actually was an inmate, motioned Jake to come to the bed where his brother lay with a white sheet covering his upper torso.

Duke's heavily tattooed arms and neck, messy graying hair and unshaven face caught Jake's attention before he saw the intravenous drip bottle, the heart monitor with the wavy lines that signaled each feeble squeeze of the heart, attached to his bed. Duke's face looked pale.

"Hey bro," Jake said softly. Duke's demeanor was unchanged, as if he had not heard his younger brother. Jake wondered if he was alive, but the heart monitor indicated otherwise. Duke held out his right hand to his brother. The nursing assistant looked at Jake and jerked his head in a gesture to come forward.

Jake came to the bed and extended his right hand to Duke, suddenly feeling a slip of paper being placed in his palm. Jake adroitly manipulated it to fit between his two middle fingers and thrust his hand into his pocket where he could deposit the kite to read later. Such exchanges between inmate and visitor occur frequently, but only the clumsy are detected by vigilant guards.

"He wants to talk to you, but he's not real strong," said the nursing assistant. Jake leaned over Duke's bed and lovingly held his brother's shoulders and looked into his face.

"You're fucking up stuff even more," Duke told his brother in a barely audible whisper that was more than sinister. "Doin' the best I can, bro," Jake answered with a faint smile, mostly for the nurse.

"I'm sending you help," the elder brother told him. "Disappear."

Jake's face was still close, but he pulled back a little as he looked into the eyes of a man who did not seem pleased with his accomplishments the past few days. Even in Folsom, Duke was able to read about the rampage of his witless younger brother. Duke, who had the respect of the white inmates at Folsom, wanted to strangle Jake but that might really aggravate his heart that had been manipulated by a drug given by this male nurse as part of his urgent ruse to deal with Jake.

"Listen, Fuck Up," Duke whispered to his brother, "Did you ever read Plan B?" Jake looked perplexed and a bit hurt by his brother's misuse of his Christian name.

"Well, bro, I thought we was doing the right thing." If Jake could have kissed Duke's ring, he would have groveled to show his allegiance.

"Listen, Fuck Up." This time the moniker really hurt Jake's feelings. "Thanks to you, I gotta' billion dollar business going down the shitter."

"But bro," Jake protested.

Duke had enough of his idiot brother and told the nurse to take him back.

With business out of the way, Jake inquired of the male nurse how his brother was doing.

"He's in pretty bad shape," the nurse said with mock solemnity. "Come back tomorrow and we'll see how he's doing then."

Jake felt no undue scrutiny from prison guards. He felt secure for the moment. The cops were looking for a white male, 40 to 50, heavy set, rough-looking suspect, somebody merciless, a definite sociopath, calculating and methodical. Jake was careful to cover any tell-tale forensic evidence that may lead to his undoing. He believed he had left no clues at the crime scenes.

Feeling confident, Jake, stretched on the bed of his Folsom motel, called the leader of his team of traffickers in El Centro.

"Javier?"

"Amigo, que pasa?"

"Bueno. Gracias. Y tu?"

"Bueno, bueno. We izz muy reech, compadre."

The shipment had been safely retrieved and had been parceled out to the network, as had all the previous deliveries, into a string of innocuous flatbed trucks. Some already had reached their destinations. Everything had been going as planned, although Javier spared the details over the cell phone.

CHAPTER FORTY-TWO

One of Javier's two-ton flatbed GMCs was stopped on Interstate 15 as it merged northward onto the Interstate 215 in Murrieta. A California Highway Patrol officer cited the nervous driver for malfunctioning tail lights.

Something about this truck loaded with four-by-eight-foot slabs of drywall just bugged Officer Steve Mercer. As soon as the truck pulled back into traffic, Mercer called his buddy with the Riverside sheriff's drug task force, Sgt. Mark Rich.

Mercer followed the truck from a distance while Rich frantically assembled a team to intercept the truck and hopefully take a closer look. The CHP officer radioed that nobody appeared to be following the truck, as is the case of a large drug shipment that involved armed escorts. Rich and Mercer remained on the phone for 30 minutes as Rich rounded up two other drug task force members and prepared to pull the truck over again, hopefully, before it left Riverside County or got lost in northbound traffic.

Rich radioed Mercer that they were ready to stop the flatbed in Perris, a one-time historical railroad stop for area farmers that now was fast becoming a warehouse distribution center for big-box retailers in Southern California.

The task force boxed in the flatbed just as it reached the exit for Perris, and ordered the driver and his companion to follow them. The two unmarked sedans and Mercer's CHP unit escorted the frightened two Mexicans to a California Department of Forestry headquarters that conveniently had a large maintenance facility.

With probable cause and two very suspicious looking suspects, the task force disassembled the neatly stacked drywall and discovered a hidden compartment amid the cargo containing over 1,500 pounds of cocaine, plus another 500 pounds of marijuana. Rich needed a calculator to figure the street value which had to total millions of dollars. Afterwards, they very carefully reassembled the illicit cargo and escorted the truck to its delivery point, a truck stop in Fontana. On the threat of immediate deportation to vicious Mexican federal police, the Mexican drivers agreed to deliver the goods to the truck stop, as planned. The three-hour delay did cause some concern to Javier's network that was waiting. By then, the Mexicans had explained to Javier about the delay, all part of the elaborate ruse concocted by Sgt. Mark Rich. The men were placed separately in cells while the drug task force traced the next steps of their drug delivery process. Meanwhile, Javier's name and his cell phone number were getting the full attention of Rich's task force.

Jake's cell phone number was now part of the escalating investigation by one task force that was working just down the hallway with another much busier and higher profile task force.

CHAPTER FORTY-THREE
July 8, Riverside

I toyed with the idea of just bagging work. Why ruin a romantic interlude with Janelle? Soon, I kept telling myself, this story would end and I could kick back again and enjoy life. When the elevator door opened to the newsroom, I noticed everybody seemed to be exhausted and in a foul mood. The paper was pretty slim compared to other editions that were chock full of ads.

"Hey, dude. What's up?" I asked Don Williams who was pounding away on his computer with an update on Jake's trail of killings.

"You wouldn't believe. Computer crashed. Entire system went down from some virus. The techs had to call in some software experts from LA. Last I heard, some e-mail from Nigeria. Everybody got the same e-mail and nobody knows what happened. You won't be able to use the e-mail system for a couple more days until they fix it with some super-duper spam killer."

I felt wonderful, although I was worried the techs would trace the meltdown to me. I'd just say somebody used my computer when I was gone. I went through my mail and checked notes from Ed and other editors about possible follow-up angles.

I dashed out a message for Ed about my day's assignments and decided to disappear from the newsroom for as long as possible. If the Nigeria connection weren't grounds for firing, I knew my sleeping with a major source certainly would be enough reason to can my ass immediately. I could close my eyes and see Janelle on my bed waiting for me. They could fire me this second and I could care less.

I made my rounds through the courthouse and then drove out to the sheriff's precinct to see Sgt. Heacock. The receptionist cleared me to walk back to the sergeant's office where he greeted me with some obscene hoots.

"Heard you had a good time last night, old Skipper!"

Why was I feeling embarrassed? I tried to ignore the teasing but Heacock kept at it. "How was she? Bet she just wore old Skipper out!"

"C'mon, give it a rest."

I changed the discussion. "What's up?"

"Not me," answered Heacock. And then I had to endure another round of teasing.

"Who's that Don Williams? I thought you were our main guy on this story. He's some piece of work."

"I'm still on the story, don't worry. Don's a great reporter."

"He's a lot tougher than you."

That hurt. "Yeah, he's good, but I'm better."

Heacock kept asking about Williams, and wanted my word that he could be trusted.

"That Williams demanded everything on the record. Wouldn't take jack shit on background. Everything had to be properly attributed. Real jerk."

As I heard this, I felt that I let the cops manipulate me because I was too close to my sources. Not to mention the little secret deal about my attempted murder.

"I just need to know if I should continue talking to Williams or stick with you, Skip. You're our guy and I don't want to screw you outta' the story."

"Hey Sarge, keep doing what you're doing. But I appreciate you not cutting me out of this story."

I was beginning to feel trapped and compromised as a journalist. Each time I compromised my ethics I seemed to dig myself a deeper hole. I had to keep the ultimate prize in sight. I had to push to wrap up the story by reporting the killer's capture.

"Sarge, you work with me and I'll work with Don. But I can't tell you not to talk with Don. He's the lead reporter now because of all the shit about the threats spray-painted on the truck. The paper's worried about my safety so my byline stays outta' the paper until the guy is caught."

Heacock didn't look too happy about dealing with Williams.

"Look Skip, we need your help again. McLaughlin's going to be here any minute. Go get a doughnut and a cup of coffee in the lunch room and we'll come for you."

I was being sucked in deeper and deeper. How could I refuse?

I headed down the hall and chatted with a few detectives who asked me about Janelle and whether we would marry once the case was solved. That was a subject I had to change pretty quickly. One detective told me about a big drug case the narcotics task force had just uncovered, but swore me to secrecy until they made a big arrest.

This was always my problem. I had great contacts that kept me informed about stuff, but I could never publish any of it until it was old news. I made myself a note to call the detective in a few days.

"Skip, we gotta' get this composite out," McLaughlin said, not bothering with any cordialities when he and Heacock joined me in the lunchroom. "This has gotta' be in tomorrow's paper." He tossed the sketch, which skimmed and floated neatly in front of me, except upside down.

I picked up the sketch and studied it for any similarities I might recognize. It was pretty generic stuff: middle-aged guy with scruffy beard, more like two or three days growth, wavy hair not far past the ears, pudgy face and menacing eyes.

"Who's this?"

"Can't tell you, now." McLaughlin said.

"You've got a name?"

"We're not ready to give you a name, yet," Heacock replied.

"C'mon guys, I need a quote from you. This stuff is so much more powerful coming from you."

"How 'bout this? 'We are confident we are close to apprehending this suspect.'"

"That's just brilliant." I folded my notebook and stuffed it into my pants. I'd use their stupid quote and push the sketch to my bosses.

"Where did you get this?" Don Williams didn't seem too happy the sketch I handed to him.

"I got it from Heacock."

"I just talked to that SOB and he never mentioned the sketch."

"He doesn't trust you."

Williams laughed. "So, do you trust him?"

"Man, he's a good cop."

"Sure, Skip. You know good cops don't trust journalists."

I wanted to help the cops, but Williams was right. I needed to keep this professional. I knew I was too close to this story for my own good.

"Send me a few grafs on what you have. I'll give the sketch to photo," he said, jerking his head toward the photo department. He held up the sketch and studied it for several minutes. I could tell he was not thrilled. With me or the sketch.

CHAPTER FORTY-FOUR

Sgt. Mark Rich was just handed the same sketch of the suspect. It came with more details, however. The advisory about the gray Toyota Tundra caught his eye. He was retrieving all the cell phone information and calls logged to Javier and a particular character named Jake Murphy. According to the Department of Motor Vehicles, they both had residences in El Centro. And this Jake character had recently purchased a gray Tundra in San Diego. Jake's driver's license mug shot looked vaguely like the face on the sketch, but Rich had been on too many wild goose chases to immediately draw any connections.

Javier Mendes and Jake must have been blood brothers by the number of calls they exchanged. And some of those calls appeared to have been made in the Riverside area, with the last one coming from the Sacramento area

Rich had a lot of background checking to do before finding out the full story on these two characters that seemed to be involved in a huge drug smuggling operation. The tracking device on the flatbed truck had only led them to some apparent small-time drug dealers in San Bernardino and Riverside counties who seemed to be running a wholesale used car lot. That told Rich that he needed to focus on Mendes and Murphy.

As Rich dug deeper on his computer, aided by a huge warehouse of law enforcement databases, he discovered that Jake Murphy, who only had two DUIs, was listed as brother to Marion Murphy, a convicted killer doing a long time in Folsom and affiliated with the notorious AB.

Where was Jake now?

A call to state prison officials was not particularly helpful. He needed some juice from somebody who could push the right buttons.

Rich's decision to walk down the hall to Heacock's office, which seemed to be occupied nowadays as much by that federal deputy marshal as the sergeant, was just one of those unbelievable moments in law enforcement that always makes for great entertainment in television and movies when happenstance solves the big case.

Heacock and McLaughlin were deep in conversation when Rich opened the door with a quick "Gotta' minute?"

Rich handed the DMV information sheet on Jake to Heacock, who then tossed it toward McLaughlin.

Heacock and McLaughlin looked at Rich as if he were handing them a restaurant tab for food they had never ordered, much less consumed.

"Gray Toyota Tundra." That was all Rich had to say.

"Get another copy and have the team show it to Ernie Salas and Terry Crawford," Heacock said.

"Dude, I'm fuckin' busy," Rich said with irritation.

Instead, Rich sat down in an empty chair and began his story on how Jake Murphy popped up on the drug task force radar screen. The looks on Heacock's and McLaughlin's faces turned from mild interest to astonishment.

"Well, there's more," Rich said.

Jake's whereabouts in Sacramento, according to his last cell phone call, posed a logistic problem for the three men who sat 480 miles away.

"I can't get Folsom people to give me squat on Jake's brother," Rich complained. The thunderbolt struck McLaughlin first: maybe Jake was visiting his brother, who was a big shot-caller there.

"What's the number?" McLaughlin asked Rich for the prison's inside line. As McLaughlin spent precious minutes going through the prison administration trying to find somebody with whom to talk, Heacock blanched and muttered a string of curses that startled McLaughlin and interrupted his conversation with a prison assistant administrator who had just picked up the line.

"Do you know what the fuck we did?" Heacock told Rich and McLaughlin, who cupped the receiver and was nearly at a point of hanging up after all his trouble.

"Skip!"

"Oh, shit," McLaughlin said, apologizing to the female on the other end of the phone who had no clue what was going on.

Heacock's mind could see the sketch of the suspect on Page One the next day and a big story about closing in on the killer and their suspect suddenly disappearing and never to be seen again.

"We've gotta get Skip to kill the story," Heacock said.

"That's your shit storm," Rich said. He was nearly apoplectic about how the drug dealer he just tracked down was about to be prematurely exposed at the hands of two idiot colleagues who had a penchant for publicity and some absurd affinity for this lame-ass reporter named Skip.

"Jake was at the prison," McLaughlin told Heacock. "His brother is in the prison hospital's intensive care with a heart attack. Jake was told to come back tomorrow."

"We have PC?" Heacock asked McLaughlin.

McLaughlin talked to his supervisors, who in turn talked with the federal attorneys, and was ordered to take the earliest flight to Sacramento where he would meet FBI and federal marshals to intercept Jake as soon as possible. Rich was invited to accompany McLaughlin to work the drug end of the caper. Heacock got Dominguez to start the paperwork to obtain a warrant for Jake's arrest for murder.

"I've gotta' get to Skip," Heacock said, frantically trying to find Skip's cell phone number amid the clutter of his desk.

CHAPTER FORTY-FIVE

"I can't tell you why Skip, but you can't run that sketch tomorrow," Heacock told me as I was headed home.

"Sarge, it's done. I can't do anything. I'm walking to my car in the parking lot. I'm off the fucking clock!"

"What?"

"I don't know what's going on with you guys. First, you make a big fucking deal about the sketch and now you want to take it back."

"Skip, my friend," Heacock pleaded. "If you run that fucking sketch we're going to lose our guy. You want that?"

"You're onto the suspect?"

"I can't tell you much more than that, Skip."

"Sarge, I'm sorry but I don't think I can help. I'll try, man. You know the old saying, you can't unring a bell once it's struck."

"Fucking bell, my ass. Forget it, Skip. I'll remember this. I'll get the sheriff to call your boss pronto!"

"Oh, man, Sarge, I'll ask, but don't expect nothing.'"

I headed back to the newsroom and approached Don's desk where he was pounding out his story. When I explained the situation, he just stood up with the sketch and headed off to the editor's office.

I sat at my desk and waited for the execution, preferably a bullet to the back of the head. It didn't take long for the editor to open his office door and wave for me to join him.

"What's this all about," Milton began, easing back in his chair and waiting for me to lay out the story.

"Well, I was just making my rounds this morning," I began. "I had this hunch that Sgt. Heacock and Deputy Marshal McLaughlin might have something fresh on the case, and . . .".

"Skip! Tell me about the sketch!"

"Well, apparently the sketch has generated a new lead and they are tracking down this suspect right now."

"Goddammit, Skip! That's the fucking reason they give you a fucking sketch so they can catch the fucking crook!"

"I know."

"Who else has the sketch?" the editor snapped.

"Just us."

Milton was not convinced. "You tell me they are looking for the world's most vicious killer and they give the fucking sketch to you as an exclusive? Only little ol' you?"

"I guess so."

"Seems to me," the editor growled, "these cops are a bunch of disorganized, desperate idiots."

He was about to tell Don to kill the sketch and any reference to it, just in case this really was a life-or-death situation, when his secretary called to tell him the sheriff was on the phone.

Milton smiled at me as he picked up the receiver. He seemed to be enjoying the moment, listening intently and staring directly at me—only his smile quickly changed to a glare.

"Tell you what I'm gonna' do, Bud," he said

"I'll kill the sketch, but we're going to use Heacock's quote. That's the best I can do. Now, you've got to give us first crack when you nab the suspect. Deal?"

The editor hung up and leaned forward on his desk. "Didn't want to run the sketch anyway 'cause I hate sketchy sketches. That's good for TV but not for me. I want both of you guys to hang out in the newsroom until the paper comes off the press just in case they catch the suspect tonight. Is that clear?"

Don and I hung out and waited in the newsroom, just in case the story broke. I sat by the police scanner when the night reporter left. Don and I didn't talk. He worked at his desk, probably writing an outline of the big story if the suspect was captured. I felt totally compromised.

CHAPTER FORTY-SIX

Two businessmen were inexplicably bumped from their Ontario to Sacramento flight. Rich and McLaughlin took their place just as the door to the delayed Boeing 737 was closed.

Rich made sure airport security was on the lookout for Jake's Toyota Tundra, just in case he left it at the airport. It was a base that Rich wanted covered at all costs. Once aboard the plane, the two lawmen sat silently and catnapped on the flight, and were allowed by the flight attendants to leave first before the other passengers.

A deputy marshal waited for them in the baggage claim area of Sacramento's airport, decorated by towering stacks of old luggage in some sort of art-deco design, and led them to his waiting sedan on the curb with its flasher lights blinking.

"There's no way of knowing just yet where your guy is," the friendly deputy told McLaughlin and Rich. The suspect could have holed up at some friend's house or was staying in any number of area hotels or motels. "He is supposed to come back and visit his brother."

That was worrisome. Had Jake been tipped to their plans? Would he still show up? They rode silently through the night traffic toward the prison, gazing at Sacramento's downtown skyline. At the brightly lit prison, the trio was escorted to an office where they waited for a detail of prison guards to brief them on security procedures, and a possible means for capturing Jake without incident.

The morning that lawmen hoped would be Jake's last glimpse as a free man saw the prison come to life with scores of dayshift guards turning out, and the start of a tedious process of caring for and feeding an army of noisy malcontents and sociopaths.

McLaughlin and Rich took position at the prison's visitor center parking lot in a Dodge Caravan with dark tinted windows as they monitored each carload of people scheduled to visit. Visitors come to share their news with inmates about life's normal routines of children attending school, family members struggling with jobs and mortgages or rents. But there are some who are there to pass illicit "kites" that contain coded messages of street deals in the offing or those gone bad, all causing mischief on both sides of the prison walls.

There was still no sign of Jake. Rich kept an empty plastic jug in the Caravan in which both men could urinate to save them having to leave the van and risk blowing their surveillance.

McLaughlin noticed a late model white Mustang convertible with the top down as it pulled into the parking lot. They watched the driver finish a hamburger and toss the yellow wrapper onto the pavement.

"Well, I guess we could get this guy for littering," Rich mused. The man sucked on a straw connected to a big cup that he also tossed onto the ground. "This jerk is really pissing me off," Rich said. He stared at the man, studying his features and trying to make sense of a fat middle-aged slob who didn't quite look like the nebulous sketch he was holding.

The Mustang driver, wearing sporty sunglasses, got out of the car and began walking in a slow shuffle toward the visitor reception building. A wrinkled yellow polo shirt made the 6-footer's pot belly seem to protrude even more. He had a close-cropped haircut, and his thick calves moved his ivory white legs in a casual, but purposeful stride. And he had a pair of flip-flop sandals that made him look like a doofus. This man didn't appear to be a guy who spent much time in the sun, but he seemed to fit in with the average redneck trying to dress comfortably for the California summer heat.

"Whaddaya think?" Rich asked.

"Could be."

McLaughlin called his people inside the prison to alert them about the man approaching the door. Jake had not made much of an impression the day before so prison officials were of little help in identifying the now high-priority target.

Jake entered the visitor center and made a beeline toward the men's room. That detour raised a momentary alarm with the two guards poised to escort Jake into an office where he would be greeted by waiting lawmen. It was more than 10 minutes before Jake emerged from the men's room and joined the long line of visitors waiting to sign in.

Jake, not the gentlemanly type, stared openly and admired a handful of waiting women in short skirts and low-cut blouses who had dressed as sexily as possible to impress the love-starved inmates they intended to see. It took forever to reach the check-in counter where Jake handed his driver's license, plus printed his name and signature on the log sheet.

Unlike the others who waited to be called, Jake was referred to two helpful and friendly guards who frisked him for weapons and contraband, something Jake remembered that nobody had done the previous day. He was then guided through the security door, which quickly closed and locked behind him.

"How's my brother?" Jake asked, just making idle conversation.

"Just fine," said one smiling black guard whose biceps bulged beneath his uniform blouse.

The route Jake was taking was not the same one he remembered from his previous visit. But Jake was oblivious to what was transpiring as he was led into a small room with table and chairs. The two prison guards stayed with him, and opened the door for McLaughlin and Rich who each found a chair at the table. Both lawmen had to check their weapons at the prison gate in cubbies reserved for each California county's lawmen.

Jake immediately sensed trouble.

"Hey, Jake," McLaughlin greeted the man with a smile. He introduced himself and Sgt. Rich. Rich's affiliation with Riverside County Sheriff's Office alerted Jake that he was going to be there for just a bit longer than he anticipated.

"Jake," Rich began. "Do you normally carry an assault rifle and about $40,000, give or take a few bucks, in your Toyota pickup?"

Rich and McLaughlin were satisfied to see the muscle in Jake's jaw twitch in reaction to the question, although the man's face remained impassive. Rich showed Jake the warrant for his arrest.

"I ain't saying a word, fucker. And I wanna' lawyer."

Jake stuck to his word as the cops discussed all the nefarious things he'd been involved in. He ignored the remark that he would rot in Death Row 100 miles to the west at San Quentin unless he cooperated. He wanted his lawyer, although he had no idea if his brother had one on the payroll.

McLaughlin and Rich headed toward the hospital to chat with older brother Duke, finding the patient in his bed and looking ashen and barely conscious. His graying, shoulder-length hair was disheveled and his bushy beard gave him the wild look of a homeless Skid Row derelict.

"Murphy," McLaughlin roused the patient whose eyes opened and closed at the sound of his name. His bushy beard had streaks of black among the long gray hairs that nearly covered the top part of his chest.

"We have your brother Jake in custody for murder and all sorts of other crimes." Duke's eyes opened and shut again. "Murphy? Did you hear that? We got your brother."

His eyes opened as he slowly tried to lift himself to his elbows.

"Ahhh, shit! That pissant mutherfucker." Duke's words were growled as loud as he could muster, but the extra dose of morphine and nitroglycerine his so-called male nurse had given him to induce symptoms of a heart attack were not working exactly the way he intended. In fact, Duke, a man who actually had a bad heart as yet undetected, medically speaking, was in cardiac distress. His eyes widened and then closed. He looked fairly furious. His heart monitor began issuing a continuous noise as the monitor signified a flatline heart rate.

"Do you think Jake will be able to go to the funeral?" McLaughlin asked Rich with a smirk.

Rich was busy taking notes of Duke Murphy's last words. They left him as the hospital staff mustered to the rescue. The male nurse who cared for Duke had a lot of explaining to do after the autopsy, and when he was done answering questions, the AB's shot-callers had a few more.

Jake was escorted by prison guards to an area outside the main gate where he was turned over to McLaughlin and Rich, who by then had retrieved their weapons and were ready to handcuff and shackle their man to drive him to the Sacramento County jail. Jake's only words were: "When do I get to see my brother?"

"Somewheres south of Hell," Rich told Jake, giving him the news about his brother's latest heart episode. Jake's eyes watered after he heard the news, but didn't give the lawmen the satisfaction of saying a word.

Heacock, weary from his sleepless vigil and aware of the minute-by-minute surveillance and arrest of Jake, was at the point of mental collapse when Rich called to say they needed to arrange transportation of their suspect back to Riverside.

So much to do, Heacock thought. Word was spreading quickly throughout the department about Jake's capture, too quickly for the sergeant to call the department PIO. True to his word, the sheriff called the newspaper editor as promised with the breaking news, which by then was late in the afternoon and quickly approaching deadline when the paper budgeted all its high-priority stories and prepared the best for Page One.

The editor peeked out his office and scanned the newsroom.

"Where's Skip?"

The managing editor scrambled to find other line editors and one began calling Skip's cell phone. It rang and rang—at Skip's desk. A desk mate answered Skip's phone with the polite greeting: "Skip's phone."

"You're not Skip!" the managing editor screamed at the reporter to whom he was staring at only 20 feet away. The startled reporter hung up the phone, shrugged his shoulders and resumed writing his story for the upcoming deadline.

"Get me Williams!" the editor yelled. "Find Skip!"

CHAPTER FORTY-SEVEN

There are only a few occasions when I feel completely vulnerable. One is when I am hunkered down on the toilet, my pants at my ankles, and am reading the sports pages as I deal with the business at hand.

"You in there, Skip?"

Do I answer?

"Yeah, what's up?"

"Milt needs you right now! I think he got a break on the killer." I couldn't identify the voice, but I think it was one of the news assistants.

When I emerged from the men's room with a folded newspaper under my arm, I felt like the entire newsroom was watching me slowly walk to my desk. Did I do something bad by taking a critically needed potty break at the wrong time?

The managing editor was waving at me and nearly tripping over vacant office chairs as he moved toward my desk.

"Skip! Skip!"

"What?"

"They got the killer!"

This was not exactly how I planned to break my blockbuster story. Everybody, except the little old lady cleaning the newsroom knew about my story before I did.

"Get the fuck outta' here and get to the sheriff's office!" Milton screamed at me from across the newsroom.

My mind still was not functioning properly. I was moving, but my brain was in slow motion.

"I must see Heacock ASAP!" I told the sergeant's secretary once I got to the sheriff's station.

"I don't have a lot of time, Skip," Heacock said as he ushered me back to his office. Detectives were sitting on their desks and in a jovial mood over the huge development and gleefully waved to me as I passed and entered Heacock's office.

Drained from his frantic dash out of the newsroom, I plopped down in the couch and took a deep breath. "Where do we begin, sarge?"

For once, I felt confident about writing this story. I was ready. I knew the details without referring to my previous stories to jog my memory.

My job was to capture the moment of Jake's arrest and the steps that led police to Folsom. This was a different kind of arrest, and I was finding Heacock more than candid about talking to me for a change. There was no reticence, no hesitancy in giving me the color I needed to flesh out the story, particularly the drama of when Sgt. Rich linked the drug interception to Jake and tracked the man down to Folsom. I was interviewing Heacock when McLaughlin and Rich called the sergeant. I begged Heacock to let me talk to each of the men who were too tired to complain or button up.

I called Folsom and got details about Jake's dead brother. I talked to the wounded and now nearly recovered Terry Crawford and picked his thoughts about prison gangs and how he felt about Jake's arrest.

Back at the newsroom, Angela, overjoyed that her life would return to some normalcy, even called me and relented to a brief interview about the toll Jake's actions had been on her life.

Ed was sitting next to me as I wrote, then took key elements from my story and updated the paper's Internet website with the latest developments, knowing the story could not be held as an exclusive overnight.

Before I realized it, I saw the newsroom clock and was shocked to see that it was past midnight, far beyond the normal deadline for breaking stories at 11:30 p.m. The newsroom had slowly emptied of people, leaving only the key players to help Ed and me finish up the main story that was long enough to fill two open pages of newsprint.

I watched Ed work through my story with the speed of a laser beam and change tenses and words that made the story read so perfectly. I did not put my byline on the story, as today's crop of reporters routinely do, because of the flap the other day over the editor ordering me to stay low profile.

I noticed that Ed had not yet put my byline on the story, as was customary when finishing up with the editing. I worried that my big story would be attributed to a staff effort instead of just me. I was too proud to request the byline from Ed who muttered to himself as he edited, mouthing words while he read or typed.

Bylines are the only sexual attraction in journalism. Give a reporter a byline and he will work long hours for next to nothing until he becomes so disillusioned over his sorry life that it ceases to mean anything.

A byline is the first thing a reporter reads after the headline and story's placement in the paper. It is a badge of honor and jealously sought and protected.

I waited for my seal of approval from Ed who seemed troubled by one point.

"Skip, what about that topless dancer you used as a source who was the impetus for this federal investigation?"

"Uh, Ed, she's fine."

"Skip, I mean you don't have any quote from her. Don't you think we need something?"

Too tired to argue, I pulled out my cell phone and hit redial on Angela's cell phone. It rang four times and was about to go to the answering mode when Angela answered.

"Angela. Skip. Hate to bother you so late. I'm still writing this story. Were you asleep?"

"No, Skip," Angela said wearily. "I'm teaching tango lessons in the living room. It's late. What time is it?"

"Almost 12:30 a.m. I need to talk to Janelle."

She seemed pissed. "Hold on." I could hear her knock on Janelle's bedroom door and wake her. "It's Skip," she said as she handed Janelle the phone.

Janelle immediately became concerned. "What's up, lover?"

"Everything's cool, 'cept I need your help in the story. My editor wants a quote from you. You know, how you were the one that got the ball rolling in the U.S. attorney's office before Dan was shot. You know? All that stuff."

"Well . . ." Janelle seemed hesitant about cooperating. She was too groggy to come up with anything useful. "Look sweetie, I trust you, just make something up. You're the writer. I'm the dancer. I hope I can see you tomorrow. I love ya," and she made sweet kissing noises over the phone that I hoped Ed did not overhear.

I wanted to close the conversation with a "love ya" in return, but that would not be a good idea with Ed sitting two feet away. "Thanks a load and bye."

I jotted down something in my notebook.

"Well?" Ed asked, waiting to insert the quote.

"I've got it."

"Just dictate it to me. I've got a good spot for it. What's her name again?"

"I've got it

Janelle Jones, who months ago approached federal authorities about her suspicions of gang involvement in the entertainment industry and was then placed in federal witness protection for her own safety . . .

Ed interrupted. "You don't want to identify her as a topless dancer? That's great stuff." Ed was mimicking a gyrating dancer and his mind was visualizing her twirling tassles attached to her nipples.

"No, Ed, she's still in fear of her life." Ed seemed satisfied with that explanation, and waited for me to resume my dictation.

"Where was I? Okay. She said she was overjoyed the investigation had resulted in the capture of the suspect.'"

"Okay, Ed, here's the quote: 'Every day I was afraid this man would come after me. Now I can resume my life and try to find some sort of normalcy.'"

"Okay," Ed said, typing the last words. "Not really compelling, but it'll do. She didn't say anything about returning to the stage and shaking her booty?" Ed was giggling in delight. I was worried about the concocted quote.

Ed, getting pressure from the copy chief to finish the story or go just home, read through my story one more time. "It's ready," he yelled. The copy chief was cursing and screaming, then called his editor in the composing room to paginate the story and send it to the press.

My heart sank. Ed seemed to read my mind as he turned to me with a sly smile. He typed my byline atop the story with a flourish.

"Nice work, Skip. I'm so proud of you."

"Thanks, Ed. You pulled it together for me. I owe you big time."

"Now, get out of here. Go home! We have a huge day tomorrow."

I knew he would be busy with Jake's court appearance in the morning and the hastily scheduled press conference afterwards in front of the courthouse.

"I think I want to hang around and see the first paper come off the press."

"Suit yourself. I'm going home."

CHAPTER FORTY-EIGHT

I got a few hours of sleep and awoke at 6 a.m. feeling ready to tackle the world. I did my mandatory push-ups, pull-ups and sit-ups before getting back to the newsroom. Running a mile for myself and another mile for the Corps would have to wait until the afternoon.

At press time, my sources were unclear whether Jake would be arraigned in state or federal court. There were so many state charges that could be filed, but they would encompass jurisdictions in Riverside, San Bernardino, San Diego and Los Angeles counties.

My first call was to the U.S. Attorney's office to talk to the information officer, guessing correctly that the case was going to be first handled by federal court. The arraignment was set for 1:30 p.m. that afternoon. I briefed the morning editors and alerted the photo department so they could send a photographer. Federal court does not allow press photographers inside the courthouse, so we needed to find out how Jake would be brought to court.

"You wanna perp walk, eh?" Heacock said over the phone when I asked. "Nice job on the story, but I'm not sure we're gonna have Jake here in time for the court appearance. All these folks schedule this shit without talking to me."

I was worried when Heacock told me that they were still arranging for some special flight from Sacramento.

I had a hunch the U.S. Marshals Service would dispatch a small plane from its air wing to airlift Jake back to Riverside and land at the small Riverside Municipal Airport. The editors thought that was a good gamble, and sent me and a photographer to wait at the airport.

I was beginning to worry that my bet wouldn't pay off until two black Suburbans pulled up to the tiny terminal and drove onto the tarmac.

When the Suburban's four occupants—holstered Glocks on their belts—got out and stood by their vehicles, I kept scanning the skies for any approaching plane. A small jet began its approach from the east and neatly touched down on the small runway. The plane taxied on the ramp up to the terminal and the waiting vehicles as the men stood by. I watched the door open and the staircase unfold to the tarmac. Two men quickly scampered down the steps and stood next to the plane, waiting for the next people to disembark. And then this big pudgy guy in an orange prison jumpsuit, his hands cuffed to a waist belt, leaned through the hatch and looked around the tarmac before carefully stepping down the ladder.

I could see McLaughlin and another cop grab Jake's right arm.

I needed a closer look at this Jake character who didn't look like any notorious killer I ever heard about.

"Hey Skip," McLaughlin called out.

"Semper fi, Frank!"

McLaughlin tossed off a crisp salute and laughed. I could see Jake recognized my name because he stared directly at me.

"Fuck you! I want to kill you! This is all your fault! When I get out I'm gonna' chase you down with a lawnmower!"

I wrote that down. "Do you have any other comment?"

My editors sent the photographer and I to the hearing to just wait until anything happened. Four other waiting journalists spent their idle time reading my Page One story. Don Williams showed up and sat next to me.

"When did you finish last night?" Williams asked.

"I went home about 1:30 a.m."

"They're ready," an attorney told the waiting journalists, as marshals appeared and ushered in the handcuffed and shackled Jake.

I moved down toward the front of the courtroom. I overheard Jake complaining to his public defender about my presence in the courtroom.

Three federal prosecutors sat at their table in nicely pressed blue and black suits and whispered to each other as they waited for the judge to appear.

The clerk answered her phone and nodded to the bailiff who opened the chamber doors to let the federal judge enter as all in the courtroom came to their feet. Without ceremony, the judge asked if the defendant's name was Jake Murphy.

"Yes, your honor," his counsel replied, also identifying himself.

"Your honor," he began. "I've only had a few minutes with the defendant and really know nothing about the case except for the tremendous amount of media coverage. I request that we set our next court appearance in two weeks."

The judge checked his calendar and suggested several dates until all the attorneys could agree.

"Your honor," the lead prosecutor said. "We have just filed charges and request that the defendant be held without bond until we can set up a bail hearing."

"The defendant will be held without bond," the judge said. "Anything more?"

The attorneys rose and said in unison: "No, your honor" and the hearing was over. One minute, maybe two minutes, I thought, and it was over.

Jake was talking to his federal public defender as the prosecutors filed out of court with a covey of reporters on their tail.

"Before you start asking questions," the lead prosecutor told me, "we're having a press conference outside that will answer all your questions."

I walked down the step and stood around the cluster of reporters and photographers who were gathering.

U.S. Attorney Frost, dressed in a gray suit and red and black striped tie, walked down the steps flanked by a dozen men, two of whom I recognized as the sheriffs of Riverside and San Bernardino counties.

"Let me know when you are ready, ladies and gentlemen," Frost announced, allowing the television crews to get their sound technicians ready to roll. One by one, the television reporters waved they were ready to roll.

Frost thanked each of the law enforcement officials, the FBI, the U.S. Marshals Service and his team of assistant U.S. attorneys for the hard work that had finally paid off. He named each of them. They each waved and mouthed "thank yous" to Frost. He rattled off a laundry list of crimes committed by Jake's motley bunch of henchmen and Jake's alleged criminal acts.

"I want to announce that a federal grand jury has indicted Jake Murphy on multiple felonies. Ladies and gentlemen, Jake Murphy's actions forever altered the lives of many families and a number of victims. I would like you to see and hear from just two brave young women who have endured so much pain and trauma."

The attorney turned toward the courthouse doors. Janelle and Angela, dressed in business suits and wearing floral scarves around their necks, walked out on cue. They looked righteously vindicated as they held hands and carefully walked down the steps to the microphones and stood on either side of Frost.

Something deep inside my stomach began causing a huge problem.

And the gurgling got worse when Janelle waved at me and Angela gave me a big happy smile. I was afraid to look at my colleagues, but smiled and nodded at the women.

"I cannot leave unsaid," Frost continued, "the tremendous cooperation we received from the news media, particularly one reporter from the Riverside area." Here it comes. I felt dizzy.

Please don't say my name, I thought

"Skip Easley," Frost motioned toward me, "was the target of this vicious gang of thugs who sent an assassin who almost murdered Skip at his apartment. Mr. Easley chose to withhold reporting this attempted murder and instead worked intensely and tirelessly with our investigators as they pursued this labyrinth of lawlessness and deceit."

Frost seemed to like that "labyrinth of lawlessness" phrase. "We have not yet found this cowardly would-be assassin and suspect he's been dealt with in the same fashion as so many of Jake's cohorts."

The dizziness returned.

I knew Don Williams was confused because he kept looking at me as he took notes. The damage was not complete. Angela also thanked me for my support and cooperation, and said how she felt her dead husband could now rest in peace.

And then, it was Janelle's turn. "Skip, you're the man!" and she mouthed a kiss at me.

The worst was yet to come.

"Skip, I want you to know that you didn't let me down when we first met earlier this year in Washington. You're just a DOLL, and I so appreciate you loaning me your little dog, Ginger, when I was at an emotional . . . I was so goddamned afraid that those suckers would nail my ass!"

I was actually praying. Please God, strike her speechless. However, she seemed energized and was talking about what a great reporter I was when Frost cut her off with a "Thank you Miss Jones."

As you can imagine, the press conference involved a lot of questions about me and Jake. Frost cut off the questions when they got too detailed about Jake's crimes.

The official entourage returned to the courthouse. Janelle waved at me and yelled that she would see me later. Not before she posed for more photographs. Angela finally dragged her away.

All the reporters then pounced on me. Of course, they wanted to know all about my attempted murder. I now knew what it was like to be interviewed. And I felt sorry for all the assholes I ever nailed to the cross of public opinion.

"I can't say anything at the moment," I heard myself say, and I needed to find a quick exit to flee this disaster. I grabbed one of the thick packets of papers being distributed to journalists by a federal attorney. I stood there and thumbed through what looked like 30 or more pages of criminal acts and allegations.

"You're on page 16." Don Williams told me. I found the page and scanned the lines for my name.

"Oh, my god."

Don just turned and left me in my state of panic and hustled back to the newspaper with the staff photographer who seemed totally confused.

Soon Janelle excitedly bounded down the stairs and hugged me tightly. She gave me a moist kiss on the lips. I momentarily forgot my predicament.

"Babe, I think I'm in a lot of trouble at the paper"

CHAPTER FORTY-NINE

"I don't understand, lover," Janelle told me as I took her back to my apartment.

"I thought you would be the big hero. You got the story, what else do they want?" What could I say? It's wrong to fall in love with my source, and it's worse than sinful to sleep with her.

"Look, sweetie, stay here and I'll be back in a few hours. I've gotta' go back to the newsroom and face the music."

It was hard to park my car at the newspaper and trudge toward my career's execution. When the elevator door opened, I saw the busy newsroom with people dashing from desk to desk. A few looked up at me as I walked to my desk.

Taking out a piece of company stationery, I pulled out a ballpoint pen and scribbled my resignation in eight brief words, then signed and dated it.

"Come in, been expecting you, Skip," Milton told me.

I handed him my resignation and mumbled my apologies for disappointing him.

Milton called in Don Williams, who quickly sat down next to me and began writing on a yellow legal pad.

"Don's writing the story. Obviously. He just needs to know about the shooting at your apartment and your involvement with Janelle and Angela."

The editor picked up a spiral notebook with the company logo on the cover and handed it to me.

"Ever read this?"

I opened the newspaper's code of ethics and conduct manual, and quickly found the rules for Conflicts of Interest that Milton asked me to locate. Journalists were expected to conduct themselves with professionalism and refrain from any actions that might be construed as a conflict in their reporting, it said. Moreover, the company required its news staff to fully inform supervisors about any actions they take in gathering news and to consult editors should any questions arise about fairness, impartiality, accuracy or dealing with official sources.

Any journalist's conduct pertaining to a story must be without reproach and never endanger the reputation of the newspaper.

"Start from the beginning and tell me everything, and I want to hear all about this dancer who you seem to be so attached to," the editor said in a firm yet fatherly manner.

"Janelle?"

"No goddammit! Marilyn Monroe! Jeez, Skip gimme a break!"

"Oh, man," Skip moaned. "You hafta see her to understand."

Don Williams came to my defense. "Skip's right. She could force Mariah Carey to sing a higher octave."

"Okay! Let's blame it on the chick!" The editor covered his eyes with his hands.

"I could be in Baja now and sipping a six-pack of Coronas and hauling in a 62-pound halibut. That goddamned Mike Bradley sent you to me and you've ruined me and my paper. I owed Mike a big favor, and all I got was a hosing from a primadonna wing nut with a hard on for a . . ."

Milton could not find the words. "This confidential source is a TOPless DANcer you've been screwing!"

Milton ended his tirade and began dictating his resignation to his secretary. He wanted me to hear what trouble I had caused.

"I don't really want to know, but tell me EVERYTHING."

"Well, it's a long story . . ."

"Don't spare the details."

After I was done, he opened his desk drawer and tossed an envelope at me.

"Here! Now, get outta here!"

It was my payroll check that included all of the overtime I had accrued except for the six hours I logged the previous night. Just $2,382.93, a sorry sum that would have to last me until I could find another job.

The security guard was ready to escort me out of the newspaper. I'd heard about these rare occasions. It was like some military general ripping off the stripes of his best soldier.

I saw Ed on my way out of the newsroom. I wanted to say something to my mentor. Ed shook his head and just did a 180-degree turn and headed into the photo department, closing the door behind him.

How could I ever thank the man who saved my career and pushed me toward this story? Disappointing Ed was excruciating

I found Janelle watching the television news in my apartment. Her smart black business suit was hanging in my closet. All she was wearing was a gray T-shirt inscribed with "My Guy's M-16 Is Bigger Than Yours!"

Janelle probably ordered that online.

"How did it go?"

I fell onto the couch and showed her my last payroll check.

"I also have $5 in my wallet, and about $2,000 in my checking account. I think we have enough to buy some gasoline to dash out of town."

"Gimme that five bucks, son," she teased. "Janelle's gonna' give you a lap dance you'll never forget!"

It was a short dance and a long night. A knock on the door the next afternoon was a welcome interruption. I found a small Federal Express box next to the apartment door. I opened it carefully.

Inside was a rusty pair of pliers.

ABOUT THE AUTHOR

Marlowe J. Churchill is a retired newspaper journalist who resides in Riverside, California. He previously resided in the Seattle-Tacoma area, which plays a part in this novel. He covered police, military, and court issues for many years and is the author of The Riverside National Cemetery Story: A Field of Warriors. He is married, has two daughters, three step-children and five grandsons.